THE HERO OF MY *Love Scene*

BY NICKI GRACE

STARRING:
Kody Benton & Winter Daniels

GUEST APPEARANCE:
Jessica Hensley from **THE RIGHT TO MY WRONG**
&
Chloe Fosters from **THE LOVE OF MY PAST, PRESENT**

ISBN: 979-8-9869087-2-4

"I NEED A BREAK FROM MY FIVE KIDS."

Winter gawked at how big his dick was because... it was huge. Instinctively, she wondered if he knew how to use it but quickly decided no.

Nothing against the guy, but in her sexual experience, big dicks didn't equal big orgasms.

If she was being completely honest, regardless of the size of a man's package or the position they delivered it in, it never got her anywhere.

Therefore, the dick before her may as well have been nothing more than a prop like those used at her job, "Movie Box Studios" appearing useful on set but useless in reality.

However, capabilities aside, she had to admit it was impressive. Bouncing around and swinging back and forth like it was parting the way for a famous celebrity to come through.

Who knows, maybe the guy it was attached to was famous, or at least pretended to be as a day job because he had the look. Tall and muscular with a chocolate complexion and a flirtatious smile, his aura screamed, "star" or "groupies apply here."

Still, she doubted he was famous, although his dick could be. The guy it was attached to was a male dancer hired by her friend, Jessica, as a celebratory token for Chloe's bachelorette party.

She giggled as the dancing dick brought to mind a hand-held compass with the arrow, pointing and shifting uncontrollably in all different directions.

There was a second dick present. It belonged to the other male dancer of the night. Although it wasn't as big, it too was impressive.

But instead of being fun and extra bouncy like the compass dick, this one was more well-behaved and of the no-nonsense variety.

It pointed straight out and barely bounced. It was as if it refused to have a good time and had been brought to the party against its will. Every move the dancer made that attempted to send it in any position besides forward-facing was met with a challenge—talk about stubborn.

If it wasn't clear before, it was clear now. She was most definitely tipsy... possibly, even drunk.

With that being said, at least she was in good company because inebriated was the current status for most of the women in the room.

About 20 feet ahead was Chloe, the bride-to-be, and one of Winter's best friends. Chloe had her wild meter on full blast. She was dancing and waving dollars in the air yelling, "Sexy Chocolate! Sexy Chocolate!" at the top of her lungs with two other girls.

Having their wish granted, one of the chocolate eye candies took a break from the group of girls he was entertaining and started heading their way. He was most certainly making sure to keep all eyes on him as he strutted, twisted and danced his firm ass all the way over to Chloe and her backup screamers.

As Winter sat there lounging, drink in hand and enjoying a much-needed break from all the excitement, she was thankful they were in the penthouse suite of a five-star hotel.

The noise level coming from this room would have earned them non-stop complaints. Approximately fifteen of Chloe's closest female family and friends were scattered around the beautiful lavish suite that housed a living room, dining room, kitchen and three bedrooms.

The party was being held in the living room area. It was a grand layout that offered more than enough space to accommodate their needs. Impeccable decor in golds, silvers and whites offered an expensive, bold look to the room.

Floor-to-ceiling windows and an oversized balcony provided incredible views of the city. Thankfully the windows included curtains because no matter how high up they were, this party needed no chance of falling into the category of public viewing.

Modern but classic couches that were a staple in the suite's daily decor hugged the walls. They had been pushed aside to make room for three round tables that could seat up to six women each.

In addition to the round tables, there were three gold mini-tables placed in close proximity. One displayed the cake, the second held bridal presents, and the third was home to various gag gifts such as tiny bottles of alcohol and keychain dildos.

Once the space requirements were met, the hotel spared no expense in providing proper servers for the event. The staff was responsible for serving, cooking and cleaning before, after and during the party. Winter could tell the staff was operating at the top of their game tonight.

They made sure everything remained immaculate. If an empty glass, loose napkin, or random trash was dropped or left behind, it was instantly collected, then discarded.

In addition, the staff kept drink refills continuous. Although a short list of finger foods, the menu was fresh, delicious and of the highest quality.

The music was blasting, and good vibes were present.

Things had already been in full swing for over two hours and it seemed that the party could continue for just as long.

Taking the final sip of her third apple martini of the night, Winter realized how good she felt. Her whole body was warm and completely relaxed. As she savored the sweet, yet slightly sour taste on her tongue, she couldn't remember the last time before tonight that she'd had a drink.

She would need to remember to make this a regular thing. A yummy alcoholic drink would be a welcomed delight as a way to unwind after a long work week.

Continuing to scan the room and observe the male dancers earn their tips, she spotted Jessica. She was re-stacking gifts that had fallen over or shifted out of place.

Jessica was an event planner and responsible for this fabulously X-rated event. Based on her all-over-the-place movements, she was still very much on event planner duty.

One would think that she would take a moment to enjoy the party, but Jessica was a host through and through.

She was all about details and keeping things in order. Some would call her uptight, but that wasn't entirely true. She was actually fun, kind and simply loved her job. Probably more so than Winter loved hers, and that was saying something.

Jessica was known to enjoy the planning more than the event itself, and even though this event was the bridal shower of one of her dearest friends, it was no exception.

Looking up to see Winter watching her, Jessica gave a quick thumbs up and moved on to another task.

A few feet behind Jessica was the bar area. Winter noticed one of the servers holding a tray and leaning against the bar staring at her.

Another staff member behind the counter was making more drinks, so it was a safe assumption that the guy undressing her with his eyes was waiting for them to be ready so he could bring them over.

Their eyes locked, and he winked at her; in return, she offered a kind smile.

He probably thought her smile meant more than it did, but he would be mistaken. She had dated some very handsome men, and although the stories started differently, they always ended the same.

Not tonight, buddy.

Tonight was reserved for fun and friends. Her only interest was making sure that Chloe had the best night of her life. She wasn't looking for any men to flirt with or even date at the moment.

Last she checked, her love life had flatlined and Winter had no plans to try and resuscitate it. Instead, she was taking a break, a sort of hiatus from relationships, and that break included sex.

She wasn't bitter about it or even saddened. It was simple, really, as of about a year ago, she'd had the realization that her focus was way too locked in on trying to find "the right guy."

Not wanting to be the type of woman, always looking for a man, she decided to try something new.

That new thing was to try nothing at all. Just enjoy life and all the great things it had to offer. She was tired, anyway. One way or another, true love would find her; it was all about timing.

If it didn't... well, that was a worry for another day.

The reference to timing as it pertained to love made Winter think of her mom, who passed away from cancer a couple of years ago. It was a horrible loss for Winter as she experienced it much too soon, behind the loss of her dad to a stroke the year before that. She missed her parents deeply and often thought of them.

Their love was of proportions greater than she had ever

seen. The way they took care of each other and enjoyed one another's company was something more commonly seen between best friends instead of husband and wife.

By watching them, she learned how powerful and fulfilling true love can be. It was something so magnetic, words couldn't describe it. If she could find love that came anywhere close to what her parents had, she'd consider herself the luckiest girl in the world.

To accept anything less would not only be a disservice to herself but disrespectful to her parents' memory and all they had taught her.

Winter was really close to her mom. They'd spent a lot of time together going antique shopping, watching movies and having great conversations.

Their favorite movies were "The Breakfast Club" and "Girls Trip".

Whenever Winter would get sad or feel down, she would visit her mom, and they'd pop in a movie and eat loads of junk food until Winter felt better. Her mom always knew what to do and say to get Winter through tough times.

When she asked her mom why she chose Winter as her name, her mom said it was her favorite season.

However, Winter knew that her mom was biased toward the season because it was during a cold, snowy day in February that her mom's car broke down, and Winter's dad, a stranger to her mom at the time, pulled over to help. They'd been inseparable ever since.

When Winter would vent about struggles in the love department, her mom would make her feel better by reminding her that, just like her name, everything had its season, and her season for love would come.

Well, it hadn't come, not for love anyway. It seemed every relationship she entered ended in disaster. When she was younger, she thought that by now, being 31, all areas in her life would be in order.

It's not that she was one of those people that presumed entering into her thirties would magically make everything okay. It was just that from early on, she had planned and made choices that she assumed would have gotten her everything on her checklist of life.

She'd always been a great deal more serious than most of her friends once they graduated high school.

Instead of partying and procrastinating, she picked up second and third jobs so that she could pay off college debts and buy her first house as soon as possible.

She wanted a job in the film industry and landed her dream position about seven years ago when she started working as a prop master for Movie Box Studios.

To date, she had paid off her college debts, landed the dream job and gotten the house. But the guy... seemed to be missing in action.

Assuming he was having trouble finding her or maybe she wasn't open-minded enough, she decided to cast a wide net with her dating choices.

God forbid if her potential guy fell through the cracks because he was unemployed, underemployed, wasn't tall enough, romantic enough, or seemed a bit weird in the beginning.

She even had a couple of long-distance relationships because love knew no bounds, and if she never tried, she would never know.

Basically, she let the fear of losing her dream guy before getting to know him drive her, and she had paid for it dearly.

Her dating choices over the years were poor and, sometimes, downright comical. Her attempts to roll with the punches and move on to the next guy who might give her the love story she so desperately wanted was a big mistake.

Instead, she kept reliving the same dating horror stories that left her in the role of the hopeful leading lady and rotated the position of leading asshole to different men.

To be fair, it wasn't always the guy's fault; she was just as guilty for choosing such poor mates, to begin with.

Once, she dated a guy named Carl, who she thought was going places. Sadly, the only place he was going was from his mom's couch to hers.

As an excuse for his couch-living lifestyle, he told her he was only living with his mom as a temporary arrangement until builders finished the construction on his five-bedroom house.

The problem was that Carl happened to leave out a few minor details. There was no actual house being built, only a hypothetical one, and due to his poor credit score, he didn't even qualify for a loan.

When confronted about this, he called it being a visionary and said that his only fault was wanting a woman he could build with. In the end, she didn't know if he was a compulsive liar or just delusional but decided to let him sort it out alone.

Then there was Greg, a magician. True, it was an odd job, and the idea of it didn't exactly make Winter giddy, but he was sweet, charming and very funny.

They met at a local comedy club and connected over their love for old-school comedians. They dated for close to two years, and she fell in love with him.

Things were going so well that she felt certain that there were wedding bells in their future. Wanting to be the supportive girlfriend, she didn't bat an eye when he suddenly stopped being interested in having sex with her. His job was hectic, he'd said. With so many tricks to learn and places to perform, it was really messing with his drive.

She idiotically accepted his explanation in hopes that improvement was right around the corner. Besides, him no longer wanting sex didn't stop his charming words and romantic gestures, so, in her mind, he was worth fighting for. She eventually found that he was using all that romance and charm to slide out of her bed and into everyone else's. He was a serial cheater who was as equally talented at pulling rabbits out of hats as he was with pulling excuses out of his ass.

Next was Alex. Maybe, just maybe, things could have worked with Alex. He was a good guy and did well for himself. There was just one problem. His dick was too small, minuscule, really.

He had some kind of condition that affected the size of it. She felt really bad for him and tried to tough it out. In an attempt to keep her happy, he was more than eager to engage in oral stimulation, but he was terrible at it! Like Guinness World Record bad.

Coming to the conclusion that never having experienced an orgasm didn't mean she had to keep being a victim to his tongue of torture, she cut her losses. After it was all said and done, she, or more so, her vagina, moved on and couldn't be any happier.

Eventually, and rightfully frustrated that yet another love dream had turned into a nightmare, it was time to call it quits... at least for a while. It seemed no matter what sacrifice she made or how promising the guy seemed, it never worked out. Her heart and mind needed a rest.

When or if the right guy came along, she would deal with it then. Her biggest fear was that she would fuck it up.

Being lied to and let down repeatedly had its way of making her doubt most things guys say. Her track record proved she gave men way too much benefit and not nearly enough doubt. Therefore, she wasn't sure she could trust her own dating judgment.

But love was tricky. She had to balance protecting her heart while not becoming a woman that let their past hurt dictate their future, but that was hard. Somehow fixing her broken heart time after time made her weary, and she was always waiting for the other shoe to drop because eventually it would drop and kick her in the ass.

The server depositing another apple martini in front of her broke her thought process. She looked up at him. It was the guy that'd been staring at her.

Now that he was up close, she could see his teeth were in dire need of some dental attention.

"Having a nice night?" he asked.

She smiled and said, "yes, it's lovely. I've been looking forward to this so I could get a break from my five kids. The single mom's life is a hard one," she lied.

She saw his expression change like someone had thrown cold water in his face.

Trying to cover his reaction, he said. "I'll bet, well, enjoy your night." Then, he picked up her empty glass and almost ran away.

She giggled to herself. He couldn't get out of there fast enough. She raised a glass to basically his trail of dust and then took a giant sip.

The night remained something for the memory books for another few hours. Little by little, the party downsized until no one was left but Chloe, Winter, Jessica and Chloe's Twin cousins, Talia and Tina. The girls were in Chloe's bridal shower and also staying overnight, putting the three luxury rooms to use. The bride-to-be had one room, the twins shared a room and Winter and Jessica had the third room.

Deciding it was time to turn in, Winter headed towards her bedroom for the night. Jessica was already in their room asleep because being the wedding planner meant that she had busy work tomorrow. Talia and Tina had gone to their rooms about an hour before with the intent to return but never did. It seemed that Talia went to pee, but because she'd had quite a few drinks, Tina found her asleep sitting on the toilet.

That just left Chloe and Winter. Last Winter saw Chloe was about an hour ago. Chloe was sitting in a chair on the balcony at the time, having an in-depth (and more than likely) raunchy phone conversation with her fiancé, Derek.

As she walked across the living room, she ran into Chloe. Literally almost ran into her because Chloe was running towards Winter with her arms open and collided with her. Embracing Winter on impact, Chloe was obviously still drunk and riding on her happy emotions. Winter had sobered up a little while ago because she had let her fourth drink of the night be her last.

"I thought you were on the phone outside on the balcony?" Winter asked, holding on to Chloe more so to keep her steady than anything else.

"No, silly," Chloe replied, swaying a bit. "I went to my room a little while ago, and had to have a private chat with the soon-to-be Mister if you know what I mean." Chloe attempted a wink that manifested in her basically closing both eyes for about 5 seconds.

"Enough said," Winter responded.

"I just love you guys so much," Chloe slurred. "This was the best night ever! Thank you for everything, Wint."

Then she leaned in close and said, "don't tell everyone else, but you know you are my favorite season?"

Winter smiled. Chloe had been saying that quirky line to her ever since they met in 4th grade. It was her cutesy way of telling Winter that she was her favorite person.

"Your secret's safe with me," she said. "You know we'd do anything for our best friend in the world, the magnificent Chloe Fosters. Oh wait, I meant Chloe James."

Chloe giggled, "It does have a nice ring to it, doesn't it?"

"It does."

Chloe let go and extended her arm upward and to the left.

"Guess I'll head back to my room now. Tomorrow, a weeding awaits."

Grabbing her friend by the shoulder and positioning her body to the right, Winter said, "no, Chloe, your room is that way. And yes, a wedding awaits tomorrow, not a weeding."

Chloe hiccuped and said, "Oops, my bad," and walked very unbalanced toward her room.

The next morning, there were people everywhere, getting the girls ready for the big day. Once again, all the action took place in the living room. They were being styled and made runway beautiful by a highly ranked beauty team provided by the hotel.

As far as the prepping went, everyone was getting the same services, just in a different order.

For instance, while Chloe, the overly pampered bride, was getting a pedicure and manicure, Winter, the maid of honor, was getting her hair done, and Talia and Tina, the bridesmaids, were getting their brows waxed and eyelash extensions applied.

Jessica, who couldn't hold a position in the wedding party because she was the wedding planner, ensured that everyone stayed the course, and all items were delivered on schedule.

Winter was surprised that no one had a hangover after such a wild night. Chloe and her cousins must have been some pro drinkers because once the alarms went off and they had finished their in-suite breakfast, Chloe, Talia, and Tina were energetic and ready to tackle the day.

"Hey, Winter," Talia said, sitting utterly still as to not cause a mistake with her brow shaping. "How'd you sleep?"

"Good. Not as good as you, though. I heard you fell asleep on the toilet."

"Girl, yes! One minute I was peeing; the next, Tina was shaking me. I have no idea when it happened. I should have been more responsible like you and sat my ass down a whole lot earlier."

"I only sat down because I was hurting from the whiplash I'd developed watching those dicks swing around."

At that comment, all the girls laughed.

"You're right," Tina chimed in. "Now that you mentioned it, I think my neck hurts, too."

"Mine too," Chloe and Talia added in unison.

They all laughed again and then settled back into their scheduled steps of the bridal party beautification process.

Nearly every thirty minutes, one of them switched stations until each of them had been plucked, packed, painted and primped. If it was in the name of beauty, then it was done.

The outcome was four women who looked red carpet-worthy. As they took tons of selfies and group photos, they would forever remember that for Chloe's wedding, they looked like beauty queens.

Even though Winter loved it, she wasn't interested in being primped to perfection again anytime soon.

She was more laid back in her style and preferred minimal makeup.

Full-fledged makeup was ok when the occasion called for it, but it wasn't her go-to for day-to-day.

Even still, she did look amazing. Her lavender dress was simple and elegant, and the silver, light studded shoes were a flawless touch.

Odd, though, the shoes fit a little snug. Taking them off and checking the size, she saw the eight printed inside the shoe label, plain as day. Shrugging it off, she figured maybe they would be okay after walking in them a bit.

By the time the wedding began, the heels Winter was wearing were killing her feet. They were evidently too small, and she found herself wincing with every step.

However, not wanting to create any issues on Chloe's special day or give Jessica a full-on aneurysm concerning one tiny detail being out of place, she decided to tough through it.

Besides, whose fault was it that this size eight fit her like a size six?

It's not like Jessica hadn't dropped off her dress and shoes and told her to try them on weeks before the wedding to make sure everything fit correctly.

Winter had tried on the dress, but got sidetracked and totally forgot about the shoes.

When Jessica checked back with her, she told her everything was fine, assuming it would be.

She was very wrong in her assumption.

Taking the walk down the aisle to stand in her designated position, Winter forced herself to smile through the stinging in her eyes as a tear threatened to roll down her face due to the extreme discomfort.

Not giving in to the pain, Winter gracefully made it to her position, managing to quash the impulse to yank off her shoes and throw them into the crowd.

She stood tall and proud, and just by looking at her, no one would ever know she was wearing size eight torture devices. To keep her mind off the matter, she mentally cursed the shoe company repeatedly.

However, when Chloe entered the room, Winter momentarily forgot about the pain.

Her friend looked gorgeous and very chic—like a flawless, golden brown doll created for the sole purpose of being admired.

Not a hair was out of place.

Chloe's high cheekbones, full lips and exotic light brown

eyes were the picture of perfection. Her classic look paired well with the timeless elegance that the entire theme displayed.

Winter couldn't help but hope that she, too, would know what it felt like to be a bride one day. Until then, she knew of no one more deserving of love than Chloe. Her heart swelled with happiness for her friend.

As Derek and Chloe read their wedding vows and made promises to love, cherish and honor one another, Winter was grateful to have such touching words to cover her tears because the pain of her feet was back at the forefront of her mind.

When the wedding was over and the reception was in full swing, all bets were off. Winter tossed the shoes aside and danced the night away. Mimicking Winter's display, Talia and Tina joined in, tossing their shoes to the side as well and jumping on the dance floor.

Even Jessica joined in on the dancing and abandoned her planner responsibilities when her favorite song came on.

Jessica and Chloe cleared the dance floor as they shook their asses and performed a fun dance routine they had come up with for the song.

The whole time, the crowd watched and cheered them on.

All and all, it was a really fun night, and just like the night before, Winter ended up tipsy. Thanks to the twins urging her to try a drink that they swore "didn't contain much alcohol."

Whether they were honest or deceptive in their attempts to include Winter in the good time they were having, she didn't know. However, after consuming two drinks, she was no longer sober.

Luckily, she was taking an Uber home, so she didn't have to worry about driving.

As the night came to an end and all the goodbyes were said, Chloe left for her honeymoon with Derek. Winter exited the building shortly after Chloe, hugging her friends goodbye and promising to text when she made it in.

When the Uber driver, Keith, she thinks that's what he said his name was, pulled up in front of her house, he looked back at her.

"Ma'am, do you need any help?"

"No, no," she said, waving his question aside. "I'm fine."

She pushed the door, which felt like it weighed a ton, open and stuck one wobbly leg out onto the ground.

She was no longer highly tipsy, but sober also wasn't an adequate description. When she was completely out of the car, she was surprised at how well she was standing.

Putting one foot in front of the other, she began what seemed like a long journey to her front door.

Continuing her left foot, right foot rhythm, Winter mentally cheered herself on. If she could keep her focus, she might make it to the door without falling flat on her face.

In what seemed like a far off distance behind her, she heard the Uber driver pull off.

Almost instantly, she regretted shifting her concentration even that slight bit. She put another foot forward and stepped onto the raised concrete that had been an eyesore on her walking path for years.

Too late to catch her balance, she stumbled forward and fell. She was grateful that on instinct, she had put her hands out. It provided a cushion to the fall, and all the weight was placed on her right hand.

Carefully, she got up and made it the rest of the way to the door. She was so tired, and all she wanted was to crawl into bed and sleep forever. Inside, she went to the bathroom and checked out her hand.

Besides the fact that it was really tender, it didn't look too bad. A few light scratches here and there that bled, but would likely not leave a scar.

Too tired to do much else, Winter typed out a quick "home now" text to her friends, wrapped a small cloth around her injured hand, and fell into bed.

Winter woke the next morning to banging.

What is that? And what will make it stop?

Turning over slowly and opening her eyes slightly to avoid letting in too much light, she looked at the clock. The display read 8:45am.

She had a terrible headache.

What was in that drink?

She was going to kill those damn twins the next time she saw them. She loved them like family, but she was still going to kill them.

Mentally, she thanked Chloe for having a wedding and reception on a Saturday. She most certainly couldn't go to work feeling like this. Having Sunday as a buffer to wind down from a wild night was exactly what she needed.

That and an ibuprofen, because in addition to the spinning in her head, Winter's right hand felt stiff and achy. She looked down at it, and the memory of her falling came back to her. Goodness, she felt awful.

BANG! BANG! BANG!

Then there was that. The loud, irritating noise. She sat up and almost toppled out of bed. Dragging herself to the window that faced the neighboring house, she peeked out of the blinds and immediately saw the culprit.

Workers were doing construction on the house that had been on the market for a few months now. Two guys were on the roof, and several others were unloading boxes and windows off of trucks.

If she wasn't feeling so yucky, she might have taken longer to enjoy the view. Almost all of them were wearing tanks and sporting arms that would make a girl want to ask for hugs in lieu of hellos.

BANG! BANG!

The guys on the roof were at it again. Making all that noise when a girl just needed some sleep.

Talia and Tina are already in for it. Adding the two roof guys to my kill list shouldn't be such a big deal.

Winter sighed.

May as well get the day started.

Possibly when she'd made herself a quick bite to eat and taken a pain pill, she would feel better.

Because, for now, a cup of coffee was the only thing that would keep her from murdering those damn men on the roof.

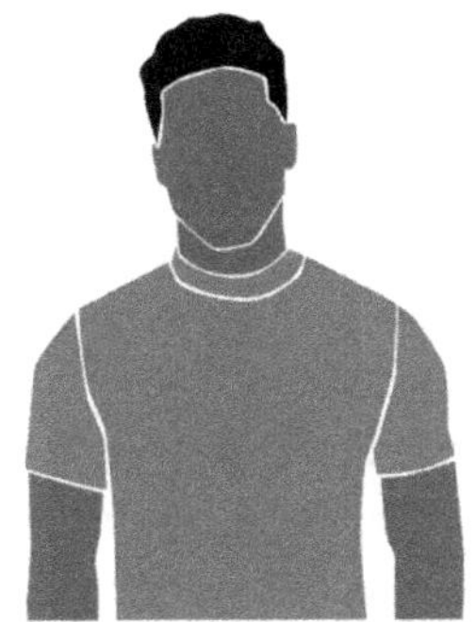

CHAPTER THREE

Kody

"THAT'S WHAT I LIKE TO HEAR."

Kody was in a good mood—an exceptionally good mood. This was to be expected when he began a new home renovation project, and with this house being almost a complete gut job, his exceptional mood would likely last all week.

Nothing against new construction homes because his company, Haven Construction, did handle contracts for both, but renovations were just somehow different.

Truth be told, they were the reason he started the company in the first place.

Something about seeing a home go from "waste" to "worth" really made him feel accomplished, which was a good thing because this current project would require his third move in six months.

Moving around that often was very inconvenient, but it was also rare, so he didn't mind. Usually, work within his company kept him in one state at least eight months at a time, instead of shorter intervals like he'd been experiencing lately.

Six months ago, he was in California, building a new community with his team. Four months into it, he had to relocate to Texas because one of his employees, Paul Dorsey, had gotten hurt on vacation skiing in Colorado.

Being one man down wasn't normally a big deal, as they

had enough employees to get the job done, but Paul was one of their managers, so Kody needed to step in to oversee a project until Paul came back.

Shortly after Paul returned, Kody got more bad news. Arlo Pereira, an employee at the Georgia location, was resigning. Arlo was moving back to Brazil to take care of his elderly parents that had gotten too sick to take care of themselves.

Kody hated to see him go. Arlo had been an invaluable member of his team for four years, but Kody fully understood the reasoning. Family was important, and he respected Arlo that much more for his decision.

However, it left a spot that needed to be filled, and who better to fill it than the boss himself?

Technically speaking, Haven Construction was a company he owned with his cousin and business partner, Jackson Knolls. But the idea of starting the company and the type of work they handled was his own.

Kody often thought back and wondered where the time went. What had started out as a small construction company in California ten years ago had grown quite considerably.

When Haven Construction first opened its doors, they were a ten-man crew, including the owners, Kody and Jackson, of course, and eight additional men to help them with projects.

Jackson handled most business management tasks, like acquiring new clients, putting in bids, contracts, etc. While Kody spent more time out in the field, participating in the actual labor and overseeing the team.

Things continued on this way for the first five years of the business, with changes made only to the crew as they had to slowly hire more guys to keep up with the workload.

As the sixth year rolled in, one of their California clients asked if they would be open to building a new single-family home community on the thirty acres of land he owned out in Texas.

Accepting the work while simultaneously building new clientele in Texas, work got so busy that Kody and Jackson decided to open a second location.

Two years later, new business was acquired in Georgia while Jackson was visiting Atlanta on vacation.

Long story short, after a year of hiring workers temporarily to handle the workload in Georgia, they landed five additional mega-sized contracts that prompted the need for a third location.

Now, with a branch in California, Texas, and Georgia, things were very busy. Each location employed a little over 75 construction workers full-time and had a full team of administrative staff.

It seemed the continuous word of mouth from their high-quality work had made the company take leaps and bounds that caused it to quickly expand, and with Kody and Jackson being such sagacious businessmen, they seized every opportunity. As a result, Haven Construction had become very successful.

In addition to the company's success, they'd made investments in stocks and some of the construction properties. They believed it was never smart to keep all of your financial eggs, so to speak, in one basket. Fortunately, that way of thinking paid off for them.

At this point in their lives, both men could easily stop working every day and become the types of CEOs who showed their faces solely to put out fires, sit in on meetings or randomly monitor staff.

But both men loved their work and employees too much to simply become a name behind a desk.

Therefore, Kody and Jackson continued to maintain their

respective roles in the company and worked interchangeably whenever the need arose.

Kody was no stranger to setting up contracts or taking the occasional business meeting, and Jackson was equally ready to throw on a hard hat and get his hands dirty whenever necessary. They made sure to stay heavily involved with what was happening within the company from day-to-day.

About two years ago, shortly after opening the Georgia location, Jackson decided to relocate from California to Georgia.

He wanted to keep an eye on how things were unfolding down there and help the process along. In full transparency, he didn't have to be there.

He didn't relocate to Texas when they opened that branch, and he handled most of his business for Haven Construction through email, conference calls and video chats.

In the rare instances, face-to-face meeting were necessary, he could easily catch a flight.

His real reason for relocating to Georgia was because he'd met Erica—a sassy, sweet beauty from Jamaica, he claimed, was the love of his life. They'd gotten married the previous year and couldn't be happier.

But Kody was single, and it was easy for him to move around. He enjoyed the travel and figured he'd stop doing it whenever it became too much.

He technically lived in California, but he was barely there. Much of the time, he was only there for a couple of hours, it seemed, to change clothes, shower and get some sleep.

When he was in Texas, he either stayed at hotels until the project was complete or stayed inside the actual renovation property if it was a long-term contract, deemed livable, and the investor agreed to it.

By staying at the renovation home, he was often able to get the work done faster so that the investor could get it sold.

He and his crew could work on the home Monday through Friday, and in the evenings or weekends, he would continue work on the house himself, tackling small projects like installing new fixtures or painting.

It just so happened that they'd gotten a new contract for a home renovation in Georgia, with the option to live in. With Arlo no longer on staff and it being Kody's favorite type of construction, he figured, why not?

It would be a nice change to be closer to Jackson and work on a live-in renovation property. However, he hadn't moved into the contracted property yet.

Instead, he was staying at a nearby hotel while they installed a new roof. If he finished the roof by Sunday, he planned to officially move into the property then.

He easily recognized the potential the house had to offer. It was a small ranch style home with three bedrooms and two baths located in a beautiful community in the Atlanta area.

Restaurants, apparel stores, food markets and banks were all within walking distance of the neighborhood.

Kody felt that he was really going to enjoy his time here. The people were hospitable, and the food was delicious. Although he hated eating out so much, as he truly did miss home cooking, it was an unwritten part of the job description that he made the best of.

Currently, he was sitting at a local restaurant called Quaint, waiting to meet with Jackson. They were going to talk over the details of the new property Kody was working on.

Quaint was a nice place that carried a retro vibe that made him think about something you would see on a 1970s sitcom. However, the colors were more vibrant, and the style of decor promoted a modern edge.

It housed red and gold booths and tables that provided a great view for customers to look out and take in the city.

Kody's eyes traveled to the family of four, a few booths ahead.

The man and woman, who he assumed were the mom and dad, were chasing a little girl who looked to be two around the table, while a little boy, slightly older, stared intently at the colorful images dancing energetically across his tablet screen.

It warmed Kody's heart to see a family together, enjoying one another. He wanted one day to have a family of his own, but he wasn't in a rush. If his parents had taught him anything, it was that good things come to those who wait.

He had been in love once, but nothing even close since. It certainly wasn't because he couldn't find anyone. He often approached (or was approached by) women that he didn't mind getting to know.

Yet regardless of who approached whom first, for one reason or another, it never panned out.

Maybe he was too picky, like all his friends accused him of, but in his mind, most of the women he met just didn't fit.

They always seemed to aim to be what they thought he wanted and didn't present him with much of a challenge.

Kody wanted a woman that had things going for herself and could keep him on his toes.

Falling for someone should be fun, enticing and real. So far, it just wasn't in the cards, but that was fine; he was patient and had no doubts that he would find her one day.

Until then, he poured all of his time and passion into his work. He asked himself questions to determine what would make each house stand out from all the rest.

For instance, what made things flow better in a home? What was most appealing? What features did families need?

Questions like these sparked a vision of what the completed home should look like. Then he would take care to include those special touches on his projects.

Such as a built-in nook for sitting and reading or staring

out the window. Mudrooms for families to unload all their outside accessories before entering the home, or a storage closet underneath the staircase.

Bottom line, anything that he felt helped to make a house a home.

Every home he worked on brought back memories of how life was growing up. He was an only child raised by what he liked to think of as the world's best parents.

His mom was a doctor, and his dad was a lawyer, and they gave him a wonderful life. The only thing that would have added the cherry on top would have been having a sibling to share all the great times with.

Luckily for him, where siblings were absent, Jackson was present. They were cousins, but acted more like brothers. They were ridiculously close and regularly at one another's house, having fun or fighting.

Which, of course, was to be expected of kids growing up.

Even still, despite a few hiccups over girls, sports or random other trivial reasons, they got along great. They enjoyed similar things, and that made for an easier bond. Both Kody and Jackson liked to work with their hands and build.

Unfortunately for Kody's parents, that meant the boys spent a great deal of time around the house breaking things in the name of fixing them.

Kody smiled to himself as he remembered how he and Jackson would shadow his dad, a natural handyman, wherever he went. They wanted to know how everything worked and cornered him with endless questions on the process.

But Kody's dad was a patient man. It was likely from his dad that Kody obtained his naturally calm and relaxed personality. His dad was not at all annoyed by the boys' curiosity.

He answered all their questions with care and enjoyment. He even explained the process in great detail and allowed them to perform some repairs if the job was simple and safe.

Kody and Jackson were amazed when they helped fix things. They'd run to Mrs. Benton and brag that they did the job on their own with no help from Mr. Benton. Always, she'd laugh and pretend to believe them.

The one difference between the two boys, which turned out to be a benefit, was that in addition to doing repairs, Jackson also enjoyed business. Learning how companies stayed afloat and made their money was an intriguing topic for him.

Quite naturally, after college, when Kody presented him with the idea of going into business together, Jackson jumped at the chance.

Kody's parents couldn't have been more proud that their two boys (as they always referred to them) had started a business together.

Sadly, a few years after the launch of Haven Construction, Kody lost his parents in a car accident. With Jackson having already lost his parents during his college years, he knew the sadness Kody faced all too well.

Kody's parents were like his own, so their absence didn't leave him unscathed. But as the saying goes, what doesn't kill you only makes you stronger, and their bond was proof of that.

The only family they had left was their grandmother, and they made it a point a few times a year to go out and visit her.

Not having much family made family a big deal to Kody, and he would do anything for them.

The cook interrupted Kody's thoughts when he hit the bell, informing the waitress that another order was ready for pickup.

Once she retrieved the tray, she turned to look at Kody and gave a flirtatious smile as she made her way to his table.

Placing it down in front of him, she asked if he needed anything else.

"No, I'm fine. Thank you," Kody said.

She gently placed a hand on his shoulder in an all too familiar way and said, "If you think of anything, *and I do mean anything,* just let me know."

Yeah, he knew what she meant alright, but he wasn't taking the bait. Instead, he gave her a responsive nod and left it at that.

He was used to women flirting with him. If he were younger, he would have invited her to his place and timed himself on how fast he could have gotten her underneath him.

But now, being thirty-two and having done a whole lot of living and learning, he was no longer interested in how many notches he could get on his bedpost.

Of course, he still liked sex; he loved it, actually, which was why it was all he cared about for most of his young adulthood.

Driving women insane from pleasure, giving them multiple orgasms and even having girls offer to do his work in college because they wanted one night with the talented Kody Benton.

His sexual reputation most certainly preceded him, and he loved it and what it did for his ego. He was probably just as addicted to the praise as the sex itself.

But it got old. It also got complicated because, more often, women would want a relationship, and he didn't. Eventually, when his narrow way of thinking caused him to lose out on someone special, he stopped living his life chasing skirts.

The time had finally come where the adrenaline rush of one-night stands or a rotation of "friends with benefits" no longer held his interests.

He wanted a woman that could offer him more, and from the obvious "please fuck me" vibes the waitress was giving him, he could tell she wasn't it.

When she stepped out of his line of vision to go check on another table, he saw Jackson standing there, smiling way too hard.

"If you need anything, and I do mean anything," Jackson said in a mocking, breathy tone.

They both started laughing, and Kody stood, pulling his cousin in for a hug.

"If it's not the man himself. How are you, Jackson?"

"I'm pretty good," Jackson said, taking his seat as Kody did the same. "Obviously, not as good as you," he added, nodding in the direction of the waitress.

Kody brushed the comment off. "Whatever, I'm starving," he said.

"Yeah, I could eat too," Jackson agreed. "I am obsessed with the pastries at this place. I used to come by here a few times a week just to grab one."

"And Erica is ok with that?" Kody asked, giving Jackson an unconvincing look.

Jackson had high cholesterol and was supposed to be trying to get it under control.

From what Kody knew from their last conversation, Jackson had made some progress in the right direction, but the numbers still weren't in the normal range.

"She isn't, but I don't tell her. Plus, you see that right there," Jackson said, pointing out the window.

Kody looked in the direction he pointed.

"Well, that big building there is called a hospital, and if anything happens, they can fix me up good as new."

"I don't think it's that simple, Jackson, and even though you may be my least favorite cousin, I think I'd like to keep you around."

Jackson smiled, but it didn't quite reach his eyes.

Adopting a more humorless tone, he said, "I know, but don't worry. Remember, I said I used to come by three times a week, now I'm down to only once a week. Baby steps, little cousin, baby steps."

Jackson regularly referred to Kody as "little cousin" even

though he was only eight months older than Kody. When they were kids, they would fight over Jackson's use of the word "little" when referring to Kody.

As they aged, Kody let it go and told Jackson that if he wanted to be known as the one between the two of them that would be arriving at senior status first, he could have it.

But he also realized that Jackson meant it in love. He always tried to protect Kody and look out for him, even though Kody had no problems looking out for himself.

"That's what I like to hear," Kody said. "Tell me, how is Erica?"

"She's good. She told me to give you a kiss for her, which you know damn well I will not do. But mostly, she sends her love and wants you to know she still hasn't stopped trying to find a woman to marry you off to."

Kody chuckled. "Yup, that's Erica."

Erica was constantly pushing Kody to get married and start a family. At one point, he attempted to appease her by going out on a date with a friend of hers named Michelle, who lived in California.

They seemed to hit it off in the beginning, but after a couple of months, it was clear they were not a good match. Michelle was attractive, highly educated, goal-driven and confident.

He loved those things about her, but at the same time, she was a little too serious for him. Activities such as board games, bowling or playing laser tag didn't interest her.

She more so liked dates that were, as she would call it, "fancy." Couples cooking classes, museums and broadway plays were more her style.

Even though he didn't mind dates like that, he also enjoyed fun. No holds barred, kid at heart, friendly, competitive fun.

Kody and Jackson continued catching up while Kody ate

his meal. When he was done, he sat back in the chair, ready to get down to business.

"Let's talk about this new renovation I'm working on," Kody said.

"First, here's your copy of the complete file on the property," Jackson said. He passed Kody a folder with several documents inside. "Of course, I still have to get permits for the additions you want, but that file contains the whole project in a nutshell."

"Great," Kody said, tucking the folder into the work bag he brought in with him. "I'll look over the file later, as I already know the basics. Such as the fact that it's a seven-month contract, and he is fine with me living on site during the process. Is there anything else I need to know?"

"Not really. It's pretty straightforward, just like all the other renovations we do. I know you've already started work on it. What did you think of it?"

"It's promising. Structurally sound and in a nice neighborhood. According to the report you emailed to me, I see that it was built in the early 50s, and a lot of the features are original to the home. It's going to need the expected things, new windows, roof, flooring, plumbing, etc. Also, I think I will remove some walls to redesign the layout, giving it the more in-demand, open concept look. The good news is, we will be finished with the roof soon and then I think it will be fine for me to move into the house while the crew and I work on the rest."

Jackson gave a sly grin, and Kody knew what was coming next.

"That's good. You've had to do two giant moves these last six months. Sounds like this project would be ideal for you. At least you'd be in the same location for the rest of the year, and who knows, maybe you'll decide to stay permanently," Jackson said.

He was always hinting at Kody spending most of his time in Georgia because he lived there. The problem was, Kody enjoyed working with the different teams and changing up his surroundings.

However, Kody had to admit the idea sounded wonderful. Slow down his travel for a while and restore some permanent order to his life. He really should think about it.

As for now, he had a hopeful Jackson staring him down. He never liked to just flat out say no to Jackson. So he opted for the easy response and said, "we will see."

Jackson seemed about to say something more, but decided against it. He'd broach the subject again soon enough, Kody was sure of it.

Instead, Jackson picked up a menu and grinned mischievously. "I think the waitress that's been eyeing you needs an excuse to come over." He raised his hand and said, "Miss, I'm ready to order."

"MAYBE YOUR PUSSY IS BROKEN OR SOMETHING?"

Work on Monday morning was exactly as Winter expected, busy. As she pulled in to her reserved spot, she saw all the usual foot traffic cluttering the parking lot.

The big sign above the building that read "Movie Box Studios" was displayed in tall, bold, yellow letters.

She still remembered how she felt the first time she saw it. Nervous, unsure, and thrilled about the possibility of landing her dream job.

On the day of her interview, she sat in her car for over thirty minutes, practicing what she would say to the expected questions:

Why should we hire you? Where do you see yourself in five years? Why did you leave your last position?

They were all on her list, and she was ready to impress with her well-rehearsed answers.

However, Mr. Cordell Sanders, a 65-year-old untraditional, warm, welcoming, downright country boy to the core and the owner of Movie Box Studios, didn't ask her any of that.

Instead, after their initial introduction, he looked at her and said, "Would you like to see a movie?"

She spent the next few hours watching the setting up and

filming of movies from various genres. She was so taken by everything as she watched scenes from romance to comedy come to life before her eyes.

Somewhere around the seventh setup, Mr. Sanders turned to her and said, "you're hired."

Winter was shocked. Didn't he need to know things? What if she couldn't meet all the demands he had? Seeing her expression at his offer, he laughed.

"Don't worry, Winter, I looked over your resume. Combine that with the genuine excitement and passion I see in your eyes, you're a perfect fit. You don't need to know everything right off the bat for this position. It's a learn as you go. And from what I can tell about you, you're going to go far."

Surprisingly, he was right. Winter dove into her new position as a Prop Master and never looked back.

Now, seven years later, she still loved this place and all the high energy it brought with it.

Upon entering the building, she was almost knocked over by a person pushing a rack of clothes. At the last minute, she took a step back and thankfully avoided the collision.

Yelling on their headset to someone named Terri, they didn't even notice that they almost knocked someone over.

Winter just shook her head and started yet again for her office. About halfway there, her assistant of five years, Lisa Chan, fell into step with her.

Lisa was an Asian woman in her late 20s who was single and had no kids.

She was more Americanized than her parents, and she made it known that she preferred it that way, by often referring to their way of living as "perfect for them but too old school for her."

She was a funny girl, who Winter loved because of the honest and sarcastic tone she brought to the office.

Her humorous personality was actually quite fitting because, minus the glasses, Lisa bore a close resemblance to the famous comedian Ali Wong. Her dry humor was one of the things Winter liked most about her upon their first meeting, and now, Winter didn't think she could survive without her amazing assistant.

"How was the wedding? I'm still mad I wasn't able to make it," Lisa said.

"It's fine. Chloe completely understood that someone had to hold down the fort while I was away. I do have tons of pictures I'll be sure to share with you. It turned out just as beautiful and flawless as Chloe hoped for."

"That's nice. Chloe deserves it. Did she enjoy my gift?"

"I'm not sure she even had a chance to look at it yet, but I think it's safe to say a box full of sex gadgets is always a welcomed gift."

"I do aim to please," Lisa said, proud of herself.

"And that you do," Winter responded. "Speaking of, what's going on with the vendor for that horror movie we started last week?"

"You mean that weird movie about the serial killer who keeps killing people, thinking he is really killing himself each time?"

"Yeah, that one."

"Annoying! Our prop vendor is at it again. He claims that they don't have twenty out of our thirty requested items in stock. He is always pulling this shit. What directive do you want me to take?" Lisa asked excitedly. She loved being able to lay down the law with the vendors.

"Call their main line, using the phone in the back office. The caller ID for it doesn't reflect Movie Box Studios. Ask for Vincent and then ask him about some of those items. If he says they are not available, setup a phone meeting for me with his boss at 4 o'clock. They can't keep pulling this and expect to keep our business. I have several companies lined up that would be kissing our ass to get the contract to work with us."

"What if he says they are in stock?" Lisa said. "What directive do you want me to take?"

"I still want the meeting, but I'd like to hear Vincent's answer first."

Shooting Winter a quick glance as they kept up the pace, Lisa asked, "I'm just making sure we are on the same page here. If you plan to do the meeting, anyway, why see what Vincent has to say?"

"Because Vincent gets paid off commission to get contracts with new companies. There are rumors that he holds back inventory to entice new companies to signup so he can get a bigger payout. I need to know if these items are in stock or not, and Vincent is my way to that answer."

"That's what I thought. Okay, I'll get right on it. Anything else you need from me before I go play detective chick?"

"Nope, I think I'm good. Oh, wait," Winter said, stopping and turning to Lisa. "Get me a list of the next ten scenes that need to be—"

"Already completed and on your desk," Lisa cut in.

"Of course it is. Have I told you that you are the best assistant in the world today?"

"Nope, but save your words. I like my praises in cash bonuses."

"Will do," Winter said, entering her office.

She took off her jacket and sat in her chair. As per their conversation, Lisa left the next series of scenes that needed to be prepped on Winter's desk and a bagel from Winter's favorite cafe.

Winter ate the bagel while checking emails. After replying to all the necessary ones, she started creating her checklist for the upcoming scenes, ensuring that all the requested inventory was onsite and in proper condition.

After finishing the sixth scene checklist, an alert popped up on her computer. It read "PATT" and stood for a movie called "Pulling at the Threads."

It was about a quirky guy who finally snaps after he walks in on his wife cheating. He kills the guy in cold blood and then holds his wife hostage in the basement so that she isn't able to tell the police.

Winter didn't often sit in on the scenes, although she was welcome to. However, this movie really piqued her interest. After reading the script and creating the prop list for it, she fell in love.

Today the scene they were filming was the cheating pair having sex—as they were enjoying the aftermath, the husband walks in, sees them in the bed naked and loses his shit.

Winter made it to the area just as filming began. As she watched the intimacy play out for the cameras, she was drawn in.

Never in her own life had she ever had sex that ranked anywhere close to the level of what this scene was portraying.

The gasping, the uncontrollable moans and whimpers, it all had to be fake. And not just fake because it was a movie, fake because women didn't respond like that... did they?

Her sex with guys was always, what was the word...basic—no fireworks, no uncontrollable screaming and sadly, but most shockingly, no orgasms.

The no orgasms part was a total shocker to Jessica and Chloe.

"*Never?*" she remembered Chloe and Jessica exclaim.

"*Yikes,*" Chloe added in a sad tone. "*Maybe your pussy is broken or something.*"

At the time, Winter recalled attempting to laugh at Chloe's joke meant to lighten the mood, but mostly, it just hurt. Not because of the words Chloe said, but the fact that it was probably true.

Something had to be wrong with her, right?

Not having an orgasm from sex meant she had issues. Expectantly, Winter had tried different positions and, of course, had different partners. Still nothing. To date, all of her orgasms came from self-pleasure, and she feared it would always remain that way.

The whole thing truly baffled her because it wasn't as if sex itself felt bad. More times than not, the guy would bring her to the edge, but her body just never took the leap.

Even still, she held out hope that one day it would happen for her. She didn't want to simply believe this was as good as sex was going to get.

Winter resumed watching and enjoying the rest of the scene until she heard someone shout, "That's a wrap for today."

Winter returned to her office to finish the scenes list she had been working on. There were several scenes left, but unlike the first, these wouldn't be simple. She let out a deep breath, pulled up her inventory list and got to it.

Around an hour later, Lisa popped her head in and reminded Winter about the 4 o'clock meeting. She also confirmed that Vincent was lying about inventory availability all along.

Winter thanked Lisa for the update and prepared for her call.

The meeting only took about twenty minutes, and by the end of it, the owner was very apologetic and promised to deal with the Vincent issue. He also offered them a free year of service as a way of apologizing for any inconvenience, hoping to keep their business.

Winter accepted the deal, but would be looking elsewhere once the contract was over. There was no way she would stay with a company that had this much drama, but in the meantime, not having to pay a fee would be nice for Movie Box's budget.

She didn't finish with the last scene on her list until 10pm. Afterward, she was so tired she could barely keep her eyes open on the ride home.

The rest of the week was more of the same—late nights and early mornings.

When Friday arrived, all she wanted to do was rush home, shower, and turn on HGTV.

It was one of her favorite background noise shows. She didn't have to focus to know what was going on, but could always look up and be current on what was coming next.

She loved the big reveals. The homes were like Cinderella stories, arriving from rags to riches in a matter of weeks. She sat down with a turkey sandwich and stared at the TV.

Traditional or open concept?

That was always the question. And 95% of the time, the answer was the latter. Struggling to keep her eyes open, she waited through all the demolition issues and budget problems for her favorite part, but ended up falling asleep before the glamorous home makeover was uncovered.

Her ringing phone woke her up the next morning.

"Hey, Winter. I'll be there in about an hour," Chloe said on the other end.

Sitting up on the couch, it had totally slipped her mind that weeks before Chloe's wedding, they had planned to spend the day together when Chloe returned from her honeymoon.

Her husband, Derek, had an important business meeting in New York that he had to attend, so they'd set up a quick four-day getaway to Jamaica and would do a longer honeymoon later.

"Umm, great. I'll see you then," Winter said as she rushed to get cleaned up and into the kitchen to start breakfast.

When Chloe arrived, Winter had just finished putting

their plates on the table. Chloe plopped down in the kitchen chair that was closest to the window and squinted her eyes.

"You forgot, didn't you?"

"No, I... yeah, I forgot," Winter said, abandoning the lie. "How'd you know?"

"Because your shirt is inside out."

Winter looked down to see that Chloe was right. Taking a seat at the table, she said, "Ugh, I'm sorry, Chloe."

"It's fine. I forgot too until I got home after our honeymoon on Thursday. I was sad because Derek had to leave immediately, but then I remembered I get to spend time with you, and I had something to look forward to."

"Glad I could help," Winter said, pouring on the syrup. "So, tell me, beyond missing Derek, how's married life treating you? Any fun new changes?"

"Not really. Since we were already living together before getting married, nothing much has changed, just my last name. But I will say I love being Mrs. James."

Winter smiled at her friend, and they carried on eating their breakfast with minimal small talk.

The banging on the house next door prompted Chloe to look out the window. Done with their food, Winter got up to put the dishes in the sink and returned to wipe off the kitchen table.

"Oh wow, is someone finally buying the house next door?" Chloe asked.

"I'm not sure. I hope so. It would be great to see that house fixed up and have someone permanently live there instead of renters. It's such a nice neighborhood. I hope that a nice family moves in."

"Uh-huh," Chloe said, only half-listening. "That or some sexy single man that can have a warm Winter," Chloe teased.

"You are so silly. I think you have higher hopes for my sex life than I do."

"You're probably right and with good reason, girl. Have you seen all of this visual sexiness laid out next door?"

Chloe was all but glued to Winter's kitchen window.

"Chloe, do you need a leash? You can't be looking at other men; you are newly married."

"I'm married, not dead. My heart may be tied down to Derek, but my eyes are free to roam. I'm just enjoying the view. What's wrong with that? It's like being married to a young, sexy Denzel, but you aren't just going to ignore a naked Idris Elba strutting by, are you?"

"I guess not," Winter said, laughing and hitting Chloe with the dishtowel.

"Seriously, girl, come and see the feast for the eyes I'm looking at. Half of them are shirtless, and even their six-packs got six-packs. Good Lord!"

Winter rolled her eyes and took a glance out of the window. True, those bodies at work were a sight to see. If she hadn't had so much on her mind and been in a different mindset concerning dating or men in general, she might have enjoyed the view a little longer.

"Yeah, they are sexy," she hummed. "But a sexy guy is not at the top of my list right now. I have tons of other things to do."

"Well, you need to pencil that in, sweetie. Didn't you tell me a few weeks ago you were having some plumbing issues? Maybe one of them can plumb all your pipes," Chloe said, lifting a suggestive eyebrow.

"You are so bad! And no, thank you, I am good. Yes, it's been a while, but I don't need to pick up random guys."

"Winter, please, you might as well before you become a virgin again."

Shaking her head and pointing a finger at Chloe, Winter said, "Chloe, stop it. You're not pimping me out for your entertainment."

"Okay, fine. Let's just talk about something else."

"Finish telling me about the honeymoon. Were you in total bliss the entire time?"

Shifting away from the window to face Winter completely, Chloe placed her hand on her chest, smiled and closed her eyes.

"It was beautiful, Winter. White sandy beaches, beautiful weather, endless drinks, sex until I was dizzy and precious time with my love. I couldn't have asked for anything better."

"Aww, Chloe, that sounds so nice."

"Yeah." Chloe's shoulder's slumped, and she looked down at the table. "I never thought I would love a guy as much as Reggie, but Derek made his way into my heart."

Reginald, or Reggie as he was referred to, was Chloe's high school sweetheart, that she dated through college.

Everyone was sure they would always be together, but when Reggie got offered an out-of-state job opportunity and asked Chloe to marry him, she declined.

Although she loved Reggie with all her heart, she simply wasn't ready to be married or leave her family and friends.

Sadly, they went their separate ways, and to Winter's knowledge, they hadn't spoken for close to ten years.

Chloe was really broken up over him, but eventually, she started dating again, and five years after her breakup with Reggie, she met Derek.

Chloe continued on. "After I caught Derek cheating that first year we were together, I couldn't have imagined I would have stayed with him, let alone marry him, but that was four years ago, and I do love him. He was also very sincere in his apology and I trust that it won't happen again."

Covering Chloe's hand with her own, Winter said, "I am so happy to hear that. All you can do is follow your heart, and as long as he is making you happy, he can keep both his legs."

They laughed and moved their conversation to the living

room. After a few hours of watching movies and having a light lunch, Chloe helped Winter do some sanding on a nightstand she'd found while antique shopping.

Winter was planning on restoring it, adding some modern touches, and then donating it to a local women's shelter.

By 9:15, they said their goodbyes, and Winter figured she'd go grab some dinner from a nearby Thai place she loved.

After picking up her food, Winter walked back to her car through the almost deserted parking lot. The aroma of rice seasoned with bell peppers, basil and onions, were calling out to her. She couldn't wait to get home and devour it.

At her vehicle, she reached inside her purse to grab her keys, and a small jolt of pain reminded her of the fall she took last week. Overall, her hand was a lot better and only hurt when she pressed it against something.

Taking a second to examine it, Winter was grateful that everything looked fine. None of the cuts had reopened. She simply needed to be careful.

Reaching back inside her purse, more cautiously this time, she located her keys and pulled them out.

She heard the footsteps behind her only moments before his hand covered her mouth and his knife dug into her throat.

CHAPTER FIVE
Winter

"I'M GOING TO
KILL YOU!"

Winter was terrified. In her sudden surprise, she dropped the food and gasped.

The guy leaned forward towards her ear and, in a low, threatening voice, said, "Remove your purse and slowly pass it back to me."

This isn't happening. Not now, not here, not like this.

Winter could feel her racing heart thudding against her chest and a horrified scream clawing its way out.

Squeezing her eyes shut, she was able to push it back down.

She had to stay calm and think. Using the hand that didn't have her keys, she grabbed her purse and passed it behind to him.

Still not loosening his hold on the cold, sharp blade, he snatched the purse out of her hand.

His sudden movement made her jump slightly, but she stiffened again as the pressure of the blade reminded her that her blood could soon be covering the pavement.

Too afraid to swallow or even breathe, Winter clutched her keys tighter in her hand, hoping he didn't notice she was still holding them. If she could just stop her thoughts from racing, maybe she could think of a way to use them.

"Easy now, little lady, what's your name?" the man asked in a tone that made her skin crawl.

The pungent smell of alcohol on his breath made her feel sick to her stomach.

"Winter," she said quietly. "Please, don't hurt me. You can take my purse and go on about your business. I won't call the cops or anything."

She meant every word. If he left her alone, she would just be thankful to be alive and leave the cops out of it.

Ignoring her request, he said, "Winter? Like the season? Now, that's funny." He laughed out loud for a few seconds and then stopped abruptly. "But maybe it's my lucky night because I've always loved winter."

The man pressed his body harder against hers and licked the side of her neck. Winter held back a scream and fought the urge to vomit.

"How would you like to turn around real slow and let me get a good look at you, little Winter?"

It wasn't a question, and she knew it. He removed the knife from her throat and then placed the sharp point at her side.

This is my chance. There is no way this bastard is going to rub his grimy hands on me. Maybe I can't beat him, but I certainly won't make it easy.

Singling out one key on the ring, she positioned it forward and held it tight. Turning around, she quickly sidestepped to get out of direct range of the knife at her side and then stabbed at his face with the key, using all the force she could muster.

Although it was all a blur, she could tell when she made contact. The man screamed, and she heard, rather than saw, what must have been the contents of her purse spill out onto the ground.

She hoped like hell he had dropped the knife, also.

Not wasting any time, she ran.

"You bitch. I'm going to fucking kill you!" the man yelled.

Winter only got a few feet before the guy was on her. He was fast. A lot faster than she expected him to be.

In one powerful push, he knocked her to the ground and flipped her onto her back.

Refusing to give up, Winter fought hard; punching, kicking and screaming. Some of her blows landed, but it seemed none of them were making an impact; however, that changed when she struck his face.

Immediately, he started swearing and grunting more death threats.

The goal was to hit him in the face again, but obviously knowing what her plans were, the attacker blocked them.

She could not think of a way to escape, and a paralyzing fear threatened to overtake her.

This can't be how it ends for me.

Another wave of panic gave her a new drive, and she kneed him, trying to bite his hand, all the while twisting and turning in an attempt to break his hold and keep him from pinning her down.

Unfortunately, it didn't work; he was bigger, stronger and a lot angrier. Against her best attempts, the attacker finally climbed on top of her, placing a sweaty hand over her mouth.

"You are going to pay for what you did," the guy snarled.

Winter saw his raised fist in the air and tears stung her eyes. There was nothing more she could do. At this point, she could barely breathe, let alone move.

Closing her eyes, she braced herself for the impact.

But the hit never came. Instead, the weight of the man was instantly lifted off of her.

Opening her eyes, Winter saw what looked to be a super-hero handling her crazed attacker like a rag doll. He punched the robber in the face multiple times before releasing him.

The enraged attacker staggered back and spat on the ground.

"Kiss your life goodbye, asshole," he said, charging at the guy that Winter now considered her hero.

The robber threw a punch that the hero ducked to avoid. Then, just as quickly, the hero delivered another forceful blow of his own, that landed on the attacker's side.

Moving unsteadily, the robber let out a groan of pain as he reached down to pick up an object.

It was the knife.

Winter spotted the glint of the weapon in the shadows as the man raised it.

"Watch out! He's got a knife," she yelled.

The man sprung forward with the knife extended, but the hero sidestepped, half turned, then connected his fist with the attacker's face.

Winter heard the knife hit the ground seconds before the guy did. Howling in pain and grasping at the side of his head, he rolled over out of the path of the man towering above him.

Clumsily he got to his feet, but this time, instead of running toward Winter's hero, he turned and ran off.

Winter sat there stunned, staring in the man's direction as he disappeared into bushes. Everything happened so fast she couldn't help but wonder if it was really over.

She half expected the attacker to suddenly reappear and come charging again.

The hero came closer to her and said something. The problem was, although his mouth was moving, Winter's brain was having trouble catching up.

Suddenly, after shaking her head to clear the fog, all sound flooded in.

"Are you ok?" he asked, offering his hand.

"Yes," she answered shakily, the panic slowly retreating.

Taking his hand and rising to her feet, Winter could feel

soreness in her legs and back. Nevertheless, that was the least of her issues. Her mental state was probably way more affected than her physical.

"Thank you so much," she said, wiping at her clothes and trying to calm her nerves. "It all happened so fast. I don't know what I would have done if you hadn't shown up."

Now that the immediate danger was over, Winter feared she might start crying. Not wanting to embarrass herself, she closed her eyes and took a deep breath.

The guy smiled and tilted her face up. He must have been examining her for wounds, she assumed, and that's when she got a good look at him.

Well, hello handsome!

This man made the saying "tall, dark and handsome" a mouthwatering reality. He had broad shoulders and seemed to be almost a foot taller than her.

His beautiful brown complexion and almond-shaped dark brown eyes made Winter feel like she could get lost in them. That was until her eyes found his lips; full, soft and inviting.

As he slowly turned her face from one side to the other, she felt her racing pulse calm. The gentle touch of his big, powerful hands somehow helped her feel better every second that he remained in contact.

"Perfect," he finally said. It was odd, but Winter somehow got the feeling that he was talking about more than her being free of scrapes and bruises. "I don't see any marks on your face, although this isn't the best lighting. Are you positive you are okay? If you need an ambulance—"

"No," Winter said abruptly. She did not like hospitals and avoided them like the plague. "I'm fine. I think I'm more shaken up than anything else."

"We should at least call the police," he said, pulling out his phone.

"No, seriously, I'm fine. I just want to get home. I don't

want to spend all night being asked questions I barely have the answers to. I didn't even get a good look at the guy, and he's gone now," she said, gesturing in the direction the guy had run off.

When she looked at him again, she expected to find pity in his eyes, but instead, she was met with compassion and understanding.

"I'm Kody Benton," he said, offering her his hand for the second time that night.

"Winter Daniels," she replied, allowing her hand to slide into his. His already familiar touch was delicate and careful.

Winter couldn't help but notice how small her hand was inside of his. It was weird, she'd just met him, but he made her feel so comfortable and safe.

Reluctantly, she let go of his hand.

"It's nice to meet you, Winter. Although I wish it would have been under better circumstances."

"Me too. But..." she shrugged off the rest of her sentence. "Do you live around here?"

"No, I don't. I'm just here for a few months, taking care of some things for work."

Of course, he isn't local. He is extremely handsome, respectful, and I'm drawn to him. Fate wouldn't be that kind. The guy who'd basically hit me over the head and run was the local guy!

"Let me help you get your things," Kody said.

Winter turned to see her purse and its contents scattered around. Fortunately for her, her purse was small, and she never carried much in it.

She retrieved the small red and gold purse while Kody picked up her wallet, a pack of gum and a tube of lip gloss. Glancing around for her keys, she spotted them a few feet away.

After collecting everything, they walked towards her car

and noticed her bag of food. She picked it up and placed it in the trashcan. Her appetite was completely gone.

Returning to her car, Winter looked up at him. For a moment, they just stared at one another as if they both wanted to say something but couldn't find the words.

Being near him helped her feel less afraid and vulnerable. Honestly, Winter didn't want that feeling to end, but she knew it had to. It was time to go home.

Would be nice if he could come with me.

The thought was insane. She didn't know this man. Maybe she'd hit her head a lot harder than she originally thought.

Winter gave him a grateful smile. "It looks like I have everything. I wish there was some way I could thank you."

"No thanks needed, Winter. I'm glad I was here."

Dammit, even the way he said my name was sexy.

Reaching into his pocket, Kody pulled out his wallet and gave her his card. "In case you need anything," he said.

Taking the card, Winter slid behind the wheel and Kody, not just a hero but a gentleman, obviously, closed her door and stepped back.

Winter buckled up, turned on the engine, and backed out of the parking lot. As she was driving away, she saw him in her review mirror, heading towards his vehicle.

By the time Winter got home, her shaking had returned. In an attempt to calm her body and mind from replaying what she thought were her last moments on earth, she took a long, hot shower and then made some tea.

When the combo of the shower and tea didn't do the

trick, Winter considered calling Jessica or Chloe, but instantly decided against it.

She didn't want any pity or consoling, at least not right now, because it was too fresh. Speaking about it aloud would only make it all too real once again, and she would probably start crying. She didn't want that.

Then there was Kody, the man that not only rescued her but seemed to draw her in. But just like the thoughts from the attack, she had to push thoughts of him out of her mind, too. He'd told her himself, he was only passing through.

She'd done the whole fitting a guy into her life thing through long-distance and never again.

Wanting him like crazy or not, she would not be bamboozled by fate or play with fire because that is exactly what Kody Benton was—a sexy, tall, masculine, hard-bodied ball of fire.

She had to stop this! Maybe it was just some twisted complex, like the nightingale effect or hero worship. Her feelings for him were likely solely based on him saving her life.

Didn't books about surviving horrible events say that was a thing?

For now, she would chalk it up to that. Her feelings were just responses to almost dying and being grateful to him.

Then she thought of his lips and how his touch calmed her and knew she was lying to herself.

Regardless, she wasn't going to call him. She didn't need a man to survive this; she just needed time—time and sleep.

But her solution was short-lived because sleep offered no relief. She tossed and turned all night and kept replaying the assault in her mind.

She abandoned the idea of getting any sleep around 5 a.m. after she had woke for the third time touching her fingers to her neck where just moments ago in the dream the blade had been.

Climbing out of bed, she went to the kitchen and started

her coffee maker. While the water was boiling, she went to the living room and switched the TV on. It was still on HGTV, and a home renovation show was just beginning.

The choice between spending the next few hours enjoying one of her favorite shows or going back to bed to battle nightmares was an easy one.

Home renovation fantasies to escape my scary reality, it is.

Arriving at work on Monday, Winter was greeted by the expected hustle and bustle she'd grown accustomed to. Being surrounded by it felt like she was being embraced by a much-needed hug of normalcy from life.

"Hey," Lisa said, approaching Winter right before she opened her office door. "Julius Davenport is waiting for you in there."

"Really? Why?" Winter asked, taking a few steps away from the door as to not be overheard. "I thought his contract was all set and he'd signed off on it."

Julius was a film director in his late 60s who rented spaces at Movie Box Studios.

"Beats me," Lisa said with a shrug. "All I know is, he came in this morning and said he had a couple more things to go over and needed to speak with you."

"Alright, thanks."

Upon entering her office, she saw Mr. Davenport sitting in one of her guest chairs with his legs crossed.

"Good Morning," she said, approaching him with her hand extended. "It's good to see you. Forgive me, but I thought we finalized everything for your space rental. I hope there aren't any issues?"

"No, no issues at all. I just have a few questions."

"That's fine. Let me grab a copy of your contract."

Locating his contract in the filing cabinet, Winter sat down in the chair adjacent to his.

"Alright, Mr. Davenport, what are your questions?"

"I was wondering how many hours we would have the space for?"

Looking puzzled, she said. "As you can see, your requested time for filming rental is listed on line eight."

"Oh. I see," he said, looking down at the line she was pointing to.

"Well," he said, as if in search of something else to say. "How long are the terms for our space rental?"

Now she was completely confused. Not only was he given a copy of the contract, he definitely knew the terms of it. They'd went over it several times in great detail, as he was very specific about the timing and amount of space he would need.

"It's right here on line two. You requested fourteen months, and we agreed to the terms for a set price."

"Wow, you're right, there it is." Mr. Davenport released a weak laugh. "For some reason, I guess I thought we had agreed on a shorter period."

"No. Everything was fine with what you needed." Going out on a limb, she asked, "Mr. Davenport, is everything okay?"

He looked up at her. "I guess I better stop while I'm ahead, since I'm probably making a fool of myself."

"What do you mean?"

"To be honest with you, I wanted to ask you out on a date. I didn't know how to broach the subject, so I came up with this dumb excuse about having contract issues to discuss."

"Oh wow, Mr. Davenport, I'm flattered. Really, I am, but I don't date my clients."

"I figured as much," he said. "But I had to try. You're a

beautiful woman, and I think I'd regret it if I didn't say something. I'm sorry for putting you on the spot."

He was a nice man, and she hated hurting his feelings, but she and him... not going to happen.

"No problem," Winter said. "Please let me know if you have any issues with your contract."

Standing to leave, he said, "I will. You be sure to let me know if your dating rule ever changes."

Winter smiled, and he left. No less than five minutes later, Lisa popped her head in the open doorway.

"What did Mr. Davenport want? You need me to make changes to anything?"

"No, everything is fine. Actually, he wanted to ask me out on a date."

"Eww," Lisa said, making a sour face. "He's in his 60s and not the good kind."

"The good kind?" Winter asked in confusion.

"You know how some men make aging look like art? They get more sexy and distinguished as they mature. I've seen men in their sixties with bodies like 30-year-olds. Mr. Davenport is the old school looking sixty. You can see his age coming from a mile away."

Winter laughed. "He's a sweet old guy. I let him down easy."

Lisa rolled her eyes. "Better you than me," she said, then walked away.

Shaking her head, Winter logged into her computer and got to work, but Kody was a recurring thought throughout the day.

I wonder what he's doing? Was he thinking of me? Maybe I should just called him?

Sparing a glance at her purse, where Kody's card was safely tucked inside, Winter shook her head. She'd come too far on this dating break to just throw in the towel.

Yes, Kody may have been handsome, polite and possessed a magical touch, but despite his alluring qualities, getting involved with him was a trap. The man already came with distance issues.

Better leave well enough alone.

Winter completed her workday and was home by six. Wanting to keep busy, she got started again on the nightstand. It was going to be a beautiful piece.

Sometimes after updating the items she found when antiquing, she kept, others were sold or donated.

Since the nightstand would be donated, Winter wanted it to look extra special. The plan was to paint it gray and replace the drawer handles with crystal knobs. She was excited to see it complete and knew the women at the shelter would love it.

Winter continued working on it a little while longer before calling it a night.

After eating a plate of leftover spaghetti with two glasses of wine, she slept a whole lot better than she had the night before.

The next morning, she felt refreshed. It seemed a long day's work and two glasses of wine did wonders for promoting sleep.

Instead of waking up from images of fear from her scary encounter, Winter wished she stayed asleep and enjoyed her explicit sex dream she'd had of Kody.

In the dream, they were back in the parking lot. After a reenactment of the heroic rescue, Kody helped her to her feet and kissed her.

Unable to control the desire they both had, he put her on the hood of her car, ripped off her clothes, and she started helping him unzip his pants. Right before he pulled them down, her alarm went off.

"Fucking hell!" she shouted when she realized it was a dream.

She stared up at the ceiling, feeling very annoyed that her dreams of Kody were going to be nothing more.

Calling him is a mistake.

The mental reminder was just what she needed. Screw the attraction or the feeling that he somehow belonged in her life. He wasn't here to stay. Not to mention he was probably already in a relationship.

A guy that looked like him had to have a girlfriend or even a wife.

Just let it go and move on.

She still had his card, but refused to look at it. If she did, her heart would betray her and commit his number to memory, making her attempt to toss the card nothing more than a pointless action.

However, she needed to get rid of it. Grabbing her purse from the nightstand, Winter blindly reached around in it until she located the thick, squared shape and pulled it out.

Leaving nothing to chance, Winter closed her eyes and tore it up. Her heart was calling her stupid, but she pushed on. She wasn't going to call him, so why keep the card?

It was too risky. Undoubtedly, a weak moment would occur and she'd give in.

I have to be smart and protect my heart. Kody already said he was simply passing through. Surely, if he is really meant to be, fate will figure out something else.

Reluctantly, Winter got out of bed, walked into the bathroom and flushed the pieces down the toilet because she did not trust putting them in the trash can.

She realized with the pipe issues she'd been having, flushing a card (even one in tons of tiny pieces) was probably an idiotic move, but the deed was done now.

She couldn't take it back. Although a part of her wished she could, she knew it was for the best.

After showering, brushing her teeth and styling her hair in

an updo with a few long loose curls left to hang down, Winter went to the kitchen and started a pot of coffee.

Walking into her closet, she took a moment to find something to wear. Deciding on a light gray skirt suit, with a yellow blouse, she got dressed. Midway through, her phone rang.

"There is drama on one of the sets. What's your ETA?" Lisa said.

"I'm about to head out in a few minutes." She was buttoning up her shirt and tucking it into her skirt. Grabbing her suit jacket, she asked, "What's wrong?"

"They were filming a bedroom scene with the actor Lance True and the actress Blair Kennedy when one side of the bed collapsed and fell onto Lance's foot. Blair happened to be stretched out on the side of the bed and ended up rolling off and landed on her face. There's already a knot forming on her head. It is crazy in there. I came outside to let you know what was going on."

"Please tell me this isn't the scene with that ridiculous high bed that the director just had to have?"

"That's the one. Lance is being cool about the whole thing, but Blair is threatening to sue. I have no idea why. The knot can't make her look any worse; it might even be an improvement."

Winter ignored Lisa's comment about the actresses' not so appealing looks and said, "Dammit! They obviously didn't put the bed together, right? Are you able to get back in there to see what else you can overhear?"

"I'll try. Let me call you back."

"Great."

Winter ended the call, finished getting dressed, and abandoned the idea of having a cup of coffee. Reaching for her purse and keys, the phone rang again. Assuming it was Lisa, she put it to her ear and said, "How bad is it?"

"Well, you can put a pin in the initial drama for now," Lisa said. "At the moment, there's a fire that needs to be put out."

Winter sighed and closed her eyes. "You mean, metaphorically speaking, right?"

"No, there's an actual fire. With all the moving around, some dumbass knocked over a candle used to help create some ambiance in the scene. Last I saw, that precious bed was going up in flames. Either way, of course, we don't need you to put out the fire; some yummy firemen are coming to do that, but it's a shit storm down here, and Mr. Sanders is having a cow. I just wanted you to have a heads up on the workday fun you are entering into."

Poor Mr. Sanders, he never handled accidents on set well. You'd think he would be used to it by now with so many years in the business, but he just wasn't great at handling catastrophes.

"What in the hell is going on today?" Winter said.

"Beats me. I'm just here because you pay me to be."

"I'm glad to see all this mayhem hasn't affected your sense of humor. Be sure to get me the names of those assigned to set up that bed."

"Already did it. I also set up a meeting for you with the two of them. I knew you'd want to speak with them. Would you like two pink slips as well?" Lisa asked eagerly.

"That won't be necessary."

"Just trying to be proactive," Lisa said innocently.

"I'll bet you are," Winter replied. "Anyway, thanks for the heads up. I'll see you soon."

As Winter was hanging up, her doorbell rang.

What now?!

The last thing she needed to see was some salesman. This day was already turning out highly eventful, and it was still early. It would be great if someone could save her from this mess she was about to walk into at work.

Without asking who it was, Winter swung the door open, ready to tell whoever was on the other side that today was not the day.

But to her surprise, she opened the door and locked eyes with none other than Kody Benton.

"IF SHE'S DIGGING THE DIRT, LOOKS LIKE I'M GETTING BURIED."

Am I dreaming? I must be.

Logically, that was the only reason Kody would be standing on her doorstep.

"Kody?" she said, slightly afraid speaking would make him vanish into thin air.

"Winter?" he said, just as surprised.

They said each other's names simultaneously, then laughed.

"How are you?" she asked.

"I'm even better now," he responded with one of the sexiest smiles she had ever seen on a man. "How are you?" he asked.

The first time she saw him, she thought he was gorgeous, but now seeing him in the daylight was downright sinful, mostly because of all the improper thoughts that were flooding her brain.

Kody's attractive face displayed a strong jawline, straight white teeth, warm brown eyes and soft, full lips. His skin didn't possess even one imperfection and his low-cut hair was wavy and black.

Winter could also now see his tall frame and broad shoulders were accompanied by sculpted arms and a defined chest.

Kody was wearing jeans and a white tank top that clung to

his body in a way she one day hoped to. He stood there oozing confidence and a natural swag that she was sure made women fall apart everywhere.

He was the type of guy you would see in a magazine, then be compelled to buy said magazine just because he was the perfect visual to pair with your vibrator on a lonely night.

Get it together, Winter!

"I'm good," she finally said with a nervous nod, pulling herself from the Kody trance. "Um, how'd you find me?"

"I didn't, not knowingly anyway. That part was just massive good luck. I was returning some mail that I got by accident and—" he broke off. "This is weird, right?"

"I'd say so. You just moved next door?"

"Yes," he paused and shook his head. "Well, temporarily."

"Oh, so you're renting the place?"

"Not exactly. I'm renovating it so that the investor can sell it. Living there while working on it just speeds up the process."

"That's an impressive way to work," she said. "I'll bet your boss loves that type of dedication."

"Seeing as I am the boss, I would have to agree."

"Then I guess Impressive was right," she said.

Winter couldn't stop smiling. It was hard to believe he was actually there and despite having so much to say; she felt speechless.

She wondered if he felt the same because, although he looked more relaxed than she felt, he, too, was staring and smiling.

"I'm sorry I'm staring," he began. "Beyond being totally, albeit pleasantly surprised, to see you, I am caught off guard. Did I catch you heading to work?"

Shit, work!

Winter completely forgot about the fire she was heading to put out.

"Oh wow. Yes, I am, actually. Emergency down at the office."

She spun around to lock her front door. After securing it, she turned around to face him and saw him extending the mail to her. She pulled it out of his hands, and their fingers touched. Instantly, she felt warm all over.

"I hope you have a good day, Winter," he said.

Do I really have to go to work? Couldn't I just hang out here, run my fingers up and down that hard, sexy chest of his and finish the scene in reality that started in my dreams? Surely they could tend to the fire at work while I tend to the one here.

As if in answer to her question, the phone rang.

Pulling it out of her pocket, she glanced at the screen. It was Lisa... again.

"I'm sorry, Kody. I really have to go. But I'll stop by soon so we can talk more," she said.

"Whenever you'd like," he replied.

Winter drove to work in total bliss. She still couldn't believe that she had run into him again—the man of her literal dreams.

Sparing a glance at her mail, Winter noticed her name wasn't on any of it. They were all junk mail that contained her address, but the name area simply had "current resident" printed.

Kody really had no chance of knowing it was her.

That made her wonder if he thought of her at all since their first encounter. Or did she just become some distant memory pushed aside once he met another beautiful woman?

When she got to work, nothing looked out of sorts or anymore hectic than the normal day-to-day.

Walking into her office, she almost ran into Lisa, who was exiting. They both stopped right before colliding.

"Hey, Winter," Lisa said, stepping aside. "I was dropping

off Mr. Sanders's list of things for you to do as it pertains to this morning's incident."

"Speaking of what gives? Where's all the chaos?"

"The assistant director was able to get things under control. Blair will no longer sue, at least not anyone within our company, and after they were all patched up, filming for the rest of the week was canceled. The staff plans to reconvene on Monday to decide how to move forward."

Winter sat down in her chair and picked up the list. "At least it's all worked out," she said to Lisa while scanning the document.

Everything on the list was to be expected.

Mr. Sanders always went haywire with wanting her to double, triple and quadruple check setup procedures, staff records and company liabilities when crazy things happened.

However, when she got to number four, she was puzzled.

It read:

Gift for niece.

Looking up, she said, "Is there anything else? I need to go see Mr. Sanders."

"That's it on my end. Catch you later," Lisa replied.

Approaching Mr. Sanders's office, Winter could see him sitting at his desk, wearing earphones and completely immersed in his computer. Not wanting to walk into his office without invitation, she knocked on the open door.

Nothing.

"Mr. Sanders?" Winter called out while knocking again.

Nothing.

Winter walked in and waved her hand in front of him. Startled, he jumped back, and the force caused the connected earphones to be yanked out of the computer.

Suddenly, the room filled with eerie music, and her boss pressed a key to shut it off.

Putting his hand on his chest, he said, "Damn, Winter, you just about scared the hair off my ass."

Winter giggled.

Mr. Sanders was a country boy through and through. He was always saying weirdly comedic things that sometimes made absolutely no sense, but usually got a laugh out of people, anyway.

For instance, when he saw an attractive woman he might say, "that girl is so fine, she made my beans sprout out of season" or "if she's digging the dirt, looks like I'm getting buried."

Needless to say, everyone always looked forward to what he would say next.

"I'm sorry. I tried to get your attention a couple of times."

"It's fine. I was just so taken with this horror scene we filmed a month ago. It's scary as hell, should be a major hit at the box office."

"I'll bet. I don't want to disturb you, I just wanted to ask you about the list you left on my desk. I understand the first three items, but the fourth said something about a gift for your niece?"

"Oh, that, I'm sorry. I added it to the list so I wouldn't forget to ask you. Shopping isn't my thing, and I need a present for my niece's college graduation." He leaned back in his chair and began to reminisce. "I remember when I graduated from college, all excited and terrified, but ready to take on the world. The one thing that gave me confidence was knowing I had people in my corner cheering me on and there for me if I needed them. Of course, she knows that, but I want her to have something tangible that shows, in some measure, how proud I am of her. I'm going to see her in December and would like to take the gift with me. I was hoping you could find me something, and cost isn't an issue."

"I don't know, Mr. Sanders. That's a tall order. What if I don't pick out something that fits what she would like?"

"Trust me, Winter, anything you pick would be 1000% better than what I would think up. You'd be doing me an enormous favor."

"I guess so," she said slowly.

"Thank you and no rush. I don't need it until December 20th."

"Alright, I'll take care of it. If it's something I find online, I'll be sure to forward you the confirmation and order details. Is it okay to have it shipped here?"

"Shipping it here is perfectly fine."

"Okay. If you don't need anything else, I'm going to head back to my office to get some work done before speaking with Brian Dunn and Thomas Stroud about the bed incident this morning. Anything you want to tell me about it?"

"Nothing to add except it was all levels of drama. Hearing the words lawsuit had me so rattled you could have stuck me on the tail of a snake. I haven't gotten a chance to see Thomas, but I suspect he is where the problem lies. Word around the office is that he's been hitting the bottle pretty hard. How he ended up hired, I don't know. I'll have to talk to Helen in HR about that. But I hope I don't see him because if I do, I'm likely to stick my foot so far up his ass, he'll be shining my shoes every time he brushes his teeth."

Winter hid her laugh by covering her mouth and faking a cough.

"You aren't getting sick, are you, Winter?" he asked, concerned.

"No," she said, clearing her throat. "Just a little throat tickle."

"Good. Anyway, let me know how the meeting goes."

"I will," she said, exiting his office.

During her meeting with Brian Dunn, everything seemed to fall in line. He followed protocols as far as Winter could tell and assisted Thomas Stroud in putting together the entire bed.

However, he explained that he handled the screws and bolts for the right side, while Thomas took care of the left, also known as the side that collapsed.

Winter thanked Brian for meeting with her and told him she would be in touch with him after speaking with Thomas.

Thirty minutes later, Thomas entered her office. She could smell the faint whiff of alcohol on his breath as they said their hellos.

"Please, take a seat, Thomas."

When he did, he almost instantly zoned out, staring at a portrait of a popular 1980s filmmaker on her wall as if the man had three heads.

"Can you tell me about the incident that happened with the bed this morning?" Winter asked. "It appears you were one of two people responsible for setting it up."

"Huh," he said with a dazed look in his eyes. "Yes, I sleep in a bed."

Winter took a deep breath and counted to five before speaking again.

"Mr. Stroud. Are you okay? I asked about the bed you handled for setup on stage twelve, not if you sleep in a bed."

"Oh that," he replied with a small chuckle. "Yes, I set it up. I think it was missing some bolts or something, so I decided to wing it."

"You decided to wing it?" she asked, shocked.

She was really trying to be patient with him. This incident would likely cost him his job and she didn't want to jump to conclusions, no matter how obvious, without giving him a fair chance.

"Why didn't you notify us of the issue and report that there were missing pieces? I'm sure that you know there are protocols for matters like these."

Thomas was slowly nodding while Winter was speaking, then stopped as his eyes drifted shut. He'd fallen asleep. Right there during the meeting, while she was talking to him!

Annoyed by his blatant incoherence, Winter hit the desk with her hand.

Thomas's eyes popped open, and he jumped out of his seat.

"Huh? What? Where am I?"

He looked confused and scared, but after a few moments, he seemed to settle and sat back in the chair.

"Mr. Stroud, have you been drinking, or have you taken something?"

"I had a few beers before work, but only three because I have control." Then he looked up and off to the side and said, "Or was it four?"

Winter was pissed at not only his disrespect but his negligence. This whole thing could have easily been avoided if he were being professional on the job. She wasn't sure who hired him or how he'd been at the company this long with his clear issues with alcohol/substance abuse, but she was ending it.

As Thomas appeared to be falling asleep yet again, Winter picked up her phone to reach Lisa.

She also pulled up the number to their car service to make sure he got home safely, but his time of employment at Movie Box Studios was over. When Lisa answered, Winter said, "looks like I'll be needing that pink slip after all."

"I'm on it!" Lisa said, a little too excited.

"We have to stop meeting this way, Miss Daniels," Kody said when she opened the door.

It was two days later, and he was once again on her doorstep offering her another tiny pile of misdelivered mail. He was so handsome and mesmerizing. Looking at his face was truly the perfect way to start her day.

"I hope I didn't catch you in a rush again?"

"No rush today. I'm sorry about that, by the way. I'm a Prop Master for a film studio, and we had a major mishap on set. My assistant was keeping me up-to-date as things unfolded, but luckily no fires to put out this time," she said.

Unless you are counting the one between my legs.

"The movies, huh? Must be exciting to see everything come together, or in your case, being the one to put everything together."

"It is. It's my dream job. Fun and fast-paced, but I like the challenge."

She saw a look of something flash in his eyes, but it was gone before she could register it.

"We all like challenges," he said, smiling.

Look at that smile. I should just give him my panties now.

"Two times in one week," she said, taking the mail from his hand. "I wonder if our mailman has been drinking?"

Winter tried to avoid touching his fingers because even the slightest brush against his skin did something to her.

"Could be," he replied, letting go of the mail.

"Regardless, I'm glad you stopped by. I wanted to see you before I left for work yesterday, but I saw you talking to a guy in a suit and thought it might be rude to interrupt."

"That was the investor. He wanted to see what we'd done so far. Any particular reason you wanted to see me? Although you never need one," Kody said.

To fuck your brains out.

"I wanted to give you a proper thanks and invite you to

dinner. You know, for saving my life and all." Then, feeling the need to explain more, she continued, "I should have offered the first time you stopped by, but I guess I was a little thrown. Anyway, it's a friendly dinner, nothing extreme or fancy. You can even bring your girl."

The last part about him bringing his girl just kinda fell out. She was nervous. She didn't want to be coming on to him and find out she was making a fool of herself.

That's when it hit her.

I shouldn't be coming on to him at all. I was taking a break, dammit! A break!

It was useless, because her heart and body did not seem to understand or even care about the strict rules of her dating hiatus. They wanted this man.

Cutting into her mentally berating herself was Kody chuckling to himself.

"The only girl in my life is my grandmother. She is very sweet, but doesn't get out much. I'm sure she would appreciate the invitation, but unfortunately wouldn't be able to make it."

Slightly embarrassed, Winter looked down for a brief moment. "Sorry for assuming. So dinner tomorrow night at six?"

"I'd love that," Kody said.

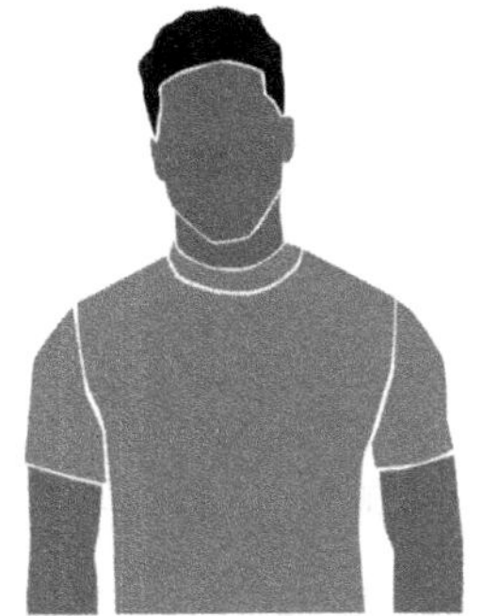

CHAPTER SEVEN
Kody

"STOP CALLING ME BOSS."

As Kody walked the short distance next door, he smiled to himself, cognizant of the effect he had on most women, and happy to see that Winter wasn't immune.

Her attraction to him made her nervous, and he liked that.

Not because the goal was to make her uncomfortable, but because he knew that it meant she liked him a lot; and liking him meant that she would have trouble staying away from him.

Which worked out great for Kody because he wanted to know everything about her.

Winter was beautiful and courageous, and he had to know more. The night they met, he noticed a strong attraction to her that he knew she'd felt as well.

Thinking back to seeing her fight for her life, and losing at rapid speeds, he could feel the anger in him resurface.

If he wasn't so good at practicing self-control, thanks to his dad and grandfather, he probably would have killed that piece of shit. God knows he wanted to.

Being a black belt in karate had its perks, but he always had to be careful. The threat level from that asshole was minimal at best, and with Kody's size and frame, self-defense, to the extent of seriously harming the guy or worse, would be questionable.

Kody was thankful to have been there at all. He'd made it back to his truck and was just about to close the door when he heard a muffled scream.

Although the parking lot was pretty empty, it was easy to not see Winter and the attacker because they were on the ground. Heavy brush and another parked car had totally obscured the assault.

The thought that he could have lost her before even having the chance to know her started a fresh wave of anger.

Then, remembering her face looking up at him, safe and alive, made him shift his focus.

After she had left, Kody had gotten in his truck and just sat there. Their brief encounter had affected him in ways he hadn't felt in a long time. He didn't know if he'd see her again, but he wanted to.

It was the whole reason he had given her his number, but after what she'd gone through, Kody didn't want to appear pushy.

What type of asshole would he be if, after a guy physically hit on her, he did the same metaphorically?

Normally, he was very upfront about what was on his mind. Beating around the bush and playing games was much too childish for his taste. Therefore, as hard as it was to let her leave and place the ball in her court, he'd done it.

But damn if he didn't spend every free minute since then thinking about her.

She was perfect.

Probably around 5 '4, slim body, enticing curves and long black curly hair. Her chocolate complexion and beautiful smile made him want to kiss her lips and then everywhere else.

That perfect ass and those nicely sized breasts, that he was certain would fit perfectly in his hands, kept his dick hard as his mind replayed bending her over his workstation on an endless loop.

Yes, he'd remembered every detail of that gorgeous face and body, and the sexual attraction was evident, but it was more than that.

He worried about her and wanted to know that she was truly okay after everything.

Thanks to fate, he no longer had to wonder. He would be living next door to her for the next seven months, and that was a very good thing.

The ball was now back in his court and although he'd take his time and try not to press her too much. Kody would get his time with her. He had to. He liked her too much.

He'd even already told Jackson about her. Well, about their encounter anyway. The next morning after the incident, he was having a phone meeting with his cousin about all of his plans for the current renovation.

Once they had things squared away and Jackson asked him what else was new, he told him about the attack the night before.

"Please tell me you handed him his ass, little cousin?" *Jackson had said.*

"You know I did," Kody said.

"I don't doubt it. I've seen you in action, and I'm sure the asshat didn't wake up feeling too good the next morning. Which is better than that bastard deserved."

"My sentiments exactly," Kody agreed.

One major pet peeve that Kody and Jackson shared was men's abuse toward women.

During their senior year of high school, a girl named Sherri Cooper was dating one of their football team members, Dean Russo.

Dean was a cool guy most of the time, but everyone knew

he had a temper. One time, after their team had lost a football game, Dean was highly upset.

His sour mood escalated when he was ready to leave, and Sherri still hadn't made it to the car.

She was a cheerleader and got held up by friends while returning some of her gear to the locker room.

When she got to the parking lot, Dean was leaning against his car with two of his team members. As the story goes, she tried to explain to Dean why she was late and kept apologizing for delaying him, but he wasn't really interested in her apology.

Finally, she'd said to him, *"Let's just go home. You'll feel better tomorrow,"* and then walked away. Dean took that as her disrespecting him in front of his friends and started hitting her.

The two team members who basically worshipped Dean didn't jump in to stop it. They were likely afraid Dean would beat their asses, too.

But after hearing the commotion from a few cars down, Jackson was glad to give Dean a taste of his own medicine.

He ended up breaking Dean's nose and might have done worse if Kody didn't arrive in time to stop him.

It was the talk of the school for weeks because the few people that saw what happened had told others, but no one that mattered was saying a word.

Dean was afraid Jackson would get his hands on him again, and Sherri was too embarrassed.

Dean's two idiot friends were already scared of Dean; they most certainly didn't want to have an angry Jackson after them as well.

When the principal, Mr. Miller, confronted Jackson about the rumors and his part in the fight, Jackson denied it.

Feeling that Dean got exactly what he deserved, Kody vouched for Jackson, saying that they left the game shortly after it ended and had no idea what everyone was talking about.

However, to ensure that the principal turned the spotlight elsewhere, Kody made up a story about seeing some guys from the other school having a heated conversation with Dean.

"Maybe that argument escalated to the fight that you heard about," Kody had said.

Whether Mr. Miller believed him didn't matter. With no evidence to do anything more, the man let it go.

Sherri, of course, broke up with Dean, and Dean stayed under the radar for the rest of the school year.

Kody felt his phone vibrate in his pocket.

Pulling it free, he checked the display. It was a call from his project manager in California, Jason Pugh.

"Hey, Jason, what's up?"

"I'm busy as hell. How are things down there in Georgia?"

"Very good. The house we are renovating is in a nice area, and I've got big plans for it."

"You always do. I know how much you love renovations. Listen, I don't want to keep you, but you know Mrs. Dorsey, the 78-year-old widow that stays in the community we do the free work in?"

"The one that always tries to pay us in knitted blankets?"

"That's her," Paul said. "Her house has a leak on the roof. I was doing some work in one of the other houses in the community, and I stopped by to check on her. That's when she showed it to me. I can repair it by replacing a few shingles, but the whole thing looks kinda bad. How do you want me to handle it?"

Kody thought a minute before responding. It made no sense to make partial repairs when the entire roof was falling apart.

Besides, Mrs. Dorsey could use a break. She had been a

strong pillar of the community for over forty years, helping everyone else. Good deeds given deserved the same in return.

"Just replace the entire roof," Kody decided. "Get Austin to give you a hand. He is really good at roof work. Write up the invoice and mark it paid like we do the others. The accountant will know how to handle it from there."

"Alright, Boss. Anything else you need on my end?"

Kody groaned. "Yeah, stop calling me Boss."

"Sure thing... Boss," Jason added with a chuckle before ending the call.

Kody shook his head and laughed to himself. Being called boss was never his thing, and his team knew it.

Years back, when they'd all started working together, he told them calling him Kody would be fine, and that it was even preferred. For a while, everything went smoothly, but then a new guy would start and refer to him as "boss" all over again.

The veteran employees would correct the new guys, but it kept happening. Eventually, it became a running joke that Kody took in good spirits.

Taking out his trim removal tool, Kody started loosening one of the original windows in the living room. This house was small, but it had a lot of windows. The good thing about that was that it gave the house tons of natural light.

Kody decided to replace the old windows with new ones that didn't have grids.

Windows with grids carried a more traditional look. Replacing them with gridless windows would produce the more modern look the investor wanted for the home.

Coming up behind him was one of his team members, Gus.

"I saw you talking to the lady next door, and you haven't stopped smiling since. Did you get her phone number or something?"

"Something like that," Kody said, his smile reappearing.

"Well, I've seen her a few times, and she is one sexy woman. If you don't ask her out, I will. Besides, she might not go for the whole tall, nicely toned body type; my style may be more to her liking," he said, patting his beer belly with a laugh.

"I'll be sure to let her know you're available, Gus."

Kody resumed loosening the window, while making a mental checklist of things that he would need to replace in the kitchen.

He'd been looking at some designs from the previous kitchen remodels he'd done, and there was one in particular that he thought would work perfectly and make great use of the space.

Plans for the kitchen reminded him he would need to decide on dinner for the night. He could grab a salad from one of the local restaurants or go by the grocery store and buy a few ready-made items from the deli area.

He wouldn't be starting work in the kitchen for a few days, so he could store a couple of salads in there to give him a break from eating so much fast food.

Even though he would be staying on the property for seven months, he didn't like to buy a lot of groceries. The goal was always to avoid becoming so comfortable on the property that he treated it like his own home.

From there, his thoughts traveled to Winter and their dinner plans for tomorrow.

I wonder what she is going to cook?

Then he realized she might not even know how to. Her plan could be to grab take out and avoid the embarrassment of making him a meal that he didn't care for. Little did she know, she could serve him gravel on a plate, and he'd happily eat it.

Yup, he may not have known what he was in for, but he knew what he wanted out of it... her.

CHAPTER EIGHT
Winter

Winter awoke Friday morning nightmare free and practically floating on a cloud. Today was the day—dinner with that gorgeous man, Kody.

Getting out of bed, Winter wondered about two things; what to cook? And what to wear?

As far as food went, Italian chicken pasta, cooked in a white wine sauce, sounded appealing. Or maybe grilled steak was more fitting and the simplicity would be something Kody would appreciate.

Winter groaned. Maybe it would have been smart to ask Kody what he wanted, but that thought didn't occur to her until now.

Considering her next decision, Winter faced the closet, taking in the endless business suits and party dresses. If she thought deciding on dinner was difficult, choosing what to wear was going to give her a migraine.

It has to be perfect.

This was a chance to make a good impression on him, because the first one was definitely less than desirable.

After all, being slapped around by some low-life, and needing to be rescued didn't exactly scream sexy, only weak and pitiful.

This time things could be done on her terms, and Winter

wanted something that showcased her confidence and walked that fine line between slutty and classy.

Besides, just because she wasn't going to have sex with him didn't mean she didn't want to turn him on.

Has it really been over a year since she last had sex?

Normally that didn't bother her so much, but to be fair, her life usually didn't consist of a Kody.

The thought made her giddy. She had never been so ready to get her workday started, so she could end it. Images of his handsome face called to her, and she couldn't wait to see him.

Opening the shower curtain and reaching for the knob, she turned it on and... nothing.

Oh no, not this again.

Winter turned the knob into the off position and back on, again nothing.

Assuming the third time was the charm, she made a final attempt, only to get the same result.

It shouldn't have surprised her at all because problems with the water had been occurring periodically for a few months now. It was either running with low pressure or it would stall, taking a few seconds or sometimes a full minute before spouting out.

Winter kept meaning to get a plumber to take a look at it, but it would suddenly start working fine, and all over again, she would forget about it.

"Think, Winter, think," she said aloud.

Checking the water in the guest bathroom didn't provide any good news, as it, too, was out of commission. She was, however, surprised that the water in the kitchen sink worked.

At least she could brush her teeth and wash her face, but unless her idea of showering was standing in front of the kitchen sink with a bucket and washcloth, she needed to figure out something else.

She could call out and spend the day at home looking for a

plumber, but that would mean some important last-minute projects at work wouldn't get finalized.

A second option would be Chloe, who didn't live too far away and normally didn't go into work until around 10am.

Maybe I could shower there before going to work?

She picked up her phone to call Chloe.

"Hey, Winter," Chloe answered.

"Hey, Clo, can I stop by and shower really quick before work?"

"Sure. Everything okay?"

"Got an issue with my stupid pipes."

"No comment," Chloe said.

Winter laughed. "Get your head out of the gutter. I mean my literal pipes. You know, the ones in the wall?"

"If you say so. You know you are always welcome to use my shower anytime, no questions asked."

"Thanks."

After a quick trip to Chloe's, Winter arrived at work and finished her daily tasks at lightning speed.

Three hours later, clear of Movie Box obligations, she moved on to search for a plumber that could come out on short notice, but had no luck.

The earliest one said they could get someone out was Tuesday. That was four days away!

Winter thanked them and hung up, opting instead to ask around at work before committing to the company.

If no one knew of a plumber that could come out sooner, then she'd call the repair company back and accept the Tuesday availability.

She knew Chloe would tell her she could come by again, but Winter didn't want to impose.

Chloe was a newlywed, and they needed their space. One favor was enough. Even if Chloe wasn't married, Winter didn't like to repeatedly cash in on the kindness of those around her.

Wanting nothing more but this day from hell to be over, she headed home around 5pm, defeated and mentally exhausted. Unfortunately, no one knew of any plumbers.

I guess that bucket and washcloth will get some use after all.

For some reason, her good mood from this morning now seemed like it had happened a million years ago.

At this point, Winter had no idea what she was even happy about, and to top it all off, she was getting a headache. When her stomach growled, Winter glanced down.

And of course, I forgot to eat.

However, her desire to get home won out over making a stop for food. It would be easy to find some leftovers in the fridge and then plant herself in front of the TV.

Winter hadn't been home longer than ten minutes when the doorbell rang. She looked at the clock on the wall; it read 5:57.

Who could that be?

Opening the door, she found Kody standing there. He was handsome, dressed casually and... there for dinner.

Shit!

Face palming and shaking her head, she said, "Oh goodness, Kody, I completely forgot about dinner."

"No problem. Is everything okay?"

"No, it isn't. My water stopped working in both bathrooms this morning, and I haven't had any luck finding someone to fix it. I may have to reschedule our dinner."

"Do you mind if I take a look at it?"

Winter's brows knitted together. "You're a plumber?"

"Amongst other things," Kody said. "I'm a contractor with an extensive background in all things home related. I can basically build a home from the ground up."

Damn! Good looks and highly skilled.

Winter had to remind herself to slow down. He was very appealing, but he was only in town temporarily, so she needed to keep her cool.

"If it's not too much trouble, I'd really appreciate it? Come in."

Kody stepped over the threshold and into the entryway. "You have a beautiful home," he said. "How long have you been here?"

"Thanks. About four years," Winter answered.

"Nice. I assume the bathroom is straight ahead on the left?"

Puzzled, she began, "How did you..." then stopped. "Oh yeah, you are living in a similar model next door. Well, have at it," she said, stepping aside and gesturing towards the bathroom.

With a nod, Kody headed toward the bathroom.

Winter watched him walk away. He was wearing a black and gray shirt with dark jeans and smelled amazing.

She, on the other hand, was still wearing her work suit, minus the matching jacket.

Glancing at her reflection in the decorative mirror she'd placed in the entryway, Winter felt a small sense of relief; she didn't look too bad.

It wasn't the outfit she had planned to wear for this dinner, but with all things considered, she could have looked worse.

Thankfully, her hair was still neat, and the skirt and blouse she wore gave her the appearance of having it together, even though at the moment she really didn't.

Winter went to her kitchen table and sat down. Her place was so small, she didn't have a dining room. Her kitchen and living room basically shared a space, separated by her kitchen island.

But she didn't mind; in fact, she loved it. She was a single woman with no kids, so it was big enough for her.

"Is today the first day you had problems with the water?" Kody asked from the bathroom.

"No. I've been having problems for months now. The water pressure has seemed to be getting weaker."

"Makes sense," he said.

"If you don't mind me asking, where are you from?" she asked.

"I'm originally from New York, but we moved to California when I was five. What about you?"

"I'm from here," she said. "Born and raised in Atlanta."

"One of those original peaches they talk about," he said in a lighthearted tone.

Winter smiled, her mind taking her to very naughty places.

"Yeah, I guess I am," she replied. "How long will you be working on the house next door?"

Kody didn't answer, so she figured he probably didn't hear her. She heard stuff being moved around in the bathroom and assumed he was trying to get to the valves under the sink.

After a few minutes, she heard him approaching the living room area.

"You mind if I check the kitchen faucet?" he asked.

"Be my guest."

He entered the kitchen and turned the water on in the sink. She could hear the gentle splash as it came out, with little force behind it.

Next, she heard him open the cabinet doors under the sink as they gave a light squeak of protest.

After another moment, he walked in and pulled out a chair to sit down and join her.

"Okay. How bad is it?" Winter asked, biting her lower lip. "Should I just toss the whole house now?"

She felt so stressed. The cost of repairing this would likely be astronomical. She should have gotten someone out to fix this months ago.

"Not the whole house. I think it still has a few years left in it," he said.

"Alright, what's the repair estimate?"

In response, Kody said, "Pass me that notepad and pen, please."

Giving him the requested items, Winter watched him write something, tear it out, fold it, and then slide the sheet across the table to her.

She looked down at it, amused. Picking it up, she opened the paper and smiled. It was the number seven. "Two things. First, what's with the dramatic note?"

"It got you to smile, didn't it?" Kody said. "You've been looking stressed since I got here. Plus, since you work in film, I assumed you could appreciate the theatrics."

"You thought right. Now on to the second." Turning the paper toward him, she said, "What's with the seven?"

"It stands for seven months. You asked me how long I'd be here. I'm here until mid-March."

Winter nodded.

It was now late August, merely days away from September. His timeline was definitely a reminder to avoid entertaining the notion of getting too close to him.

He will be gone soon enough.

If she could just keep that in the forefront of her mind, she would be alright.

Putting on her best business face, she said, "Thanks for trying to soften the blow, I really appreciate it, but you never answered the question about costs."

Noticing her shift in demeanor, Kody said, "You have galvanized pipes and low to non-existent water pressure throughout the house. This indicates corrosion in the pipes. It's currently only affecting both bathrooms, but in time it will affect the entire house. Repairs for just the two bathrooms cost somewhere between four to six thousand dollars, while a total home repair is approximately ten thousand."

Winter's shoulders slumped, and her attempt at keeping a business-like edge got traded in for her earlier response... face palming.

This was a nightmare. She had some money saved, but fixing the two bathrooms would clear that out, and she couldn't even think about fixing the whole house. She'd have to get a loan for the rest, and she didn't like loans.

She felt him gently touch her hand and looked up.

"Oh, I'm sorry," she said. "I'll just need a couple of hours to think about which route I'd..."

"It's going to be okay," he said, cutting her off before she could further explain. "I'll do the work, and I won't charge you for it."

What in the hell!? Is he pulling my leg? He has to be pulling my leg. Or joking. Yup, that's it. He's joking.

"You're joking, right?" she said to him.

Kody stared at her with a straight face. "Why would I be joking?"

If he wasn't joking, then what type of game was he playing? In Winter's world, no one did anything for free, especially not home repair work.

Either he thinks I'm some damsel in distress who can't pay her own way, or he wants me to owe him a debt.

Staring into his captivating eyes, she guessed it was a bit of both. He likely thought she was some weak-minded woman, but he would be mistaken. She could fix her own problems.

And if he thinks he can get me to owe him sex in exchange for services, he is so right...WRONG! I meant wrong!

Obviously, her body was having trouble getting with the program. It wanted in on whatever deal he had in mind and would sign on the dotted line happily, but luckily her body wasn't in control, her logical mind was, and it didn't like the idea of being indebted to him.

Realizing she had been silent way too long, she said, "Because no one does anything for free."

His response was simple and appeared genuine. "Now, you've met someone that does."

Winter narrowed her eyes. "I don't believe you."

Kody laughed. It was a nice laugh, one that helped ease some of her apprehension.

"Come on, Winter. Seriously, I don't mind. I'd love to work on the house and did I mention I could start as early as tomorrow?"

It may have been her empty stomach making her crazy, but he really did sound serious. But why? He'd already done enough.

"Really tomorrow? Don't you have your own projects to tend to?"

"Usually, I don't do much work on the weekends. If I must, I do small things on the inside of the home like install light fixtures or replace outlet covers, but I try to stay away from the larger projects."

"Now that just makes it sound like I would be working you for free on your off days. I don't think that would be a good idea, so just make me a fair offer, and you're hired."

His eyes wandered to the corner of the room where she had a huge blue and gold abstract painting, with dashes of white lines throughout. If she wasn't confident about anything else, her decoration skills made her feel proud and competent.

Lord knows she could use all the points she could get in looking less like a victim and more like an intelligent and capable woman in Kody's eyes.

He remained silent as his eyes continued to scan the room for a few seconds longer, then finally they were back on her.

"Tell me, Winter, what do you think about non-monetary payments?"

I knew it! He thinks I am some dumb woman who would easily jump into bed with him out of desperation.

Winter cleared her throat and crossed her arms. "Listen, I don't know what you think—"

Kody chuckled and interjected, "I was talking about food, Winter."

"Food?" she said, confusion halting her thoughts.

"Yeah. For instance, what were you planning on making tonight? I mean, before the whole plumbing debacle."

"I was going to make a chicken pasta, cooked in a white wine sauce."

He closed his eyes and exhaled.

"I love Italian food. I think that would be a fair trade. You cook dinner for me, let's say once a week until the job is done, and we will call it even."

"How long will the work take?"

"About a week. That would include drywall repairs and painting. But since I am only working on the weekends, it would take a month."

Winter thought about it.

One meal per week, for one month, that equated... four meals. For a ten thousand dollar job! Was he crazy?

"Kody, I truly appreciate the obvious faith you must have in my cooking, and while I do agree that I can grill and sauté with the best of them, my skills in the kitchen are not up to par for a ten thousand dollar trade."

"Isn't that my choice to make?" he asked.

"Are you sure? That's a lot of money you're missing out on."

"Winter," he said in a way that somehow came off as caring yet firm. "I'm good on money; what I don't have is home-cooked meals, which I miss because I don't have the time to do it myself. You have a problem, and I have the solution. But since you are so determined to debate this, let me just end it now. Didn't you say you owed me for saving your life?" He looked at her with a checkmate smile.

No fair!

He just pulled out the big guns. Using the "I saved your life" card not only made her feel guilty, it ended the conversation. He'd won fair and square.

However, the comment he made about not needing money stuck out in her mind.

Who didn't need money?

It sure as hell wasn't her, or else she wouldn't be in this mess right now.

Although having to spend more time with Kody wasn't messy at all, unless you counted in the hot and sweaty way that she hoped to end up.

Stop it.

Winter shook her head, pushing the sexual thoughts aside. His money and his body, no matter how alluring, were his business.

"How does dinner on Sundays around seven sound?" Winter asked.

Kody didn't even seem to think about it before responding. "Sounds good to me."

"Alright, any special menu requests?"

"Surprise me."

"Food allergies?"

"Nope, I'm good."

She watched him, oddly comforted by how easygoing he was. Most men would have jumped at the chance to have a personal chef that owed them a favor, but Kody was different somehow.

He appeared to want to put her at ease, which made no

sense because she was the one that needed to be catering to him.

"Well, if you say so," Winter finally said.

"I do," Kody replied, giving her a smile that showed off his perfect white teeth. "Speaking of food, since we had to cancel dinner, would you like to order pizza?"

Feeling her stomach almost jump for joy after being unintentionally ignored all day. She picked up the phone and asked, "Are you fine with meat lovers?"

While waiting for the pizza, they made small chit chat. It was funny, even though they had already seen each other several times, they still hadn't had proper introductions.

Winter told Kody all the general stuff about herself, such as how she spent most of her time, insights about her life growing up, and how she got started on her chosen career path.

To her surprise, she even confessed how close he was to being murdered by her the day he woke her up banging on the roof the morning after Chloe's wedding.

Kody thought that was hilarious, and according to him, it would have been adorable to see her march over and yell at his team.

It was hard not to take note of how simple it was to communicate with him.

He listened, commented, and asked questions of his own while supplying answers to the same questions on his account. Winter really liked him and couldn't believe he was single. There had to be a catch; there just had to be.

Kody was thirty-two, no kids, from a well-to-do family, and owned a very successful business.

They even had tons in common; their parents were

deceased, they both had no siblings and enjoyed many of the same hobbies. Without much effort, the conversation simply flowed, and that sent off alarm bells in Winter's head.

If he seems too good to be true, then he probably is.

On another note, Winter realized that as great as the "getting to know you" topic was, it seemed they both were steering clear of the elephant in the room—the horrible experience that brought them together in the first place.

It was still a terrifying experience that she hadn't mentioned to anyone. She was thankful when the doorbell rang because she could dodge the topic a bit longer.

After grabbing the plates, glasses and sitting down at the table, Kody said, "So, how are you?"

"Oh, I'm fine. My plumbing drama will be solved, thanks to you, and I met all of my deadlines at work. Life is good."

"That's not what I meant," he said, studying her.

She knew that wasn't what he meant; she could hear it in his tone. He wanted to know about her mental state since the attack.

"I'm fine, for the most part. Sometimes sleeping can be a challenge, but the past few nights..." she gave a shrug. "No issues."

Kody's sympathetic expression touched her.

"If you ever need me," he said. "You have my number and can call me anytime."

She looked down to avoid his eyes and, although she knew she had no reason to be, Winter felt slightly embarrassed.

"Umm, about that," she said. "I don't have your card anymore. I think I accidentally threw it away."

"Accidentally, huh?"

"Yeah," she said, averting her eyes. That was her story, and she was sticking to it.

Noticing her phone lying on the table, he pushed it closer

to her and said, "Maybe we will store it here this time, you know, so that you don't accidentally throw it away."

"Good idea," she said, picking up the phone and entering his contact info as he rattled it off for her.

Attempting to get out of the conversational spotlight, she asked, "Where'd you learn those smooth moves the night of the attack? You some famous martial artist or something?"

Kody began tracing his finger around the rim of his cup.

"Yeah, something like that. Just without the famous part. My grandfather was in the service. During his stay in Japan, he developed a major interest in Karate and studied hard until he became a black belt. He even won a few local tournaments, then continued his practice when he came back home to the states. Eventually, when he had his son, he passed it down to him, and my dad passed it down to me."

Winter was impressed.

"Wow, that's amazing and honorable. What age did you start training?"

"When I was five. Both my dad and grandfather always stressed that it was less about the actual fight and more about your mental control. Being able to center yourself amid chaos and think clearly will make a bigger impact when you find yourself in dangerous situations."

"Lucky me," Winter said, more to herself than him.

Now might be a good time to ask him to teach her some of those moves because she was clearly an easy target. However, she didn't want to talk anymore about the experience, so she was relieved when Kody changed the subject.

"Tell me more about your job. I know you love it, but what exactly does a Prop Master do?" he asked.

"In a nutshell, I break down scripts to determine what props will be needed for the various scenes throughout the movie. I'm responsible for the procurement, inventory, care and maintenance of all props associated with productions and ensuring that they are available on time and fall within budgetary requirements."

"Sounds like a lot of work."

"It can be, which is why I have an amazing assistant. There is also a team dedicated to handling the setup of the scenes. When I'm not busy creating the lists, reading scripts or researching props, I help with that part too."

"A woman with many talents. I like that. And according to what you said the other day, there are also a lot of unfortunate accidents?"

"Sadly, sometimes there are. The most recent was a bed falling apart during filming, and the actors got injured. We don't always use real items, but depending on the scene, sometimes we have to, and in this case, it didn't work out so well."

"Sounds to me like there is never a dull moment. Got any more wild stories you can share?"

Winter thought about it, then started smiling. "Once there was a scene with a dog that had a crazy case of diarrhea..."

As she told him about the funny and shocking situations that took place on set, Kody hung on every word, watching her animated hand movements and her eyes light up as she spoke of the job she loved.

"What about you?" she said when she was finally done. "Tell me more about the renovation projects. How exactly does that work? It must be tough living in a home while renovating it. I love watching HGTV and people always say renovations are a nightmare."

"It's not so bad. I don't have as much stuff as a person who actually lives in the home. Plus, I don't stay in a lot of my projects, only very select ones owned by investors."

"This is all so fascinating," Winter said. "How do you set that up?"

"Well, it has to be in the contract that they are fine with

me living there while working because, obviously, they have to keep the power on, there has to be working appliances in the home, and there can't be any safety issues like mold or damage to the foundation."

Winter took a bite of pizza, swallowed, then said, "Let me get this straight. You are saying you can live in the house like normal for the contracted time?"

"I can, but I try to keep a small footprint. For example, I only move a bed and a dresser into the house. I like to keep the areas as clear as possible because we need to work around anything that I bring in. I also rarely, if ever, touch the stove, and I only keep the bare minimum in the fridge."

"Wow. I think that would be hard for me?"

"For some people, it would, I get that. But I'm on a project to work, not to relax, so I don't require much."

"Is there seven months of necessary work in that house? Is it that bad?"

"No. For the age of the home, it's actually in pretty good condition. Any updates or repairs I have planned can be completed within 4 or 5 months, but my cousin always overestimates the contracts because of permits. With this home, I am going to tear down some walls and extend the master bath. Sometimes, waiting on the all clear before we can continue working can mess with the deadlines if we aren't careful."

"Smart planning. I love renovations."

"I can tell," Kody said. "Maybe we can walk over there in a little bit so you can see the before, and when we are done, I can show you the after."

Winter's eyes lit up.

"I'd like that," she said, then added, "Why did you say you could tell I love renovations?"

"The HGTV comment for one, and for two..." He nodded in the direction of the nightstand she had been sanding the last few days.

"Oh, my little project," Winter said with a smile. "When I have time, I like to go antique shopping, find pieces that speak to me, and restore it. Most of the time, I add modern twists to it and in the end, some pieces I keep, others I sell, and occasionally I donate items to a local women's shelter."

"That's not little at all. It's a big deal—creative and generous. I'm impressed. I do something similar out in California. There is a community for low-income families, and when I have the extra time, my team and I do free repairs and upgrades to the homes."

"Kody," she said, touching her chest, "that is so sweet."

"And so is what you do for the women's shelter," he countered.

"Yeah. It feels good to do something for others. I used to go with my mom when I was a kid to different homeless shelters and serve food. It surely kept me grateful for everything I had. Although I didn't complain much, anyway. I had a good life. My time growing up was enjoyable and memorable. I often think back on it, or rewatch some of my favorite shows growing up, to feel closer to it."

"You have a love for throwbacks?" Kody said.

"I guess you could say that. I feel like the world was safer and somehow saner back then, or maybe it only seemed that way."

"No, I fully understand what you mean. When I watch a movie from the 70s or 80s, with that horrible wallpaper, people rushing to their ringing landline phones and kids coming inside from playing hopscotch all day instead of video games. It really makes you miss it."

She couldn't believe it. He actually understood what she was saying. Not only that, he had a comment of true substance to add to it.

Most guys laughed her off or commented that nothing is different or worse in today's society. In their opinions, the only difference is that nowadays there are more media outlets to report the bad stuff.

It wasn't that she didn't understand what they were saying or even agree on some level. Social media had definitely opened the floodgates of information, but it still didn't negate the fact that memories of her childhood made her feel better and comforted.

They continued eating their pizza and talking for a couple more hours. After that, they walked next door so that she could see the current state of the property.

As Kody walked her through his plans for the place, Winter was taken in by the passion and care of the details he put into his work.

She was surprised that she didn't want the night to end. She wasn't sure if she ever enjoyed talking to a guy she'd just met this much.

He told her that he would be over at 9am to get started on the plumbing. He also promised her that the bathroom in her room would be back in full working order no later than Sunday.

In the meantime, since he would start with her bathroom first, she needed to clear her things out so he could get the work done easier.

Checking the clock, Winter decided to call Chloe and Jessica. It was about time she caught them up on the events unfolding in her life.

"Are you sure you aren't busy?" Winter asked for the second time since Chloe had answered the phone. Now that she had her friend on the line and knew Derek was home, the call felt intrusive. "I don't want to interrupt you and Derek."

"I told you, I'm good. Derek is in his office preparing for some upcoming meeting, and I was just painting my toenails. Your timing is perfect. What's up?"

Chloe was mostly quiet the whole time Winter recounted

the details of her assault, the plumbing situation and Kody's role in everything.

Every now and then, Chloe would gasp and say, "Are you kidding?" or laugh where appropriate, but nothing more than that.

When Winter was finally done, Chloe said, "First things first, I'll bet you were scared because I would have pissed myself."

Winter released a lengthy sigh.

"I think I was too afraid to do much of anything other than try to keep my life intact."

"I am so glad that bastard didn't get to hurt you. I would have had to hunt him down and kill him myself!"

"I know. I thank God for Kody being there when he was."

There was a long pause before Chloe spoke again.

"That brings me to the next thing. This sexy stallion saves you, then ends up being one of the guys working next door to you. And you didn't even mention any of this when you came over to shower the other day?! If I wasn't so thankful you were ok I'd be so mad with you right now."

Winter was instantly filled with guilt. Hiding this from one of her closest friends may have been a mistake, but it seemed like the ideal decision at the time.

"I'm sorry, Chloe. At first, I didn't want to share the assault because it was too fresh and I just wanted to forget about it."

Chloe's voice softened. "I understand. I'm not mad at you, I just hate the idea of you being alone in all this."

"Yeah, well, maybe I'm not. Kody will be living next door while he works on the house, so I don't think I will be alone too often."

"Huh? Why is he living next door? Is he homeless or some sort of charity case for his job?"

Winter laughed out loud. "Homeless... far from it, I actually think he's loaded. He has a house in California and owns the construction company with his cousin. He moves around between here and his other locations in Texas and California, working on different homes, getting them built, repaired, or whatever they need to get them sold."

"Interesting," Chloe said in an intrigued tone. Then, with sudden excitement, she added, "I like it! And I think I like this Kody guy for you. Please tell me he is single?"

"No, no no. You calm down Chloe James! I don't need you trying to play matchmaker. He is single, but he is also just passing through. I don't want any messy situations or to jump in line with all the other women I assume are beating down his door."

"Don't start, Winter, you are already thinking too much. Stop worrying about the other women. You obviously like him and I am going to go out on a limb and say he likes you too, right?"

Winter leaned against her bathroom wall and thought about it.

"I think so," she said hesitantly. "I mean, he is offering to do the plumbing work for free."

Chloe was silent for a long moment and then said, "Winter, you must have missed a step. You told me about your plumbing issues and that you hired him to fix it. Somehow, you didn't mention that he was doing it all for free."

"Yeah," Winter said sheepishly, "I skipped that little detail."

"Do I need to come over and slap some sense into you? Of course, he likes you! This man is about to throw away thousands of dollars just to look at your ass, and you are saying you think he likes you!"

"It's not completely free. I will at least make him meals once a week."

At that, Chloe started laughing so hard it sounded like she

dropped the phone, but Winter couldn't fault her. The whole arrangement did sound pretty lopsided. Which begged the question again...

Why would he do this for free?

Chloe finally settled down and said, "For what he is doing, you need to open a restaurant for him, and don't forget to add yourself to the menu of available options."

Winter rolled her eyes.

"Only you would have a ton of sex jokes," Winter said.

"I think anyone in their right mind would," Chloe responded playfully before continuing in a more sober tone. "Seriously, though, it's clear he really likes you. So what if he may leave soon? That's why they made cars, planes and phones. You are basing your reactions on the fact that your past attempts at a long distance didn't work out. Don't do that to yourself."

Winter sighed.

"I know you're probably right, but I just need to think about it some more. Opening up only to be crushed repeatedly isn't easy."

"I get that, sweetie," Chloe said. "That's why, in the meantime, you will have me pushing you out of the nest, again and again, my little birdie. I'm not letting you grow all cold and distant. Yeah, love hurts, but so can being alone if you don't want to be."

It all made perfect sense, yet Winter was still being cautious.

"I hear you, Chloe, and I'll try. That's the best I can give you."

"That's all I'm asking for," her friend replied. Happy that she had won this round.

Winter glanced at the time again. It was getting late.

"Sorry to cut this short, but I need to call Jessica. I'm sure she, too, would like an update on my life."

"Don't bother," Chloe said. "She'll be calling you."

"What did you do?" Winter grumbled.

"I was texting her while we were chatting," Chloe said. "No way is she going to sit this love story out. The way you two met and now with him living next door, she wants all the details."

Sure enough, Winter's phone beeped, indicating an incoming call.

"And there's Jessica," Winter said. "You want to be added in?"

"Nope, got to go. I'm about to surprise hubby in his office with a happy ending." She giggled mischievously. "Later."

Winter switched over to Jessica, and as soon as she said hello, Jessica blurted out, "Oh, Winter, it's just like the movies. Tell me everything!"

For the second time that night, Winter dove into the story of how they met, reconnected, the plumbing drama and how she feels about him.

After hearing responses that sounded identical to Chloe's and catching up on what was new in Jessica's life, they ended the call.

Smiling to herself, Winter thought about how much she loved her friends.

They were kind, honest, hilarious, and a whole lot crazy, but she wouldn't have it any other way. A chat with them always made her feel much better and more open to taking risks.

Taking a risk is actually how they all became friends.

It was in fourth grade that they bonded over setting up a boy that was bullying them. He was a fifth-grader named Terrell Nash but went by the nickname Terror.

He was a lot of trouble and spent most of his time harassing all the other kids in school—making them cry or stealing their lunch money, was all part of his day-to-day.

It was Chloe who finally said enough was enough. She'd found Winter in the corner crying because Terror had snatched off one of her favorite hair bows during recess and wouldn't give it back.

Chloe decided since he liked to steal, maybe she could give him something a lot more valuable to take.

Chloe knew where their teacher kept her purse. It was in a closet in the back of the classroom on the top shelf.

Therefore, the next day, having Winter stand guard, Chloe snuck in and made it to the closet.

Using a step stool that was in the corner, she retrieved her teacher's purse, wallet and, for good measure, a pack of gum.

Terror kept his book bag on a table outside during recess, so she planned to slip the items in and later tell a teacher that she saw him do it.

However, on her way out, still holding the wallet and gum in hand, she saw Jessica, who was at the blackboard, erasing the lessons from that morning.

Jessica was a straight-A student, labeled teacher's pet, and was always used as an example of how the rest of them should behave.

Chloe didn't care for Jessica for those reasons alone, and now Miss goody two-shoes was probably going to rat her out.

To her surprise, Jessica said nothing. She merely stared at Chloe, wide-eyed, and after a moment of just looking at each other, Chloe figured, "What the hell?" she'd come this far.

So she tucked the items into her pockets and walked back to the door to go outside.

Successfully planting the evidence in Terror's book bag, she waited until recess was over and then ran up to the teacher, telling her what she saw.

Of course, Terrell denied taking anything. He was outside the whole time he swore to the teacher.

Chloe assumed the teacher might ask the class if anyone

else saw Terrell take anything, at which point Winter was supposed to step forward and say she did.

But to Chloe's horror, the teacher didn't do that.

Instead, she went to ask Jessica if she saw anyone inside the classroom while she was cleaning the board. And of course, Jessica said she did see someone.

Chloe rolled her eyes and was ready to surrender when Jessica said she saw Terrell sneaking away with the stolen items.

Needless to say, little Terror got in some major trouble, and Winter got new friends.

They had her back then, and they still had it now. Chloe and Jessica were right, she should stop being so scared.

So what if love didn't work out well for her in the past? That didn't mean she should go out of her way to avoid getting to know a great guy.

Maybe if nothing else, he could end up being a good friend that she hung out with when he was in town. He was the type that was impressive on and off paper, and that was a good thing.

With his business mind and easy-going nature, he was definitely a good person to know. That's when Winter officially decided she and Kody could be friends.

No one could ever have too many friends, could they?

Even if he was a friend, she wanted desperately to sleep with. That didn't have to happen, right?

She could play it cool and just go with the flow.

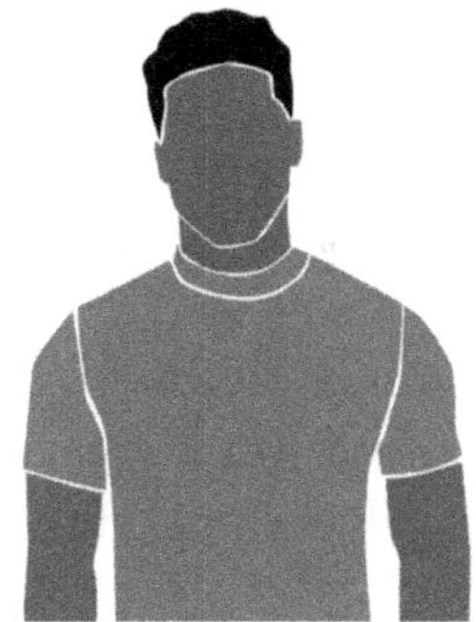

That was one of the most enjoyable evenings Kody had experienced with a woman in a long time... that didn't include sex, of course. For the past few years, every date he had was predictably the same - small talk, then sex and sometimes not even in that order.

But in the last few months, it hadn't consisted of anything because he hadn't had the time or interest to entertain women he knew he could never be serious with.

Kody's last date was five months ago with a girl named Keisha. She lived on the other side of the community he lived in, and they often exchanged pleasantries when he was checking his mail and she was out walking her dog.

Keisha repeatedly hinted at them going out, but Kody wasn't convinced it was a great idea. True, she was attractive, had a very nice body, and seemed sane enough. Yet somehow, she gave him a weird vibe.

However, having nothing concrete to base his internal hesitations on, he finally caved and asked her out to dinner.

In the end, he should have just listened to his instincts. After their second date, it became clear why she wanted to get to know him. She was a divorcée who was only living in the neighborhood because she got the house in the settlement.

The problem was, she couldn't afford to live in the

upscale, gated community and keep up with her lavish lifestyle at the same time.

Therefore, Keisha was hoping to get remarried soon so that someone could keep her living the life she had become accustomed to.

She assumed Kody must have made a pretty decent living because he had a home in the neighborhood. She was right about that assumption, but wrong that Kody was going to be husband number two.

The magnet effect money had was something that he had become familiar with after running into his fair share of women who wanted to become Mrs. Benton for all the wrong reasons.

Generally, his looks alone were enough to grab a woman's attention, but when they discovered he was pretty well off, they pressed the idea of having a relationship harder.

Usually, he could tell the type from a mile away, and if they did get past his radar, it wasn't long before they revealed themselves in one way or another.

Kody thought back to another woman he was getting to know who was attracted by the number of zeros she assumed were in his bank account.

They were at his house watching a movie, and she asked to use the restroom. Pointing her in the direction of it, Kody continued watching the movie.

After hearing a small noise coming from his home office, he walked towards the sound. She was on the phone with her friend with her back towards the door.

He heard her tell the friend that she was looking for his bank statement because she could tell he had money.

He had to give it to her. She was bold.

Impressed with her courageous action, Kody gave her another minute to continue her search.

She wouldn't find anything, of course. Anything

pertaining to his personal finances was in a safe across the room, hidden by a decorative table.

Casually leaning on the doorframe, he'd said, *"I think you'll have better luck if you look through the papers to your right."*

The woman nearly jumped out of her skin and Kody still smiles to himself when he thinks about that story.

Yes, he had definitely met his share of women he referred to as "goal minded." Which was why he could tell that Winter was so different.

It's as if she called out to him without even saying a word. Activating his protective mode to want to be there for her, spoil her and do anything to make her smile.

He had already broken his own rule of mixing business with pleasure, but he simply could not resist. He wanted to make sure she was taken care of and that the job was done right.

Being a contractor himself, he'd heard the horror stories of crappy work and unprofessional service. He did not want that happening to Winter.

Kody was so moved by not only her beauty but her drive, creativity, genuine kindness and strength. She wasn't looking for handouts from him or anyone else. He admired the hell out of that in a woman, and it just made him want her even more.

Money already wasn't a big deal to him; he simply wanted to spend it on a woman that he cared for and felt deserved it. And even though he had just met her, he could tell Winter Daniels was one of those women.

The last time he felt this way was in his mid-20s. Her name was Latisha, but everyone called her Tish, and she was something special. Sadly, though, she met the wrong version of Kody. That version was younger and dumber and didn't know something amazing when he saw it.

Even though he wasn't looking for a good woman, only a good time, Tish changed all that. The way she carried herself, her goals, her perspective and overall aura broadcasted her as not typical.

At the time, her mature stance on the world and how she lived in it was a significant contrast to his immature ways and "live life like a party" attitude.

Nevertheless, they enjoyed each other's company and after a year of dating, Kody had fallen hard for her.

Then one day, Tish did what he considered the unthinkable. She invited him to the wedding of her best friend. After that, it was all downhill. His mind switched from rational to irrational faster than ever.

He became entirely convinced that she would want to be a bride next.

It was likely his own paranoia, and her invite was innocent. Still, in his adolescent mind, she was basically asking him to plan his own wedding instead of merely attending one.

Because he wasn't a total asshole, he didn't leave her hanging. He still accompanied her to the wedding, but afterward, he slowly started to pull away by calling less and not asking her on dates.

Tish confronted him about it a few times, but Kody shrugged it off as being busy. Eventually, Tish stopped pressing the issue and faded away completely.

For the years that followed, Kody hadn't gotten that initial spark he did with Tish, with anyone else, and he assumed he'd never get it again, but now he had.

In every way that he could imagine, he wanted Winter. The only drawback was that she had walls up. Kody could see it in her eyes, and it displayed through her cautious actions.

For instance, claiming she threw his number out by accident didn't fool him. It was merely how she avoided getting too close.

For now, she saw Kody as bad news, a man that couldn't be trusted, but in time, he would prove to her that she could.

Sitting at a table abandoned by the work crew a few days ago, he scrolled through his planner. He needed to prep a list of tools he would need and assign timelines for when he would have each step done.

Thinking over the details, it dawned on him that he could move faster if he got someone to assist.

Already reaching for his phone, Kody knew who he'd ask.

Tim Minter, a long-time employee, welcomed overtime and usually kept his weekends free in case the company had any extra projects. With three kids already and a set of twins on the way, Kody understood Tim's reasoning.

He would give Tim a call and let him know he needed a hand. Giving Winter one less thing to stress over before he returned to California had become a priority.

Damn, what happens when I leave?

That thought was a surprise. Yes, he wanted her, but he shouldn't be so troubled by the thought of leaving.

Surely, if a deeper relationship formed between them, the distance wouldn't destroy it, would it?

It destroyed you and Ashley.

The reminder gave him pause. He'd met Ashley in Georgia the previous year, and their relationship fell apart not long after it officially started.

But Winter isn't Ashley.

And thank God for that, because Ashley was a headache. Kody picked up his notepad, abandoning his useless wondering and instead focused on the now.

It was clear the plumbing would be a lot of work, but he wouldn't dare tell Winter that. He didn't want to give her any reason to shy away from him.

The next morning, Kody was up bright and early. When the doorbell rang at 8:15, indicating Tim had arrived, they immediately got down to business.

Kody explained the timeline and phases he wanted the work completed in. Then he went outside to help Tim unload the truck and carry tools, pipes and drywall over to Winter's yard.

When everything was complete, they walked up the three stairs that led to Winter's front door.

Winter opened it before Kody even had the chance to knock.

"Well, good morning, beautiful," he said to her.

She was wearing gray and purple drawstring shorts and a white tank top that read, "I'll just sleep it off." Her hair was up in a high ponytail, with a few loose pieces that were doing an adorable job of framing her face.

He wanted to throw his damn work bag to the side and work on her instead.

Winter smiled, said good morning, and invited them in.

Standing in the entryway, Kody put down his work bag and introduced Tim.

"We are ready to get started," Kody said.

"I see, and ten minutes early, no less. I was making some coffee and saw you guys walking over from the window. Would either of you like a cup?"

"We just had some," Kody replied.

"Okay. Well, you know where the bathroom is. Please let me know if you need anything."

Nodding, both men headed toward the bathroom, and Winter walked into the living room.

It only took moments before the clanking and banging noises of repairs flooded the house. Kody was thankful that her house wasn't huge because it meant they would get to the pipes easier and seal things back up faster.

About an hour into working, Kody realized they were missing a part. Going into the living room, he spotted Winter sitting at the table typing away on her computer. She looked up at him and smiled.

"Sorry to bother you, but would it be okay if we ran to the warehouse to get another part we need? It could wait until tomorrow, but we are working at a good pace, and I don't want to interrupt that. The warehouse is only fifteen minutes away, so it won't take long."

"Fine by me," she said.

He briefly considered leaving Tim to keep working while he was gone. He trusted Tim and had no reason to doubt his professionalism or Winter's safety around him. But he could never do that.

Her attack was still a fresh wound, and being left with a man she had just met wasn't a good call on his end. If he wanted her to open up, he needed to make her always feel protected.

Kody and Tim retrieved the necessary part from the warehouse and returned to Winter's in under an hour.

Around 1:30, things were looking so good with the plumbing that Kody was certain he would have her shower ready by the time he was done working for the day.

Entering the living room to tell her the good news, he saw her busy moving around in the kitchen. She obviously didn't hear him come in because she didn't look up.

He watched her for a moment, enjoying the view of her small curvy frame advance around the kitchen as she stepped this way and that, putting food on a white tray.

Every time she leaned down, one of her long black curls

would fall in her face. He could easily get used to seeing her every day.

Finally, he said, "Winter, do you have a second?"

Picking up the tray, she came around the island and sat what looked to be chicken wraps on the table.

"Sure, what's up?"

"I have good news. We are almost done with the plumbing for your en suite bathroom. We will need to finish the drywall tomorrow, but you are welcome to use your shower tonight."

Winter released a grateful sigh.

"Thank God!" she said. "When you first walked in, I thought you were going to say you ran into some issues and I would be without my bathroom for another week! But thank you for that, and now I have some good news for you."

Kody was taken aback. Seeing her was good enough news for him.

"What is your good news?" he asked.

"Lunch is ready."

Kody's brows lifted. "Lunch?"

"Yes, lunch. You didn't think I was going to let you work and not feed you two, did you?"

"Winter, you didn't have to do that. We would have—"

She waved a hand to cut off his response.

"It's no trouble, and it provides the perfect segue into what else I wanted to ask you. What do you think about dinners twice a week instead of just once? Maybe Saturdays and Sundays?" She looked down sheepishly before continuing. "It seems unfair to have you work here and then have to go order takeout at home alone."

Kody nodded slowly, unable to stop the smile tugging at his lips.

"I think your new offer sounds great."

"Wonderful! Now you can have lunch whenever you're

ready, and if seven works for you tonight, I will see you for dinner."

That evening, he was on time, as usual.

Winter had just started setting the table when he arrived. He offered to give her a hand, but she declined, saying most of the work was already done.

She told him to make himself comfortable, and he did so by looking around the small, but cozy living room.

On one side of the fireplace there were built-in bookshelves that displayed various objects such as books, tiny decor pieces and artwork.

Neatly in the corner of the bottom shelf were several board games. Kody leaned in to take a closer look.

"I see you have trouble and monopoly. Those are two of my favorite games."

"They may be your favorite, but I, Mr. Benton, am the champ."

Kody tossed her a challenging look over his shoulder.

"Oh, really? I'd like to see you prove that," he said.

"Careful what you wish for," she responded.

Coming around the kitchen island, Winter placed two plates on the table. "Dinner is ready."

They dined on perfectly seasoned steaks, paired with mashed potatoes and a spinach salad. The food was delicious, and before he knew it, dinner was over and they had relocated to the couch.

"What were you like in high school?" Kody asked.

Winter thought about the question, then said, "I was a mess to put it simply. Completely consumed with all the teenage girl drama—moody and thinking my world was over every time the slightest negative thing happened. My good friends, Chloe, Jessica and I were cheerleaders, and that was fun. But overall, I would never want to live through those years again."

He loved watching her talk and reminisce. The way her eyes widened, her hands moved in excited animation, and even the joy in her voice captivated him.

"I remember you telling me about your friends. They sound nice. Chloe is the one that just got married, right?"

"Yes, and Jessica is the event planner who organized it."

Kody nodded, then said, "Do you ever want to get married?"

He could tell she was caught off guard by his question. She blinked a few times before clearing her throat. "I do," she answered slowly. "But who knows, relationships can be so tricky."

Not when it's with the right one.

"True," was all he said.

"What about you?" Winter asked.

"I'd love to be married one day," he said, noticing once again the brief surprise that covered her face, but she straightened it quickly, switching the subject.

"Wait," she said, nudging his leg. "You didn't tell me about how you were in high school. Let me guess, you were a jock and a real ladies' man?"

"Sadly, that describes me. I spent way too much time enjoying the glory of being the "it" guy and a lot less time understanding that being "it" could do nothing for me. I didn't apply myself as much as I should have and got in trouble a lot."

"No judgments here. None of us were our best selves in high school. Any high school sweethearts?"

"Nope. As you said, I was a ladies' man, so I wasn't interested in dating just one girl."

Winter nodded as if his immature ways in high school were still alive and well in the man he was today.

She then confirmed his suspicions when she said, "Yeah, that doesn't surprise me."

"I'd never deny the truth," Kody responded. "That was me from high school and basically until my mid-20s."

"Okay. So why should I believe it's not you now?"

Kody sat back and studied her, wishing he could take her into his arms and remove every awful experience from her life. Clearly, those experiences had tainted her view of men, or at the very least, relationships, and she deserved better.

"Something you should know about me. I don't beat around the bush. If I ask it, I want to know it. If I say it, it's because I mean it, and if I think it, it's usually because I'm going to do it."

Winter shifted as if the temperature in the room had gone up several notches, which meant she understood him perfectly. If he wanted it, he got it, and what he wanted was her.

Winter narrowed her eyes. "So you are saying you used to only be about sex and games, but now you have matured and left that life behind?"

"Bingo," he said.

Winter shrugged. "If you say so."

"I do say so. And let's get the spotlight off of me. Did you have a high school sweetheart?"

Winter shook her head.

"I dated a few different guys, but nothing serious."

"Interesting," he said.

Winter shifted on the couch to fully face him. "How so?"

"Well, just like I seem like such a bad boy to you. You strike me as a good girl. One that is very old-fashioned in her way of doing things. I could see you staying serious with one guy throughout school, attend college together and then get married."

Winter threw up her hands.

"I guess that does describe me, simple in the things that pertain to life and love. I mean, I wasn't like you, just having sex with everyone. I actually stayed a virgin all throughout high school."

He noticed she quickly averted her eyes as if she said something or gave some insight into herself that she didn't mean to.

Smiling, he said, "Then that settles it. You are as much a good girl as you seem."

"Whatever," Winter responded, playfully rolling her eyes.

"No, seriously," Kody reassured her. "I think that's cool."

Somehow, that made her even sexier to him. He wished, at that moment, he could kiss her, yank her down to the floor and have his way with her. But he knew he couldn't, now was not the time.

But soon.

Suddenly, Winter snapped her fingers as if remembering something. "You said earlier you enjoyed board games. Want to play a few rounds of trouble?" she asked.

Kody thought the game title accurately described their situation, because if she stayed this close to him for too much longer, trouble is what she'd be in.

CHAPTER ELEVEN
Winter

"EVERY TIME I
SHOWER, I'LL
THINK OF YOU."

The next day was more of the same—loud noises as Kody and Tim worked on the house. Winter was grateful that she had been able to take a shower last night and couldn't shake the feeling that she needed to do more to prove her gratitude.

Already she had added in lunch and dinner on Saturdays and Sundays, but perhaps there was something more that could properly convey her appreciation.

Perhaps sex would be the perfect thank-you gift.

The thought entered her mind before she could stop it, like a reflex ready to wave the white flag and give in to every sensual desire she had.

After much effort, Winter successfully pushed the thought aside. What she gave Kody wouldn't be sex, no matter how starved for intimacy she was.

However, it would be something special. Now all that was left was to figure out exactly what that could be.

At dinner that night, they enjoyed chicken curry with garbanzo beans, onions, and peppers over a bed of jasmine rice.

Winter asked more questions about Kody's company and how it all got started. The goal was to keep him talking, not only because his job fascinated her to no end, but she loved hearing his voice and staring at his lips.

I'll bet he's a good kisser.

Her fantasy of him lying her on the table, brushing soft kisses all over her body, before having his way with her, played on an endless loop inside her head throughout dinner.

When it came time for Kody to leave, Winter gave him a hug that was far from innocent. Mentally blaming her "accidental caresses" to his arms and chest on the alcohol.

His hard body framed against hers almost made her abandon all will power and yank him down for a kiss. But right before she threw caution, and her panties to the wind, Kody leaned down, kissed her on the cheek and said goodnight.

The next morning, standing in her completely repaired bathroom, Winter prepped a quick text for Kody.

> Winter: Thanks again for the repairs. Now, every time I shower, I'll think of you.

Immediately, she closed her eyes and groaned. Her choice of words sounded way too flirty, even though technically she would think of him, because he fixed it.

That made sense... right?

Hitting send before she could talk herself out of it, Winter placed her phone on the bathroom counter and finished getting ready for work.

The day progressed slowly. A norm for when the studio team was wrapping up projects.

Set up days were always exciting. Cleaning up, however, was a complete bore, and Winter spent most of the day overseeing and signing final walkthrough documents..

Around noon, Lisa stopped by Winter's office. "Hey, Winter, you got a minute?"

"Sure, what's up?"

Lisa came in and sat down. Then leaned back and closed her eyes.

"Umm, are you okay?" Winter asked, confused.

"Yeah, I'm fine, just hiding from Mr. Sanders."

"Why?"

"I had ten minutes left on my break. He found me sitting at my desk and started this long conversation about how he had the perfect guy for me. I was a little intrigued at first, and then I found out he was talking about his nephew, Dylan."

Lisa made a face to match the obvious disgust she had on the inside, and reflexively, Winter did the same.

Dylan was Mr. Sanders' forty-something year old nephew who was always trying to hook up with someone. The task seemed simple enough, but it was a challenge because Dylan was gross.

He was immature, dressed poorly and had no ambition. Even worse was the fact that he'd lived in his uncle's basement for the last four years and liked to flaunt his relation to the boss, hoping to get dates.

Dylan flirted with every girl and tossed around outdated pickup lines to, as he called it, "seal the deal."

Winter once had the unfortunate experience of being subjected to his company for an entire hour.

Not wanting to be rude, Winter tried her hardest to wait him out, praying that he would see a girl in a short skirt walk by that he couldn't bear to ignore.

However, after Winter made a comment about being sleepy and Dylan said, "I know you are tired because you've been running through my mind all day," her patience vanished.

She put her phone to her ear, faked answering an emergency call, and excused herself to her office, where she hid out for the rest of the day.

Not too heartbroken by her absence, Winter heard through work gossip that Dylan moved on to one of the director's assistants.

"Enough said," she stated to Lisa. "Hide away."

Turning her attention back to her computer, Winter realized she hadn't checked her phone since she got to work. When she glanced at the screen, she immediately began smiling.

> Kody: You are very welcome. I'm glad to hear you'll think of me in the shower; my skills are the reason you are wet after all.

Winter bit her lip and grinned harder.

Should I reply? Or make him wait?

If she responded, Kody would likely say something that had her getting wetter right there in her office. No shower required.

Winter sighed, and for the millionth time, reminded herself to keep things light.

There is only friendship in our future, nothing more.

Nevertheless, the idea of sex with Kody wouldn't depart her mind so easily. It was thrilling and new, which turned Winter on and scared her at the same time. Which was odd. Winter wasn't a prude and sex definitely wasn't scary.

Possibly, it was just that her attraction to him was unlike any she'd ever had. She wanted him, and every day Winter felt as if her desires would override her logical reasonings to stay away.

"What has you smiling like that?" Lisa said, staring at Winter suspiciously.

Winter cleared her throat and put her phone away.

"Oh, nothing."

"Yeah, right, either it's a man, or the test was negative," Lisa said.

Winter laughed out loud.

"Not that it is any of your business, but I'll give you a hint; it isn't a test."

"Good, it's a man!" Lisa stated excitedly, sitting forward in her seat. "Do we like him?"

"It's not like that. We are just friends," Winter said, trying not only to convince Lisa, but herself.

"Boo," Lisa said. "I need to hear about some real love. Staging all these scenes are really messing with my mind. I need to either experience my own fairytale or live vicariously through someone else's romantic reality."

Winter shrugged. "Sorry to disappoint."

"No biggie. I've got work to do, anyway. I think I have successfully dodged Mr. Sanders, so I'm going to help them bring in some equipment from outside."

"Why? Are they about to start another scene?" Winter asked. "I didn't see anymore on the schedule."

"No. It looks like it's about to rain, so they want to move some things in."

"Oh, wow. Then they'll have to move it right back out for tomorrow, huh?"

"Not likely. I checked the forecast. I think it's going to rain all week."

"Damn. Sucks for their budget."

Lisa nodded and stood. "Yes, it does," she said, moving towards the door. Lisa stuck her head outside of Winter's office and peeked around, first checking to the right, then to the left and, for good measure, the right again. "Alright, I think I'm good. Later."

She was gone before Winter got the chance to say goodbye.

Winter considered the conundrum for the setup team. If they couldn't do the outdoor scenes for the rest of the week, that would create a pile-up of work for next week, which wasn't good because next week was already full.

But that was a problem for next week, no need to borrow stress. Instead, she could use this downtime to locate an acceptable gift for Mr. Sanders's niece because she still had no idea what to get.

It did indeed rain for the rest of the week. But anything that pushed the intense heat of August out for some cooler weather was worth the gloomy, gray, water-filled days.

Especially since Winter had other things to lift her spirits.

She and Kody had been texting and chatting on the phone all week. He made her laugh, and hearing his voice made her feel alive in indescribable ways.

The problem was quickly becoming that she couldn't get enough of him and every encounter they had left her wanting more.

Besides, it wasn't as if she saw him a lot this week. Rainy days kept him and his team mostly indoors doing repairs.

It appeared Winter was throwing her own advice about not getting too close, right out the window.

Then again, they hadn't done anything more than talk and enjoy one another's company, so maybe there was still hope for her.

It was nice being his friend, and besides the flirtatious comment about the shower making her think of him, there hadn't been any more naughty notes exchanged.

Winter finished her dinner and placed her plate in the sink. Walking over to the nightstand that was now ready for a fresh coat of paint, she decided to work on it for a few hours before getting ready for bed.

She turned on the TV, and instantly, HGTV came roaring to life, providing Winter with the inspiration and background noise she needed to work.

The hours ticked by and Winter half-listened to the episodes as they played out. Every now and again, she paused briefly to see the house before the remodel and then again once it was complete.

As a new episode began, Winter took another break.

This couple wanted a home with a long list of features, including at least four bathrooms, five bedrooms, a large kitchen, an office area, a deck, a pool and a large space for entertaining.

As the show host took them around to see homes that had the potential to meet the couple's many requests, Winter felt an uneasiness creep in.

The home the couple was currently touring had nearly fifteen bolts on the door. The husband made some comment that the previous owners must have been obsessed with security and the wife laughed it off like it was some joke.

Wanting to feel safe was no laughing matter in Winter's mind, and the comment caused her to glance up at her own door.

One measly lock stared back at her.

After her whole ordeal, she should have considered making sure she was a lot safer in her own home.

May as well add figuring out how to better secure the premises to the growing list of ways to protect herself. She already had to find a way to stop those awful sporadic nightmares and learn to defend herself on there.

Apparently, she truly had her work cut out for her, and sadly, she didn't want to face any of it.

Winter woke with a jerk. The man with the knife had her.

She shoved at her covers and realized...

No, he doesn't. It was just a dream. A fake, no possibility of becoming a real danger, dream.

No one had her. She was safe in her bed at home. The glow of her nightlight was bright enough to cast a glow in every corner of her small room.

No one else was there.

Taking a few deep breaths, her eyes darted towards the clock; it was 11:30.

She was safe and everything was fine. If only her heart would get back into her chest, she would be able to collect herself.

It was only a dream.

But it felt so real—his breath on the back of her neck and the cold, sharp blade at the front. He held it with just enough pressure to slice her clean open if she made the wrong move.

"Not real. Not real," she said aloud.

Then she heard it, a sound at her window. Getting out of bed hesitantly, Winter tiptoed over to the window. Gathering her nerves, she risked a tiny peek out into the dark, rainy night.

Nothing was there. More importantly, *no one* was there.

Maybe it was just a loose branch or thunder in the distance. The news did say that there would be a major thunderstorm rolling in.

Getting back into bed, Winter did three rounds of slow, steady inhales and exhales, then closed her eyes.

Drifting back to sleep, Winter saw it again... the knife! And it was at that exact moment that a powerful bolt of lightning cracked the sky.

Shaking and beyond terrified, she grabbed her pillow, and suddenly the room went absolutely dark.

"No, no no no no," Winter said, retrieving a large flashlight from her nightstand drawer as a tsunami of terrifying questions swam around in her head.

Did someone cut my power? Are they trying to break in? Will sitting in bed like an idiot give them ample time to do so?

Shining the flashlight at her closed bedroom door and tightening her grip on the pillow, a new panic set in.

I need a weapon. How in the hell do I not have a weapon? All I have is a stupid flashlight! What can I do with this? Hope the light catches his eyes and momentarily blinds him so I can get away? This is ridiculous! He'd stab me to death while laughing at me.

And there it was, her entire pathetic demise. The intruder may as well take her now. She wouldn't fight, hell she couldn't fight.

I only have a fucking flashlight! Winter once again reminded herself.

"Calm down, Winter," she said aloud, but hearing her own voice offered no reassurance because it sounded shakier than ever.

First things first, she would check the window again. Maybe the power went out throughout the entire neighborhood. If that wasn't the case, she would make her way to the kitchen and grab a knife. A big knife.

Then again, maybe switching the order of things and getting the knife before checking the window would be smarter.

What if someone really was trying to break in?

She was wasting time.

The window was closer than the knives in the kitchen, and Winter figured if she exercised caution and moved quickly, there would be nothing to worry about.

Winter placed the flashlight on the nightstand and picked up her cellphone in its place. If there was someone out there, at least she could dial 9-1-1 as she ran down the hall and out the front door screaming bloody murder.

She released a huge breath.

No one had singled her out. The entire neighborhood was dark, which meant that no one had power. Finally, getting her nerves to accept that there was likely no threat, Winter almost screamed when her cellphone vibrated in her hand.

The sudden movement caused her to bump into the nightstand, and the flashlight fell to the floor. It landed on her foot and Winter let out a curse as it rolled from side-to-side, bouncing light off the walls.

After picking up the flashlight, Winter looked at her phone and saw an indication for a text.

Kody: Are you okay?

Winter: No.

More should have been said, but Winter was having trouble getting her bearings.

She was not okay.

Maybe in five minutes, when her nerves were no longer on edge, she would be, but for now, she wasn't.

This was no time to play strong. She was afraid and even sleep offered no escape. Mistake or not, she couldn't take it back now.

Suddenly, Winter heard knocking at her front door and Kody's voice calling her name.

Yanking up the flashlight, she rushed to open it.

Coming inside, Kody placed his hands on her shoulders before caressing her face and cupping her chin. "What's wrong? Are you alright?"

Winter could only nod.

Had this man run over to save me... again?

"What happened?" he asked.

Embarrassment was beginning to set in and Winter fidgeted, adjusting the flashlight to avoid blinding either of them.

Choosing her words carefully, she said, "The thunder must have woken me up. Then with the power going out shortly after and sounds of what I think must have been branches hitting my window, I guess I just got scared."

There was no way she would tell him about the nightmare. This entire ordeal was pathetic enough. The power going out shouldn't scare her the way it did.

She had spent many nights alone in this house without power due to weather issues. If it was manageable then, it should be manageable now.

Yeah, but that was before a man held a knife to your throat.

Looking up at him, she asked, "Did you literally drop everything to rush over here?"

"Yeah," he said, as if she should have known he would. "I was up working when the power went out and I wanted to make sure you were okay. When you said you weren't, well..." he lifted his hands, letting his presence speak for itself. "I don't even think I shut the front door."

Winter didn't know what to say. No man had ever seemed to care about her this much.

"Listen. I'm going to go next door and get a couple of

things and lock up the house. I will be back in less than two minutes, alright?"

Winter nodded, and Kody exited the house.

She turned around, shining the light throughout her living room. There was nothing out of place, and no vengeful man with a knife had been lurking in the darkness.

But seeing she had nothing to fear still didn't settle her unease. Hearing the thunder crackle and pop in the distance, she prayed Kody would get back quick.

Her prayers were answered when he walked back into her house less than a minute later, carrying some big, bulky object. Kody placed it on the floor and pressed a button.

Instantly, the entire entryway, including her kitchen and living room, were illuminated.

"Wow," Winter said, looking around. "It's kinda like the lights are back on."

The light was so bright, her flashlight became nothing more than a glow stick in comparison. She switched it off and was once again thankful that her house wasn't that big.

"The power just went out a few minutes ago; I'm surprised you already had something like this," she said.

"I keep it on the truck. It's useful for when I'm working late or on a site that doesn't have power yet."

"Thank God for your smart planning," she said.

They moved to the couch and sat down.

"Cute pajamas," he said.

"Thanks," Winter replied, looking down. She was wearing an all-red set, with white letters that read:

Nap time are my happy hours.

"What were you working on?"

"Computer work from a few of our past projects," he said.

"I hope the outage didn't cause you to lose something you can't get back."

"No, everything is fine. I'm always prepared." Kody faced her. A more serious tone to his voice. "Tell me again what made you say you weren't okay when you texted me?"

"I already told you, it was the thunderstorm. I think everything caught me off guard. Why are you asking again?"

He touched her hand and said in a tone that somehow proved he knew she wasn't being completely honest. "Because I feel a person should have to look you in the eyes when they are being dishonest with you," Kody said.

Winter exhaled audibly. "Okay, you got me. I had another nightmare."

His gorgeous brown eyes softened.

"Why didn't you call me, Winter? I told you, you can always call me."

Now, on top of being pathetic, Winter felt guilty.

"Yeah, but people say that. They don't really mean it. It's just a common line that people use. Usually to fill the silence."

"Winter, I told you. If I say it, I mean it."

He pulled her into his arms and kissed her forehead.

Is this really happening?

Winter was too afraid to move. Kody was still practically a stranger, yet somehow, amid her inner chaos, his embrace had the power to give her peace.

If she was dreaming again, this wholeheartedly beat those horrifying nightmares where she felt cold and alone under the control of a ruthless attacker. She now felt warm and safe.

His kindness and care on a matter so delicate gave Winter the courage to open up and talk to him about her reoccurring nightmares.

She fell asleep in his arms and slept soundly until the beeping sounds of appliances and random devices sprung back to life, indicating the power was on.

CHAPTER TWELVE
Winter

It was Sunday, and Winter was preparing the last originally agreed upon dinner for the work Kody had done.

However, she wasn't broken up over it because they had already decided to continue hanging out.

Kody not only had taken care of all the plumbing, but he had been there as a shoulder for her to lean on. Her nightmares had reared its horrific head often over the last few weeks, and every time she needed him, he came without question.

He'd stay as long as she needed him to and kept her mind occupied by playing board games, watching movies or just talking.

Kody never pushed for sex, and she liked that; in some twisted way, it made her want him more. But the pain of how hurt she would be if things didn't work out kept her in line... mostly.

Winter still cuddled close to him and enjoyed the gentle kisses on her forehead and cheek he'd often give her. But shockingly, she still hadn't kissed him.

Nevertheless, she could tell that it was a fight she was about to lose soon—might be tonight, even.

Turning off the water in the kitchen sink, Winter marveled at how great things looked. Everything worked perfectly and you couldn't tell where the new drywall and paint started and where the untouched parts ended.

Kody and Tim finished up around 11 a.m. that morning. Kody said he needed to shower and take care of a few work things before joining her at 7 for dinner.

It was now 6:50, and Winter was making the sauce for some homemade hot wings. Tonight's dinner was created to fit the mood. With it being the end of September, football season had started, and she and Kody were excited to watch the game.

Winter loved football.

Dressed in her Atlanta Falcons jersey and a cute pair of fitted black shorts, she carefully poured the sauce over the wings before adding them to a platter.

The doorbell rang, and she went to let Kody in.

"Smells good," he said, joining her in the kitchen. "Need me to do anything?"

"Nope, I got it. Go sit down. I'll bring the wings and beers to the table."

After getting them all set up, Winter turned on the TV and blasted the volume. This evening the living room would be as loud as the stadium itself.

Once done eating, they moved their cheering and shouting over to the couch.

During a commercial break, Kody said, "I need to ask you something."

Winter turned to him, a big smile on her face. The Falcons were in the lead and she couldn't have been in a better mood.

"What's up?"

"Would you like to go out to a company function with me? One of the investors we work with hosts an annual party that Jackson and I attend. It's next Saturday, and I would be honored if you were my date."

Winter's smiled widened.

"I'd love to. What time?"

"I can pick you up at seven?"

Her brows narrowed. "Pick me up? I can walk next door, and we go from there."

"You could, but you won't because it is a date, and I—" he said with emphasis on the word, "—am going to pick you up."

She loved his gentleman qualities.

"Excuse me then, your way sounds great. I'm surprised you're asking me out on a date. I just assumed you preferred not being seen with me in public," she said jokingly.

"That couldn't be further from the truth. You are gorgeous, and I think you know that."

He picked up his beer to take another sip.

"Thank you. And you, Kody Benton, are also very handsome," she said, giving him a flirtatious smile.

Placing his beer back on the coffee table coaster, Kody sat back on the couch and said, "Well, well, what do we have here? I think that is the first time you have verbally admitted your attraction to me."

Winter frowned. "Really? Surely, I have told you."

"Nope."

"What about when…"

"Nope."

"There was that time," she attempted yet again, words fading on her lips, as she couldn't recall an example.

"No," Kody said. "You smile, you avert your eyes, you even sigh in that way you do when you really want something, but you feel you shouldn't have it. But you never say it. Don't worry, though, Winter, I already know you want me."

"Do you?" Winter said, crossing her arms. "How?"

He watched her for a moment before speaking, causing her to shift uncomfortably to avoid his sexy, poker-faced gaze. "Come here," Kody suddenly said.

Winter moved closer and Kody placed his hand on her

exposed thigh, gently tracing one finger up her soft, chocolate-covered skin. Then he moved closer, wrapped his arm around her waist and lifted her onto his lap.

Stopping mere inches from her lips, he said, "because I want you just as bad."

Then their lips met.

Soft and teasingly at first, then more intense and passionate. Her mind was exploding.

Daaaaaammmmmmnnnnnnnnn!

Kody was a magnificent kisser.

Winter felt tingles all over her body, and the yearning in between her thighs was growing stronger with every second his mouth was on hers. She didn't want to stop, didn't want to pull away. She could stay like this forever.

"That was nice," she said when they finally had to take a breath.

"It was," he agreed.

Winter licked her lips, tasting the traces of him that were still there. The game was back on, but suddenly it didn't seem to matter as much.

"Why is it you've never tried to kiss me before?" she asked.

Kody's response was simple.

"Because you weren't ready."

Winter thought about it. She couldn't argue. He was right. If he tried too soon, she may have kissed him, but would likely have regretted it almost instantly.

She promised herself over a year ago that she would start taking her time, and tonight she felt she had done that. Kissing him felt right, and she found peace in that.

Leaning forward and staring into his eyes, she said, "Thankfully, I am now," and kissed him again.

It was date night, and Winter felt exhilarated. In her mind, the events of the evening would play out to be so romantic and blissful that she may as well be starring in a fairytale.

Holding the phone to her ear and standing in front of her closet, with dresses strewn about the room, anxiousness was setting in.

"What type of dress should I wear to this event?"

"That's easy," Chloe said. "One that says fuck me."

"Clo."

"Fast."

"Clo."

"And hard."

"CHLOE!" Winter said, stomping her foot.

Chloe laughed, then said, "Fine! Since you are such a prude, let me think about it." After a few seconds of silence, she said, "I got it! Wear that glamorous teal number you wore to the Gibson's charity event. Kody will have to use all of his restraint not to attack you on the dance floor."

Winter imagined it. Chloe was right; it would be perfect. The dress had a v cut around the chest area; it hugged her curves while simultaneously achieving a flowy effect.

It was the ideal combination of sexy and classy and was sure to make a good impression. The look on Kody's face when she stepped out in that beauty would keep his eyes locked on her all night.

"I agree," Winter said into the receiver. "I also think wearing my hair up will add a nice touch."

"Doesn't matter," Chloe said. "Once the night is over, he's going to ruin that hair."

Laughing, Winter said, "Does your mind ever leave the gutter?"

"Not really. I think I've started getting mail there. Anyway, as usual, I have to go, tons of work to do."

"Alright, Clo. Thanks so much."

"Anytime, sweetie. Love you."

"Love you too," Winter said, ending the call.

The next night, Kody arrived on her doorstep looking every bit of the striking gentleman he was.

He wore a dark blue suit that fit his body so perfectly, Winter was certain it was tailor fitted. As Kody walked her down the stairs and toward the vehicle, he held her hand.

Then, once at the massive, shiny, black SUV, Kody not only opened the door for her but helped her in, placing one hand on her waist and the other on her ass.

Be strong, Winter. Be strong.

Walking around to his side, Kody got in, buckled up and they were off.

The buttery leather seats were warm and inviting, and the inside of the vehicle was just as impressive as the outside.

Wood grain trim, an extraordinary sound system and highly detailed touchscreen, currently showing an image of which door was open, commanded attention.

Winter assumed the SUV must have been top of the line and had no idea that vehicles like this were available to be rented.

"This is nice," Winter said once Kody slid behind the wheel and began backing out of her driveway. "Where did you rent it, if you don't mind me asking?"

"I didn't. It's mine. I leave a vehicle at my Georgia and Texas location for when I'm in town. I only use it when I have meetings or don't want to drive the work van around. Sometimes I let the onsite managers use it so that it doesn't sit around for months without being driven."

"That's, uh... smart and kind of you," Winter said.

She truly didn't know what else to say. He was obviously financially well off, and somehow asking more questions made her feel as if she were prying.

So instead, she leaned back and enjoyed the rest of the ride, listening to soft music on the radio.

Arriving at the event, Winter felt glamorous and beautiful. Not just because Kody had already told her how beautiful she was numerous times, but because the place where the event was being held was nothing short of incredible.

It reminded Winter of one of those red carpet events you see on TV.

Leading Winter over to a man and woman that looked to be about their age, Kody introduced her to his cousin Jackson and Jackson's wife, Erica.

The family resemblance was uncanny.

Although Jackson carried more weight in the midsection, both men sported those tall, muscular frames and possessed the type of handsome features that would make most women look twice.

Erica was tall and exotic looking. She had a light brown complexion, dark brown slanted eyes, and high cheekbones. Her hair was cut into a sleek, black, shoulder-length bob that elegantly framed her face.

"We finally get to meet the woman Kody is always talking about," Jackson said.

Winter was surprised that Kody had mentioned her, often it seemed, to one of the closest people in his life.

They all chatted a while longer, before Kody, promising to return shortly, pulled Winter to the dance floor.

"Your cousin and his wife are really nice and funny," she said as Kody spun her around and pulled her back into his arms.

Kody spared a glanced toward Jackson and Erica. "Yeah, they are good people."

"I'm surprised you mentioned me to them."

"Why is that?" He asked, leading her slowly to the music with his hand around her waist.

"I don't know, honestly."

"You shouldn't be surprised, Kody said. "Even though I haven't known you long, you're special to me."

Touched by his words, Winter revealed how much she felt the same.

Gazing up at him, she confessed. "You're special to me too, Kody." A slow smile crossed his lips and Winter averted her eyes, searching for something to say that wasn't so emotionally revealing. "How tall are you?" she asked.

"6' 2, why?"

"I was just curious."

"Don't worry, the far distance from your lips to mine won't make me kiss you any less," Kody teased.

Winter laughed.

"You are charming and handsome, but your belief that I want a kiss from you is a little presumptuous, if you ask me." Winter said teasingly.

"Lucky me, I wasn't asking," Kody replied, leaning down to kiss her.

It was soft and sweet and made her weak at the knees.

When the song was over, he led her out onto the balcony, where the view literally took her breath away.

Winter had never seen downtown Atlanta from an angle like this, with its dramatic skyline and overflow of tall and short, nicely lit buildings. Kody put his arms around her, and they silently watched the busy city before them.

"I'm not complaining, but don't you have more people you need to mingle with?" Winter suddenly asked.

"Not really. I spotted the host when I came in. He was already engaged in what looked to be an intense conversation with a group of people. I'll circle back around to him in a bit."

"As long as I'm not keeping you from anything."

Pulling Winter closer and kissing her neck, Kody said, "You aren't." Then, not too far behind him, he heard Jackson calling his name. "But I'll bet that's about to change if Jackson has anything to say about it."

Jackson approached Kody and Winter with a big grin on his face.

"Winter, do you mind if I steal Kody away for a second? I have someone I need him to meet."

"Not at all," she said.

Kody gave her one last quick kiss on the lips, and then he and Jackson walked away.

Once again, Winter faced the city lights and continued to admire the stunning view laid out before her. This was nice, having a lovely night out with Kody and getting to see parts of his world.

It made her feel more connected to him. She really could get used to this.

"Beautiful, isn't it?"

Winter turned to see a stunning woman wearing an absolutely breathtaking black dress that hugged her perfect figure, and somehow, made Winter feel underdressed.

"Yes, it is," Winter said.

The woman offered Winter a small, dainty hand. "Seems we haven't had the chance to meet. I'm Ashley."

Shaking her hand, Winter said, "Nice to meet you, Ashley. I'm Win—"

"Winter Daniels, I know."

Taken aback, Winter questioned, "How?"

"I handle the guest list for the Gander Company events. It's kind of my job to know who is hanging around these things, you know?"

With a relieved smile, Winter said, "Oh, okay, makes sense."

"I see you're here with Kody Benton," Ashley remarked, lifting a brow, and Winter felt her stomach clench. The woman's tone was telling and Winter somehow knew she wasn't going to like what Ashely said next. "Not to be too forward," Ashley continued. "But from one girl to another, I just wanted to warn you."

"About?" Winter said, urging Ashley to go on.

"He's a liar, or possibly a player, whatever fits for the month, I guess."

"I'm not sure what you're —"

"I know," Ashley said, holding up one perfectly mani-cured hand. "It's none of my business, but I was once right where you are. I met him at this exact party a year ago and I really believed the relationship was going somewhere. Long story short, I was wrong and ended up broken-hearted. I don't want what happened to me to happen to you. Kody isn't the settling down type. So my advice to you is to have your fun, but don't let your heart get involved."

Winter nodded slowly. "Umm, thanks."

"It's no problem. Us girls have to stick together. Besides," Ashley said, lowering her voice. "Even though he is a waste of time, at least he's a beast in the bedroom, right?"

The woman laughed as if she didn't have a care in the world and Winter wanted to punch her. But instead, she smiled, nodded and pretended that she too knew what sex was like with Kody.

Ashley finally stopped laughing and said, "I have to get back. It was nice meeting you, Winter."

"Likewise," Winter lied through her teeth.

Then, as if she hadn't just totally destroyed Winter's world, Ashley turned around after taking a few steps and cheerfully said, "By the way, cute dress."

Winter stared out the window on the ride home, letting the questions, fears, and images of sex between Ashley and Kody consume her.

Running into Ashley had thrown her into a loop she didn't see coming. Kody appeared so genuine in his intentions toward her. But then again, didn't every guy?

Dammit, why now?

They were having a wonderful evening, and then here comes Little Miss Ashley, raining all levels of drama on Winter's parade. She didn't want to simply believe Ashley, but she didn't want to totally disregard her, either.

If Winter's past had taught her anything, it was to pay attention to all the signs.

So what are the signs telling me now?

That she liked Kody. No, more than liked— he was the type she could truly love. Her heart told her that he was honest and worth the risk, but her heart was known to confuse what it wanted with what it needed.

Breaking the silence, she said, "May I ask you a question?"

"Sure," Kody said.

"What's the real reason you did the work for me?"

Winter watched his brows furrow. "You mean besides the obvious?"

"Yes. I know," she said, waving her hand to dismiss Kody's basic reply. "The work needed to be done, but why for free?"

He glanced at her, giving her a playful grin.

"But it wasn't free. Remember those delicious meals?" he said.

"Kody. I'm serious. Why?"

He focused on the road.

"You're a smart girl, Winter. I don't think I need to tell you that I liked you from the first day I met you."

There were those flutters again.

Dammit!

She couldn't get to the truth if quivers of desire assaulted her every time he said something nice or flirty, even though she felt the same.

Toying with the gold bracelets on her wrist, she said, "I understand that. But you could have simply asked me out on a date, couldn't you?"

"I could have," Kody replied slowly, clearly trying to see where she was going with this. "And if necessary, I would have. But at the time, I had an in, so I took it."

"So it wasn't a ploy to get me to owe you something in return, something like sex?"

Kody said nothing for a long moment before commenting.

"Winter, with all due respect, I don't have to give out free labor to get a woman to sleep with me."

"Don't remind me," she said, rolling her eyes.

Kody's lighthearted tone was replaced with a concerned one. "Is something wrong?"

Winter closed her eyes, letting her head fall back onto the headrest.

This conversation was going all wrong really fast. They'd had a magnificent night; she didn't want to ruin it. She simply needed to know the truth.

What does he want from me?

Deciding to just come out with it, she said, "I met Ashley, and she had some interesting things to say about you."

"I see," Kody replied with understanding. "I'll bet she did."

"Why do you say that?"

Kody took a deep breath, then exhaled. "No reason."

"So there was something..." Winter paused, searching for the words. "of substance between you two?"

There was a delay in his response, and Winter assumed he was deciding on how much to share.

"I met Ashley last year when I came here for the annual Gander company event. We ended up dating long distance for a few months and from the start, I told her I didn't want anything serious. Even though she agreed, when it came down to it, she wanted more than I was looking for. When I broke it off with her, she was pretty mad and claimed I lied to her and led her on."

"Did you?"

"I just told you I didn't."

Winter crossed her arms. Someone was lying, but was it Kody or Ashley?

"Why didn't you want to be serious with her?" Winter probed.

"She isn't my type."

"Why not?"

Kody exhaled again.

"Why do you keep doing that?" Winter asked.

"Doing what?"

"Exhaling before you answer me. Are my questions annoying you?"

Was she trying to pick a fight? Wanting to halt this amazing night in its tracks because she was starting to get scared again? Or was she jealous that, however short-lived, he'd had something with Ashley?

No matter the answer, if Ashley was right, her fears of getting hurt were just around the corner.

Still carrying the same calm tone he always did, Kody said, "No, Winter, you aren't annoying me."

"What is it then?"

"I like you a lot, and I don't want you to see me in an unfavorable light for untrue reasons, but I have the feeling that Ashley got in your head. I didn't want more, but she did, and that's pretty much the whole story. But you are welcome to ask me anything you like, and I'll always answer honestly."

Winter didn't know what to think. He could be telling her what she wanted to hear. Or Ashley could truly be a nut job, spreading untruths about Kody due to hurt feelings.

Winter decided to err on the side of caution. If she didn't sleep with him, she didn't have to worry about getting hurt.

We can hang out, still kiss, definitely still kiss, the thought made her smile. *But nothing more. Nothing more!*

Who was she kidding? She was already in too deep and the attraction was pulling her in like a magnet. The desire for this man was so strong it almost physically hurt.

With immense frustration, Winter shifted to stare out the window.

"You alright?" He asked.

Aware that she was letting her emotions show way more than she should for a man she wasn't even in a relationship with, Winter nodded.

"I'm just tired, that's all, but I had a really nice night. I haven't done dinner and dancing in a long time. Thanks for inviting me."

Kody placed his hand on hers. "It was my pleasure."

The contact caused Winter's pulse to rise several notches.

Just stay cool. Don't envision him pulling this truck over, laying you on the hood, and...

This had to stop!

She wasn't some horny teenager. So what if Ashley referred to his sex skills as ranking off the charts? Or that he looked extra sexy tonight and harbored a dangerously captivating touch?

She could... no! She *would* keep it casual and light. No sex.

"Since we are being honest," Kody said suddenly. "Tell me why I make you nervous?"

Winter withdrew her hand from underneath his and adjusted in her seat.

"You don't... make me nervous," she lied.

Kody released a low chuckle, but as usual, he didn't push. He never did when it came to delicate matters. Which was yet another thing she found attractive about him.

"It's just," she paused. "You seem like this total package. Not only are you handsome and successful, but you are also kind and a gentleman. Then you top it all off with that sexy stare that I'm sure makes women fall apart."

As they drove, the lights from other cars and street fixtures momentarily illuminated the inside of the car. Kody glanced at her and gave her a smile that had to be saying something; she just wasn't sure what.

Winter snapped her fingers. "See like that!"

Kody played clueless. "Like what?"

"That little smile you're doing. What were you just thinking?"

Kody licked his lips and looked over at her. "Do you really want to know what I'm thinking?"

Winter faced the road. "On second thought, let's change the subject."

"If you'd like," he said.

Steering the conversation back to relationships, Winter asked, "Why wasn't Ashley your type?"

"I think we had conflicting views on the way we saw the world. Not to mention, she came from a lot of money, and it seemed she looked down on people who didn't."

Not even knowing Ashley, Winter could see how that statement would ring true. The "cute dress" comment seemed more condescending than anything.

"Care to give an example?" she asked.

Kody seemed to think about it.

"There was this incident where we were taking a walk and saw a homeless guy. He asked for money for food, and I stopped to give it to him. I only had $50 on me at the time, so I gave him that. After we walked away, Ashley started in on how that was way too much money to give a guy who more than likely only wanted it for drugs. When I told her he could just be down on his luck, she said that he's down on his luck because he was lazy."

"Lazy?" Winter said annoyed. "Everyone homeless is not lazy. Sometimes, life just throws curveballs quicker than some of us can handle."

She was thinking about the women that she knew from the shelter. Many of whom came from harsh situations and were homeless before a kind soul gave them some help to reach the next step.

"True," Kody replied. "But I'm not one to argue when I see a person has their mind set on something, so I just told her I understood her point and tried to move on."

"I assume she wasn't interested in letting it go?"

Kody shook his head.

"Nope. She even went as far as saying I should go back and check to see if the guy did, in fact, buy food."

"That's umm far-fetched. Is that why you ended things?"

"More or less."

Winter let that soak in.

"I'm surprised you were even attracted to someone so rude."

Kody's fingers tapped the wheel.

"Honestly, I don't know if she was aware she did things like that."

"I guess that makes sense," Winter said before quietly adding, "So you told her you didn't want anything serious?"

His answer shouldn't have mattered, but it did. In Winter's mind, wanting nothing serious with Ashley, equated to wanting nothing serious with her.

"Because I didn't," Kody said. Then as if he understood the real meaning behind her question he added, "However, if I really started feeling her and thought we fit well, I would have been open to things progressing."

They drove for several minutes in silence before Winter asked her next question. Kody seemed to be an open book about his past and she couldn't help but take advantage.

"Have you ever been in love with anyone?" she asked.

"Once, with a girl named Tish?"

"What happened?"

"Stupidity," Kody said evenly.

"On your part or hers?"

"Mine. I was young and didn't want anyone to "stop me from living," so I pushed her away. Being the smart lady she was, she left."

"That sucks. I'm sure you regretted that for a while."

"I did, but everything happens for a reason. What about you, any loves in your past?"

The temptation to redirect the conversation away from her pathetic love life was pulling at her. Hearing herself admit to the stupid mistakes as it pertained to her choices in men was embarrassing.

Still, sharing was only fair.

"There was one guy I loved. His name was Greg and..." Winter hesitated, "he was a magician."

Kody caught his laugh before it fully erupted. "Wait, don't tell me. Did he disappear?"

"He didn't, but his dick did, and it reappeared in another woman."

They shared a laugh at that, the ease of exchanging romantic histories continuing the rest of the ride home.

Winter was yet again made aware of how easy Kody was to talk to. Throughout the conversation, she had to keep telling herself that sex with him was off the table. Her body would simply have to stop wanting him because she wasn't giving in.

I can do this. I can be strong.

She really couldn't.

Fifteen minutes later, they were standing on her porch, kissing. What started out as a sweet gesture of him walking her to the door turned into a hot, erotic make-out session.

After Kody brushed his fingers over her cheek and thanked her again for accompanying him to the dinner, Winter couldn't resist. His touch always awakened something in her.

Finally, ending the kiss and pulling away, Winter told him she had to go. There were things she had to do in the morning.

What she really meant was... *he* was the thing she wanted to be doing until the morning.

Kody lifted her hand to his lips and kissed it, promising to see her the next day. Winter hurried inside and locked the door. Not so much to keep him out, but to keep her rapidly growing desires in.

There was Candace.

Chloe couldn't stand Candace, but she had good reason. The woman was always flirting with Chloe's husband when they came in to the cafe.

However, in Candace's defense, if there were such a thing, she flirted with most men.

She was a wanna-be actress who had dreams of making it big in Atlanta or LA, but Winter was starting to think the only TV time Candace was going to get was when they showed her picture on the news for being murdered by a vengeful woman.

"One day, someone is going to beat her ass," Jessica said. "I wouldn't mind it being me, but my last fight was in high school. I'd probably be fighting her using the windmill arms."

Jessica backed away from the table to demonstrate her windmill attack.

They all laughed.

"Yeah, girl. That's pretty outdated. You might want to fine tune your self-defense moves first," Chloe said. Her eyes were locked on Candace, who was currently leaning down so far to take a male customer's order she may as well took the order topless. "I'm all for avoiding violence, but Candace is always pushing those buttons. I even mentioned her inappropriate behavior to the manager, but nothing happened."

"Doesn't surprise me," Jessica said. "The manager is a guy, so Candace is probably sleeping with him, too."

"True," Winter and Chloe agreed.

Another waitress, with a name tag that read Brenda, came by and deposited three chicken salads on the table.

It was early November, and Chloe, Jessica and Winter were at UpDial, a popular cafe, catching up on their lunch break.

"I still can't believe I've been married for three months," Chloe said, staring at her ring.

It sparkled in the rays of sunlight that beamed through the large windows.

"Well, believe it, because you are! Speaking of," Jessica said, rummaging through her gigantic bag and pulling out a box that she passed to Chloe. "Mrs. Malcolm sent you this."

"Awe, Cat Lady Malcolm got us a gift? That's so sweet." Then, looking at Jessica with a touch of alarm added, "Is it something I will need to have cleaned first?"

"No, don't worry. She gave me the money and told me what to buy. The gift never spent any time inside her house."

"Thank Goodness, I don't want to listen to Derek with that constant sneezing and coughing all night."

Chloe's husband, Derek, was highly allergic to cats, and Mrs. Malcom, aka Cat Lady Malcolm, had tons of them.

She was a kind, highly respected woman in her seventies that lived next door to Jessica. She used to be a veterinarian who owned her own practice with her husband, Marlin.

They both loved animals, cats, especially. When Marlin passed a few years back, the only thing she had to remember him by were the two cats they owned. However, eventually, two turned to four, and then four turned to seven.

Seven cats shed a lot of hair, and no matter how much she

cleaned, that cat hair remained just as much a part of the home as Mrs. Malcolm herself.

"That's great. Tell her thank you so much for thinking of us," Chloe said.

"I will," Jessica promised. "Now, back to the details of your newly married status."

Chloe beamed. "It just feels surreal sometimes. Like, I'm still that little girl thinking about someday, and someday has already happened. I truly believed you and Winter would be married before me. Specifically, you, Jessica."

"What?! Why me first?" Jessica asked in disbelief.

"Oh, Jessica," Winter said chiming in. "don't be modest. You know you are the most put-together girl we know. You like things done in order. If married, with 2.5 kids and a white picket fence needed a visual, you would be it."

"Yes, maybe that's true, but my OCD hasn't won me any relationships that got me to the altar now, has it? Goes to show, life is full of unpredictable surprises. In this case, I'm glad that the surprise of happily ever after went to a dear friend of mine."

"Don't make me cry," Chloe said.

"It's true, you're a great friend, Clo. A little bat shit, but definitely a keeper."

"I second the bat shit," Winter added.

Chloe pointed at Winter and grinned.

"Alright, Winter, I see how you're going to be. Let's get the spotlight off me and shift it on to you. Jessica isn't dating anyone right now, but you sure are. Tell us about Kody; he get some Winter loving yet?"

"Yes, do tell!" Jessica teased, lightly poking her fork into the salad.

"Not yet," Winter groaned with annoyance. "But it's getting so hard to keep telling myself no."

Jessica eyed her. "What's the holdup?"

"Honestly, I think it's two things. One is that I like him too much. We have so much fun together, no matter if it's going out or staying in. I have never felt this way about a guy before. It was bad enough when my relationships ended in the past, but it's different with Kody. It's like things are so good with us, I'm scared sex will ruin it. What if I give in and it doesn't work out? I'm scared I will really be broken this time. I'm tired of going down the same road, you know?"

"No, I don't know. You can't live your life afraid. I'm not saying open your heart or your legs to every guy you meet, but don't let your decisions about moving forward be based on fear. You deserve to be loved, and we all know the road to real love isn't easy, so that means take your ass back down that road again and again if you have to. Unless—" Jessica paused and narrowed her eyes, "this is really about that run-in with that Ashley woman from the party last month?"

Winter shook her head.

"No, it's not about her. But at this point, my ass that you spoke of is sporting permanent tire marks from men running over me so much. It's only been three months, and in four more, he's gone, which means if I let this go any further, I am asking for trouble. I'm not saying I will never attempt a relationship again, but getting more involved with Kody, in particular, just doesn't seem like a good idea. No matter how bad I want to screw his brains out. And oh my goodness," Winter said, biting her lip, "I want to really bad."

Chloe put up a hand.

"Wait. Hasn't this man already re-piped your entire house and come to your aid with every scary nightmare you've had?"

Winter let out a small breath, nodded, and then picked up her water to take a sip.

"Winter, I love you," Chloe said, placing a hand on Winter's knee. "But you're dumb as hell. If you don't give him some ass, I will."

Winter almost spat her water out. She fully caught herself just in time, and only a few beads of water escaped. Wiping her mouth and coughing, she took a minute to collect herself.

Still laughing, she said, "Chloe, your crazy ass almost made me choke!"

"It's the truth," Chloe stated with a shrug, pouring more dressing on her salad. Then, abruptly, she stopped. "Oh, wait! I'm married now, so I can't sleep with him, but I'm going to pass the baton over to Jessica and let her do what I can't. Jessica, you've got my back, right?" Chloe asked jokingly.

"I think I can take one for the team," Jessica smirked.

They all laughed.

"Seriously, Winter," Chloe said soberly, "Don't block what could be because of past hurt. Sex aside, you like this man. I see the way you light up when you talk about him. So what if he leaves in a few months? If it's real, it will work out. Now, tell us the second reason you haven't slept with him?"

Winter finished chewing and swallowed. Her next excuse was a little embarrassing.

"This is going to sound weird, but he makes me feel like he could fuck me senseless, and that intimidates the hell out of me."

"Because of your inexperience with orgasms?" Chloe said matter-of-factly.

Winter glared at her. "You didn't have to put it so blatantly, but yes, due to my inexperience. Combine that with liking Kody as much as I do, and I feel like a shy virgin all over again."

"Oh, I know what you're talking about," Chloe said. "He gives you that speak a new language vibe."

"Huh?" Jessica and Winter asked in unison.

"The type of guy that fucks you so good he has you saying shit and you don't even know what it means?"

Winter snapped her fingers, now following Chloe's bizarre way of thinking. "That's the type."

Then they all started laughing again.

After finishing lunch and saying their goodbyes, Winter arrived back at work with a clearer head.

Walking toward the building, she pulled her sweater closed.

The early November air offered a slight chill that Winter delighted in. Falling in line with her name, she loved the colder season. Entering the building, she noticed that there were fewer people around than before she went to lunch.

"Hey, Winter," Gary called, heading in her direction.

He was the Production Assistant to a well-known director who was currently filming the sequel to a highly anticipated horror flick.

"Hey, Gary, what's up?"

"Please, tell me your day isn't too busy? We need a hand with staging to finish up a scene. Five people called out sick today and two more headed home during lunchtime. This damn bug going around is putting us so far behind."

"I don't think I'm too busy. Let me just put my purse and sweater in my office, and I'll be right over."

"Thank you," Gary said, clasping his hands together and shaking them gratefully.

Winter dropped off her belongings and headed back to help with the setup.

The flu traveling its way through the studio was a common occurrence this time of year. The constant hacking and coughing was almost like background noise everyone expected.

It dawned on Winter that she hadn't seen Lisa all day. When she finished helping Gary's team set up, she would find her assistant to make sure everything was alright.

"You want this over there?" Jeff, one of the team members, asked, holding up a square glass cube.

"Yeah. Make sure it is close to the edge of the table. It needs to be in the shot because I think it's going to be knocked over by 'accident.'"

"Okay, got it."

Winter leaned over to resume setting up the artificial plants. This scene was in an office. Some crooked lawyer was about to meet his doom, if she recalled correctly.

Her mind drifted back to Kody. The things she could do with him on that desk. She imagined him towering over her as they tore at each other's clothes, consumed by her desire for him to be inside her.

A cough behind her made Winter turn around.

It was Lisa. She looked horrible. "Lisa, are you okay?"

Lisa shook her head. "It's this damn flu. I guess I'm its latest victim," she said in a congested voice. "I dragged myself out of bed because I had to finish a project, but now I'm so weak I can't even work up the strength to masturbate when I get home tonight."

Winter started laughing, then said, "Aww, poor baby. You're about to head home now, though, right?" It was more of a statement than a question.

Coughing again and taking a moment to catch her breath, Lisa nodded.

Winter frowned. She felt so bad for the sickly woman.

"Thank you so much for coming in, sweetie. Is there anything I can do for you before you go?" Winter asked.

"Would you like the flu? I'll give you mine," Lisa offered.

"No. I think I'm good."

Lisa started to leave, but then hesitated. "Oh yeah," she said, pausing to cough several more times. "Mr. Sanders is out too. He left about an hour ago. He said something to the effect of his "nasals leaking noodles" or some odd gibberish only he understands and went home. I assumed it was in reference to his runny nose."

"Yeah, that sounds like him. Thanks for telling me. You get some rest, drink plenty of water and skip the masturbation for a few days. I'll check on you later."

Lisa dragged herself out of the staging area, and Winter got back to it. With everyone around her getting sick, she hoped that she could avoid being next, but she suspected she wouldn't be so lucky.

Within the next few days, her predictions proved true. What started out as a scratchy throat on Monday manifested into a full-blown cough with congestion and constant sneezing by Wednesday.

Winter was pushing herself to make it until the end of the week, but when she woke up with body aches and a fever Thursday morning, she had to surrender to the sickness.

Coughing and shivering uncontrollably, she made her way to the kitchen to get some tea. She didn't have much of an appetite and felt very weak.

Aware that she hadn't been feeling well for the past couple of days, Kody came by to check on her.

Initially, Winter begged him not to, but Kody's persistence won out.

As she lie in bed, dressed in three layers of clothes and covered up to her neck in blankets, Kody sat beside her on the bed, asking what he could do.

"Absolutely nothing," Winter croaked. "But you should leave before I get you sick."

Kody lightly patted the blankets. "Don't worry about me, Winter."

The cough intensified and Winter yanked the covers up higher, burying herself underneath. Kody tugged the covers down just enough to see her eyes.

Nodding his head in the direction of her nightstand, he said, "I put you some water, juice and lozenges right there. I got the key you left for me on the counter, so I will drop off your medicine, and of course, I will have my cell if you need to contact me. Are you sure you don't need anything else?"

Winter weakly shook her head.

"Get some rest, and I'll be back after work."

Kody kissed her on her forehead, his lips feeling warm and smooth against her achy skin. Winter closed her eyes, only intending to slow down the spinning room, but unexpectedly fell asleep.

The next morning, she awoke to the sounds of Kody moving around in the kitchen and feeling as if her body weighed a ton.

She went into the bathroom to wash her face and brush her teeth before taking the slow, painful walk to the kitchen.

"Hi," he said, coming over to give her a gentle hug. "How are you feeling?"

"Still not the best. What are you up to?"

"I was making you some soup. I know you still don't have an appetite, but when you do, it will be ready."

Winter smiled, then coughed. "That's nice of you, especially since you don't cook. Will it make me worse?"

"I see you have jokes," Kody said with a laugh. "No, it will not make you worse, and remember, I said I don't have much time to cook. I very well know how to."

Winter practically collapsed into a chair and shrugged. "I'm already sick. What's the worse you could do?"

Coming around to the table where she was sitting, Kody

said. "I am so glad you took time out of your schedule to come and poke fun at me, but you should be resting. I'm about to go back to get some stuff done at the warehouse while the guys work on the house. Would you like to be set up out here on the couch or back in bed?"

Winter pointed to the couch, and Kody helped her get set up, bringing all the things she would need. After Kody fluffed a pillow and covered her up with a thick, blue blanket, Winter looked up at him and tilted her head.

"You're amazing, do you know that? You really didn't have to do all this."

In response, Kody gave her that sexy smile that she had grown to love. It dawned on her that is she weren't so weak, she would be all over him.

"It's no problem, beautiful," he said.

That compliment caught her off guard. Upon glancing at herself in the mirror a few minutes ago, Winter had concluded that her looks matched the train wreck she felt like her body had been in.

But instead of commenting, she only smiled and leaned forward to pick up her tea from the coffee table.

"Before I go, I meant to ask you why you never park in your garage?"

Winter let the soothing ginger tea warm her throat before speaking.

"The garage door stopped working around eight months ago and I hadn't had the chance to get someone to come out here and fix it, but thanks for reminding me about that. It's getting colder outside and it would be easier to get in my car without having to walk out the front door."

"I was thinking the same thing," Kody replied, "Which is why I fixed it. You can park in there now."

And then he left, as if he hadn't just seized control of her heart, mind and body.

Hell yeah, Winter thought, a weak grin covering her lips. *He is definitely getting some.*

"Why do you have more money than me? I think you're cheating, Kody. Taking from the sick is not a good look."

It was a few days later and Winter felt much better, thanks to the delicious soup Kody had made and his caring bedside manner.

They were currently sitting at Winter's kitchen table, playing Monopoly and eating popcorn.

"It's not my fault you didn't buy the railroads. I told you, you can't be caught sleeping on the railroads."

Winter rolled again, landing on some property Kody owned. Silently holding out his hand for the money, she squinted at him and then gave him what was owed.

Kody picked up the dice and took his turn.

"This is fun," Winter said. "Why don't you tell me more funny stories about your childhood before this NyQuil kicks in?"

Kody thought for a moment, then his lips curved into a smile.

"You see this scar right here?"

He was pointing at the side of his jaw. Winter tilted towards him and spotted it. She had never noticed it before.

"I see it."

"I got it when I was ten and I told everyone at school it was from a pit bull that attacked me out of nowhere, and I managed to escape, but that is not what happened."

Winter leaned forward. "This sounds juicy."

"The truth is, I was a Michael Jackson fan, or more like

fanatic. I wanted to learn how to dance like him so bad. I practiced for hours at a time, trying to master the moonwalk. One day, I was really feeling confident and decided I could probably figure it out if I had a stage to perform it on."

"Oh, that makes total sense," Winter said jokingly, and not the least bit convincing.

"So, way too sure of myself, I went to the dining room table and climbed up. Everything was going fine until I decided that I should do a spin at the end of my moonwalk performance, and I fell and busted my ass, as well as my chin, falling off the table."

Winter's lips twitched, and she covered her mouth with her hand.

"You can laugh," he said, already laughing himself.

She started cracking up. "I'm sorry, it's so mean to laugh, but why didn't you just use the floor?"

"I was ten. I was an idiot. In my mind, the floor was not a stage."

Catching her breath, Winter said, "You know what? I'm laughing at you, and I had something similar happen to me. I wanted desperately to have those crinkle curls that were so popular, but my mom refused to buy me the curling tool for it. So I used a bulky curling iron and tried to create the crinkle effect. I ended up burning my neck and told all my friends it was a hickey."

"A hickey?" Kody said, shaking his head. "A hickey doesn't look like a burn mark."

"I know! But we were like eleven, I think, and truly nerdy. We had never seen a hickey up close. Even if one of my friends thought I was lying, they never called me out on it. It's not like they'd ever had one to compare it to."

Kody sat back in his chair. "Well, I hope you eventually got one so that you could see how off base you were."

"You know what?" Winter said, thinking about it. "A guy

has never given me a hickey, but they've also never given me an orgasm, so I guess I'm two for two."

Oh shit!

As soon as it came out, Winter wanted to take it back. She didn't mean to say that. She was feeling way too relaxed, and it just slipped out.

Damn you, NyQuil.

Certain that Kody's cheesy come-on line was underway, Winter readied herself, stuffing popcorn into her mouth and trying to keep a blank expression.

When men found out that she'd never had an orgasm before, they immediately began promising her endless nights of world-rocking sex and orgasms. Which is why she had learned to avoid mentioning it.

Kody was still silent, and Winter risked a glanced up at him.

"It's your roll," he said.

Winter picked up the dice.

Maybe he didn't hear me. Or maybe he is at a loss for words on what to say about something so pitiful.

They continued playing the game a few more rounds. Still, Kody said nothing, and the silence was killing her. She might regret hearing what he thought, but she had to know.

"So, you aren't going to say anything?" Winter asked.

"About what?" he said, moving his tiny silver top hat the appropriate spaces.

"About what I said."

"I don't know, Winter. I'm not really into it?"

Her mouth fell slightly open.

"Not into it? You mean you've never done..." she paused, searching for the right word, "that for a girl before."

"I have, but it isn't really my thing."

What in the hell! What type of selfish man didn't like to give women orgasms?

Collecting herself, she said, "So you get yours, but you're not interested in them getting theirs?"

Kody shrugged. "Honestly, they don't even have to give me one."

Feeling as if the NyQuil had to be affecting her hearing and comprehension, she asked, "Kody, what are you talking about?"

"I'm talking about hickeys. What are you talking about?"

"Orgasms!" she said louder than she intended.

"Oh, those," he said nonchalantly. "I can give you one of those, but I draw the line at hickeys."

Then he looked up with a mischievous grin on his face. Winter started laughing and threw a piece of popcorn at him. Kody dodged it and started laughing, too.

The following weekend, Winter was ready to get out of the house. Being cooped up, sick and feeling like death's play toy, had made her desperate for some fun.

Since she and Kody had previously gone bowling together, he thought it would be a wonderful idea to go again, but this time, as a larger group.

Kody invited Jackson and Erica, and Winter invited Jessica, Chloe, and Derek. However, Jessica refusing to be, as she called it, "the lonely wheel," invited a male friend to help even the numbers.

After the group exchanged greetings and a bowling lane was assigned, Winter headed to the restroom; an overly excited Jessica and Chloe tagging along.

Erica was at the bar, ordering everyone drinks, and the guys were doing some sort of male bonding over an upcoming football game, which meant Winter was prepared to hear an earful from her friends.

As soon as they were inside the bathroom, Chloe said, "Damn, Winter! I see why you're all hot and bothered. That man is sexy as hell."

"I have to agree," Jessica said, cracking the bathroom door

to take a peek at the guys chatting away. "Do you think he would mind being cloned?"

"I'll have to ask," Winter responded jokingly. "But don't you have a guy?"

Jessica waved her off. "Oh please, Jimmy is just a stand in."

They finished up and prepared to exit the bathroom to rejoin the rest of their party.

Before they did, Chloe halted Winter and said, "By the way, you are right, that man will fuck you senseless; I know the type when I see them. But don't worry, you'll be fine. You're just tall enough to ride that ride." Then she slapped Winter on the ass and caught up with Jessica.

It was a joyous, competitive, exciting night. They played three games, and each round was the guys against the girls.

The guys won the first round, girls the second and the third round solidified the guys as the official winners for the evening.

According to Chloe and Erica, the alcohol kept them off their game, but they wanted a rematch in the near future.

Winter wholeheartedly enjoyed the outing. Kody seemed to like her friends, and she could tell they liked him as well. He fit in so easily with his jokes and laid back personality.

They ended the evening in front of the fireplace at her house, kissing and cuddling.

The next day, still requiring time out of the house, Winter decided on dinner at a new gourmet pizza place in the neighborhood.

Upon entering the restaurant, she could already tell that she would love it.

The place was cozy with an indoor brick fireplace, spacious wooden booths and various pizza creations on display.

Winter couldn't wait to eat. Her appetite had returned with a vengeance after she got well, and she was starving.

Their waitress, a girl named Bianca, who looked to be in her mid-twenties, was perky and friendly... too friendly.

Every time Kody asked a question, Bianca was extraordinarily helpful. She gave eye contact, made additional suggestions and even offered to get him samples.

Yet when Winter inquired about anything, Ms. Perky would answer straight away—no further discussion, and barely made eye contact.

The actions were obvious enough to be understood, but subtle enough to make Winter look like a madwoman if she got snappy with her.

If Kody noticed, he said nothing, but he did repeatedly place his hand on Winter's and defer to her whenever Bianca asked him a question.

Finally, after deciding on a large pizza with extra marinara sauce, tons of vegetables, pepperoni, ground beef and extra cheese, they handed "Bitchanca," as Winter had mentally named her, their menus and settled in.

Scanning the room, Winter noticed the place wasn't too crowded, which made sense, with it being a Sunday night. Most people were probably at home prepping for work tomorrow, getting kids to bed, or watching football.

Winter wondered if they'd make it home in time to catch the end of the game.

Touching the pocket of her jacket that was hung on the back of her chair, she realized she'd left her phone in the car.

"What time is it?" she asked.

Kody stretched out his arm and checked his watch. "Around 7:30."

"Good. I'm hoping we can catch at least the end of the game."

"We should be able to," he said.

"That's a nice watch," she said, admiring the dome-shaped

accessory with its unique layers of gold and blue. "Who makes it?"

Kody glanced at it again. "This one is by Audemars Piguet."

"Never heard of them."

"It's a Swiss luxury watchmaker."

"Cool, are watches your thing?"

He smiled. "It was my dad's thing. He collected really nice ones and I think it rubbed off on me. Shortly after he passed, I remember seeing this one in a store when I was in Paris, and I had to have it. It was one I knew he would have loved."

Winter felt her heart warm. "You don't hear about watch collectors every day. What made him pick that as an interest?"

"I'm not sure, honestly. When I asked him why he liked watches so much, he'd always say the same thing."

"Which was?" Winter said, urging him to continue.

"A man only has so much time on his hands. Use it wisely and remember that as long as time keeps counting, you have no room for doubting."

Winter pondered it for a moment, coming to her own conclusions about what it meant, but not sure if she was correct.

"Those are some very wise words. Did he ever come out and tell you what he meant? Although I'm sure you eventually drew your own conclusions."

Kody smiled to himself, obviously taken back to a different period in his life.

"My dad made everything a teaching moment and, being a kid, his response confused the mess out of me. I would keep saying, "but dad, time doesn't do math," in reference to the counting part. He'd merely smile and say, "no, son, but it's always adding up." When I was older, I finally understood that he was saying life will always keep moving, so you shouldn't waste a second of it doubting yourself or living in fear. It was that piece of advice that helped me take the leap and start my own business."

Winter touched his face, and Kody turned toward her so that their eyes met.

"Your dad sounded like a smart man. He would be so proud of you," she said, meaning every single word about this incredible man that fate had inserted into her life.

Kody leaned over and kissed her then.

"Thank you," he said.

When their pizza arrived. It was every bit as delicious as Winter assumed it would be. Gourmet was certainly the right name for the type of pizza they served.

It all tasted so fresh and savory. She ended up eating four slices right along with Kody.

Fully satiated and happy, they waited for the check. When it arrived, Winter reached for it.

"Nope," Kody said, beating her to it and pulling it in front of him.

Winter gaped at him. "Kody, I never pay when we go out. Let me pay at least this time. You're kinda killing me with all the kindness here."

"You'll live," he said, placing his card into the black check booklet and sliding it towards the edge of the table.

Almost immediately, Bitchanca came back over to get it.

"Fine," Winter said with a defeated sigh. "Thank you for dinner."

"No problem."

Winter stared at him, deeply appreciating everything he had done, and wished she could do something substantial in return.

Chloe would suggest sex, which Winter now fully agreed with, but she also wanted to give him a gift. Something he could take back with him to California and it would always remind him of her.

Suddenly she thought of it—the perfect gift. So perfect, in fact, it would also solve the gift dilemma she had been facing for Mr. Sanders's niece.

The ringing of Kody's phone yanked Winter from her thoughts. Kody pulled it out of his pocket, checked the screen and put it to his ear.

"Hey," he said. Then, after a long pause, "No, I didn't. Did you need me to?"

Lowering the phone, Kody said to Winter. "Do you mind excusing me for a second? I need to get some information off a document in the truck."

"Of course not."

"Thanks, I'll be right back."

He headed toward the exit door just as the waitress was approaching to pick up the check.

A few minutes later, Bitchanca returned with the black book that contained what Winter assumed was Kody's card and the receipt. After placing it on the table, she told Winter to have a nice night, and practically skipped away.

I hope your night includes you slipping on some pizza dough.

Winter rolled her eyes and reached for her water. In doing so, she accidentally knocked the book off the table. Leaning over to pick it up, she saw it had opened, and a card fell out.

The card read.

"If you need a reservation or anything else next time, call me."

It included a phone number and below her name, Bianca Reynolds.

Winter was pissed, and Bitchanca had just lost the "anca" and was now simply Bitch!

Winter didn't even like that word. She rarely used it and hated referring to other women that way, but in this case, the title was so fitting it practically wrote itself.

She couldn't believe the guts the woman had. It didn't matter that she and Kody weren't actually together. Bitch didn't know that!

Winter was right on the edge of calling the waitress back over and giving her a piece of her mind, but then it dawned on her there was something she actually wanted more... to see what Kody would do.

She liked him and was finally ready to have sex with him, and then this happens.

Is this a sign not to go any further? Would he take the card?

There was really only one way to find out.

In truth, she couldn't be mad if he took the card; he was not hers, although her heartfelt otherwise.

Pushing her feelings aside, Winter put the card back into the book and laid it on the table.

A few minutes later, Kody returned. "I'm sorry it took longer than I expected. You ready to go?"

"Sure," she said.

Kody grabbed the booklet and opened it. Trying not to be too obvious, Winter pulled on her jacket and started buttoning it while discreetly watching him out of her peripheral.

Kody hesitated a moment.

It wasn't a long moment, and the only reason she noticed it was because she knew what to look for.

Bracing herself for his reaction, she saw him retrieve his card, a copy of the receipt, and nothing more.

Her heart got back into her chest as Kody closed the book and put it back on the table.

Extending his hand to her, he said, "Shall we?"

They were in the car now, and she kept peaking glances at him.

Could he get any sexier?!

Winter wanted him bad... very bad. As a matter of fact, she wanted him now. But being Kody, she knew he wouldn't try anything without her giving him the green light.

How could she push him? Coming out and just saying "please screw my brains out" sounded tacky and too desperate.

Besides, usually men always made the first move, but Kody Benton definitely wasn't most men. He made her feel like it was her first time all over again and, in a way, maybe it was.

It had been well over a year, after all.

Hoping to create an in, she said, "Does that happen to you a lot? Women practically throwing themselves at you, I mean?"

She already knew he would know what she was referring to. Even though he didn't know she had seen the card. The gutsy waitress was far too obvious in actions alone.

"Sometimes," he said.

"How often do you accept the offer?"

"It used to be often, now not so much."

"Why is that?" Recalling a previous conversation, she said, "Oh wait, I remember you said that you've grown out of that."

"You would be correct."

"But don't you miss it?"

"Random sex?" Kody said bluntly. "Not really. Don't get me wrong, I love sex, but at some point, you want a relationship to be about more than..."

"Sex," she said, finishing his sentence.

Kody nodded in agreement and slowed down to make a right turn.

Alright, you've got the ball rolling. What now?

Winter nervously tucked her hands underneath her legs and stared out the window, desperately trying to find a way to say "fuck me now" in a very ladylike manner.

She was just about to ask another basic question when Kody suddenly said, "Speaking of sex, I remember you telling me that a guy has never given you an orgasm before. That sounds like a much more interesting topic; let's elaborate on that."

What the hell?!

The goal was to find a way to trap him in a conversation that would lead to her getting her desires met, but right under her nose, Kody had turned the tables on her.

Winter shifted uncomfortably in her seat, but she wasn't backing down. "Okay, what do you want to know?"

"First, I have to clarify. Have you ever been able to give yourself an orgasm?"

"Yes."

"But you've never had an orgasm through sex?"

Another uncomfortable shift, on Winter's end. "Sadly, never."

"Oral?"

"Nope. But I haven't met... umm... many guys that are willing to do that."

"Interesting," Kody said slowly.

"Why interesting?"

"You said you haven't met a lot of guys that are into that."

"I haven't. They want you to do it to them, but that's kinda where it ends." Winter licked her lips. *Time to stop circling the pool and dive in.* "What's your stance? Are you that type?"

Kody glanced at her. "Are you asking if I eat pussy?"

The bold and direct response caught Winter off guard, but it was an immense turn on. She squeezed her legs together to provide some relief from the throbbing happening between her thighs.

Winter cleared her throat. "Yeah," she said, trying to sound more relaxed than she was. "Are you... into that?"

"Do you want me to be?" Was his brazen reply.

"Uh... maybe," she said.

Dammit, Winter! She thought, mentally scolding herself. *The answer was supposed to be yes! Hell yes! Not maybe!*

Kody chuckled. "That wasn't a definitive answer, but it'll do. Have you at least gotten close to cumming during sex?"

"Honestly, I don't think so."

"Why didn't you just tell the guy you weren't satisfied? Maybe he could have tried something new."

"I don't know. It sounds a little cruel. I'm sure the guy might have been doing the best he could, and here I go, crushing his ego." Deciding to go a step further to gauge his reaction and hopefully find the courage she seemed to misplace every time the topic of sex comes up, she said, "I mean, imagine if we were together and I had to say hey Kody, you're not getting me there. Wouldn't that be horrible?"

Kody took his eyes off the road for a split second and narrowed them at her. "If you don't want me to pull this truck over right now, you should avoid using me in your hypothetical scenarios."

Now they were getting somewhere. She would love for him to pull this truck over.

Smiling, Winter said, "I'm sorry, was that rude?"

"Not at all," he said cooly. "I just don't like being an example in your sexual failures."

"It was only a little joke. No need to get all sensitive," Then she added, "unless I'm hitting on a bit of truth. Maybe you can't satisfy a woman either?"

Winter wanted to push him. She needed to fulfill this sexual ache that had been building ever since they met.

Kody hummed low in his throat. "Would you like me to solve your curiosity?"

The tingling between her legs jumped several notches, and her stomach tightened.

"What if I do? I'm not afraid of you pulling this truck over," she said in a low voice.

Winter sat really still, waiting for his reply, his eagerness, his... something, but he said nothing.

"Did you hear me?" she asked.

"I heard you," Kody responded. He drove another few minutes and then signaled to pull over.

Her heart rate sped up.

Is this really about to happen? Have I made a mistake?

Questions consumed her mind and although Winter wasn't sure of the answers, she was sure that she wanted him.

Once Kody put the car in park, he hit the button to release his seatbelt and then did the same to hers. It immediately retracted, freeing her to lean forward.

Meeting her the rest of the way, Kody caressed her face gently, before tracing his thumb over her lips.

"So you've finally decided to let me touch you," he whispered, his mouth finding hers. "To taste you," he added, kissing her again, "and be inside you."

Winter moaned, and her eyes drifted shut as her breathing grew heavier. Kody deepened the kiss, this time parting her lips with his tongue, and her entire body went weak.

It was feeling so good that Winter had to get closer to him.

As if he read her mind, Kody leaned in more towards her and wrapped one arm around her waist, then resumed laying soft, heated kisses up and down her neck and collarbone.

Out of nowhere, he stopped.

When she opened her eyes, she saw him pulling her seat-belt back around her and then clicking it into the latch.

Still, only inches away from her lips, he said, "I'm all for spontaneity, but after that little joke you made, sex in a truck where space and time limit what I plan to do to you, is letting you off the hook easy and that's not going to happen."

Then he re-latched his seat belt, put the car in drive and got back on the road.

Damn, I'm fucked.

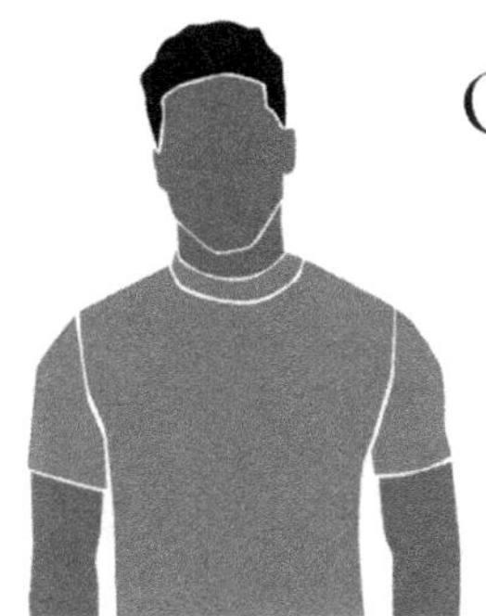

"STOP BREAKING MY HEART, FALCONS," Winter yelled at the TV.

In frustration, she grabbed her bottle of beer from the coffee table and took a large gulp.

Amused with her tantrum-like behavior that consisted of adorable pouting and animated stomping, Kody decided to add fuel to the fire and said, "What did you expect when you picked a horrible team to be a fan of?"

"Oh, really?" Winter said, turning in his direction and placing her hands on her hips.

"Yup," Kody said, taking a sip of his own beer.

"Well, Mr. Benton, would you like to put your money where your mouth is?"

Kody placed his beer on the coffee table and met her gaze. "I would love to. What do you have in mind?"

"Just a little bet. I mean, if you can handle it."

"I think I can handle betting against a team that is likely to give my team an easy win."

"Watch it, buddy," Winter warned, pointing at him. "So, here's the deal. If they win this game tonight, you have to do whatever I want. No complaints, no back outs and no hesitation. And if you win, I'll abide by the same guidelines."

Kody glanced up at the TV screen, checking out the score display.

"You sure you want to place that bet? They are already down by 12."

Winter held her chin high. "Yes, I do. I have faith in my team."

"Alright," he said. "What would you want?"

Lost in thought, Winter glanced around the house, tapping a finger against her lips.

"I got it! If I win, you have to go antique shopping with me. And I'm not just talking a couple of hours, in and out. I mean a whole day from location to location, with a stop at my favorite restaurant downtown for lunch."

"I can agree to that."

"Good," she said excitedly. "And what would you want?"

Kody picked up his beer and took another sip. Placing it back on the table, he said, "dessert."

Winter looked puzzled. "Just dessert, really? Wow, you're easy to please. But whatever, it's your choice. So what are you thinking? Cakes, cookies, pies?"

"I'll let you know."

"Alright, then. Come to think of it, that's weird that in all the cooking I've done for you, I have never made you dessert."

"Don't worry," Kody said with a grin. "I won't hold it against you."

Winter returned to her seat on the couch. The fire was crackling, and the house was nice and warm.

Kody loved seeing her like this, so lively and cheerful. She was wearing her red and black Falcons jersey with black shorts and red fuzzy socks, showcasing her team spirit.

It was in stark contrast to his basic gray sweats and sweater.

He didn't really have a favorite team; he just loved a good game. If the Falcons won, he was happy to take his loss with a smile, but if they lost... well, he had something tasty in mind.

They watched the rest of the game on the edge of their seats. Winter probably more nervous about the outcome than Kody.

When the final touchdown had been made, ensuring that the Falcons weren't going to be able to reclaim victory. Winter picked up the remote and hit the off button.

"Damn Falcons," she grumbled to herself. Then turning to Kody with gritted teeth, "Congratulations on your win. What type of dessert would you like?"

Kody laughed out loud. "Well, don't be so happy about it."

"Sorry," Winter said. "I just hate losing. Of course, I'd be happy to make anything you want. You won fair and square."

He gave her a look and then picked up his beer. Winter tossed up her hands.

"There you go again. What was that look about?"

"What look?"

"Don't play innocent with me."

Pretending he didn't know, Kody said. "I have no idea, Winter. I was just thinking about dessert."

"Good. You know what you want, then?"

"Yes, I do," he said. "But I'll let you know for sure tomorrow."

"Works for me."

With the topic settled, Kody remembered it was something else he was supposed to ask Winter about.

"I know it's months away, but what do you think of going to Jackson's for the Super Bowl? Erica is an early planner, so she's already hounding me about attending and bringing you with me."

"Hell, yeah! I'd love to go. Jackson and Erica are a lot of fun, and I'll bet they will do a better job of cheering on the Falcons with me, assuming they make it to the Super Bowl, of course."

"I'll let her know."

It made him feel good that the three of them got along so well. Seeing the happy family dynamic gave Kody even more of a reason to consider his future with Winter.

He still hadn't decided if he wanted to permanently relocate to Georgia, but he knew for sure that he wanted to be with her, long-distance or not.

They hadn't discussed relationships, but he already felt like she belonged to him.

She had opened up a whole lot since they first met, but he knew she still had a long way to go.

He was content to continue allowing her to let him know when she was ready for the next step, and he'd take it from there. And as luck would have it, a few days ago, she'd made it known that she was ready for sex.

Part of him wanted to jump at the chance. He wanted her so bad it was hard to concentrate sometimes.

But there was no way he was going to let his first time with her be in his truck—not after that slick comment she'd made.

He was Kody "Fucking" Benton. Even the mere idea that he couldn't satisfy a woman had no business in the same sentence as his name.

No, he had a better idea that was already playing out quite nicely.

As Winter was walking past him toward the kitchen, Kody grabbed her arm and pulled her down onto his lap, kissing her deeply and passionately.

Expectantly, her body responded to his touch, and he relished how soft and sweet she was. He was falling in love with her. He knew it, and he welcomed it.

"What was that for?" she asked, lightly biting his bottom lip.

"Mmm," he moaned, lowering his hands so that they cupped her ass. "I'm getting ready to head home."

Winter made a sad face.

"Awe, really? I was hoping you'd stay the night. I sleep better when you're here."

If I stay, sleeping will be the last thing you will be doing.

Kody smiled at her.

"I would, beautiful, but I have some paperwork to finish up at home and a meeting with a possible new client tomorrow."

"I thought Jackson took all the meetings?"

"Jackson takes *most* of the meetings. This client wants more in-depth details about the stages of construction as it pertains to his contract, and that is my area of expertise."

"I know another thing you're an expert in," she said, touching his lips with her fingers.

"What's that?"

"Kissing," she said, placing her lips on his.

The next morning, Kody stood in the living room, surveying the house while his team members tackled projects from all sides. It was coming along quickly.

To date, they had mended the roof, added a skylight, revamped the kitchen, renewed the porch and deck, switched out the windows, demolished two walls, and altered the fireplace.

Walking into the master bath, it was barely recognizable. It looked so different compared to the original design, bigger and a whole lot better.

Kody was in the process of constructing a lavish walk-in shower, that had required a wall to be taken down in order to increase the size.

After retrieving the necessary tools for the shower base, Kody got to work. He was thankful that construction work felt so natural to him, because he did the work almost robotically.

If it weren't for that extreme familiarity, he might have made some mistakes because his mind wasn't completely on the job.

Instead, it was consumed with a sexually shy, but otherwise highly confident, woman.

Picturing Winter's smiling face caused Kody to smile. Without even trying, this woman was making her way into his heart.

Her safety and happiness meant the world to him, and it had become a personal mission to ensure that she knew that.

That's when Kody remembered to call and verify the arrival of the concrete truck for later this week.

This house needed a brand new driveway, and at the same time, he planned to fix a small pocket of damage to Winter's walkway and surprise her.

As soon as he grabbed his phone off the bathroom counter, it started ringing in his hand.

"Hi, Jackson, what's up?"

"Damn, man, you answered fast. I know you miss me, but you can't just sit around waiting for my call."

"I'm sure that would just brighten your day," Kody said with light sarcasm. "But I was just about to call the concrete company."

"Oh, about the driveway?"

"Yeah. I need everything to stay on schedule."

"Gotcha. In that case, I won't hold you long. I wanted to know what time you had the meeting with the new potential today?"

"It's at five. Everything all good?"

"Yup. I'm writing the details of all the meetings we have

set for this month. You know, because I like to keep records of all the who, what, why, when and where in case I need to refer to it for something."

Kody cut open a box of tile and sighed. "I know how meticulous you are with the details. By the way, how does 8:30 sound for a phone conference tonight to go over the meeting?"

"Sounds perfect to me. Before I go, did you ask Winter about the Super Bowl?"

"I sure did, and she said yes."

"Thank God, now Erica can leave me the hell alone." Kody laughed. "I swear, Kody, I love that woman, but she will stress the fuck out of me when she wants something done."

"I believe you."

"Anyway, I'll let you go. I need to call Jamie and see if we need to hire a few more guys in California. Work has increased for the fourth month in a row up there. Not to mention they might end up being a boss short soon, I hope."

Jackson was yet again hinting at Kody settling down in Georgia.

What the hell? I'll throw him a bone.

"They just might, Jackson. Georgia is looking pretty good to me these days."

"Thank you, Winter!" Jackson shouted before hanging up.

Kody was so distracted by thoughts of Winter as he drove to his meeting, that he decided to give her a call.

"How was your day?" he asked once she answered the phone.

"It was great. Busy, but not stressful. I have to go in early tomorrow, so I think I'm going to eat a quick bite, watch a little TV and then head to bed."

A quick glance at the dashboard clock revealed it was 4:30.

"You do need your rest. What time do you think you'll be going to sleep?"

"Hmm, around 8:30. Why?" Winter asked in a seductive voice. "You want to come tuck me in?"

"I wish," he said, his dick getting hard at the thought. "But I'll try to call you before you go to sleep."

Kody could hear the smile in her voice when she said, "I'd like that. That way, I'll be sure to have sweet dreams. Good luck with your meeting."

"Thanks, gorgeous," he said, ending the call.

He hoped this wouldn't take long. The client, Eric Boswell, wanted Haven Construction to build a housing community on the north side of Atlanta.

Mr. Boswell had already spoken to Jackson but wanted to ask more questions about plans, materials, details of each stage, etc.

Kody was happy to answer any questions, but he knew the whole meeting was more of a formality. The man had already stated that he would sign the contract at the meeting with Kody today.

Arriving at the restaurant, Kody was given a ticket for valet parking and went inside to be seated.

Mr. Boswell arrived ten minutes later, ready to hear all about the plans and give Kody insight on his new community vision.

Two hours later, satisfied with Kody's responses, the meeting concluded and Mr. Boswell signed the contract, ready for the project to begin.

Now, with his business complete, Kody only had one thing on his mind... Winter.

He imagined her wearing one of those cute pajama sets, with her hair in the messy, curly ponytail she always wore to bed.

Glancing at the clock, he figured he could get to her house by 7:30, giving him an hour before his meeting with Jackson.

His plan was simple, really. He needed her, and he would have her.

Kody rang the doorbell and within seconds, heard Winter say, "Who is it?" from the other side of the door.

"It's me," he said.

Opening the door, he watched Winter's face go from excitement to confusion.

"I thought you said you couldn't stop by tonight," she said, stepping aside for him to come in. "Is everything okay?"

Walking inside, Kody waited until she closed the door and face him before replying. "Everything is fine. I simply wanted to surprise you."

He pulled her to him for a kiss and then stepped back to admire her pajama set.

As usual, it didn't disappoint. This one was blue shorts and a matching shirt that read, "Sleep is my hobby."

"I love seeing your pajamas," he said, pointing at the shirt.

Winter appeared momentarily embarrassed and glanced down at her shirt.

"Thanks, I love funny pajamas. They appeal to the kid in me." Then gesturing a hand toward him she said, "But forget me, you're the one looking all sexy in that suit. Can I get you anything?"

Oh, you're about to give me everything.

"No, I'm fine," Kody said.

His eyes raked over her body, and there was a brief silence in the room as the energy changed. He moved towards the living room, stopping to lean on the arched frame that separated it from the entryway.

Kody could tell Winter noticed the shift in the room, too, because not only did she not make any moves to come closer, but her signs of nervousness kicked in.

Her eyes darted from side-to-side and she swallowed, obviously searching for something more to say.

"Umm, did you get the contract?" she asked.

His reply was to the point. "Yes."

A smile broke out over her face, and she clapped her hands. "Congratulations, Kody!"

"Thanks, but it's no big deal," he said, his patience growing thin.

"It kinda is," Winter said. "More contracts means more money. What business doesn't want that?"

"I'm good on money," he said, taking a step back so that he was further inside the living room.

Winter's eyes widened, but she still made no move to come towards him. Instead, she tried to buy time.

"Well, don't you sound arrogant?"

"Not being arrogant. Only stating a fact."

"Most people aren't so nonchalant about gaining more money for their company. Kinda makes me wonder..." she said, trailing off.

Kody tilted his head. "Is there a question in there somewhere?"

He knew she would never ask him about his income. Not that he'd hide it from her if she did. But asking questions like that just didn't fit with her.

"Not one that I'm willing to ask," Winter replied in a quiet tone.

He smiled at her. "You are so fucking sexy. Do you know that?"

In response, she smiled, then bit her bottom lip.

Kody's need for her intensified then. Her lip-biting turned him on beyond measure. He undid the buttons on his suit jacket and said, "Millions is the answer to your unasked question."

He didn't wait to see her expression or hear her response. Done wasting time, Kody walked to the kitchen table. After pulling a chair out, he removed his jacket, placed it on the back of the chair, and sat down.

"Come here," he said.

Winter's reaction amused him. She stood, frozen in place, fidgeting with her hair, not knowing what to expect, and he liked it that way.

"Umm, is there something you want to talk about?" She asked.

"No," Kody said. "I don't want to talk. I want you to come and sit down."

Something was up. Winter could tell, but what was it?

Was he finally about to tell me he has a girlfriend back in California? A long-lost kid? Oh shit, maybe an STD?!

But Kody didn't seem like he came to deliver bad news. His demeanor was more controlled... animalistic... intense.

Was he about to fuck her on the table, making her fantasies a reality?

The idea was both exciting and alarming.

She'd wanted him for so long. What if he didn't live up to her expectations? Hell, what if she didn't live up to his?

Cautiously, Winter walked to the table, Kody following her the entire way with his eyes. She couldn't read him. She hated when he did that. Made his face blank, and she had to freak out on the inside like some awkward teenager unsure of herself.

It was annoying how sexy he looked sitting there confidently with his arms crossed, watching her.

Approaching the table, Winter reached for the chair next to his.

"No," Kody said in a quiet, but stern voice and placed a finger on top of the table in front of him.

Winter laughed anxiously. "You mean sit on the table, seriously?"

In response, Kody simply lifted a brow.

He isn't going to do what I'm thinking, is he? He wouldn't... He couldn't... I shouldn't.

"C'mon, Kody. I don't know if—"

"Winter, stop stalling. I can't satisfy a woman, remember? So you have nothing to fear."

Oh, he was good! He was going to make me eat those words while he ate...

Winter shivered. Even the thought made her wet.

Finding some courage, because she wouldn't let this demure woman he seemed to spark in her run the show, Winter stepped forward and got up on the table to sit in front of him.

"Now what?" She said.

Kody leaned forward and put his hand around each thigh and pulled her closer to him. "Up," he said.

Winter complied, and he pulled off her pajama shorts and underwear in one smooth motion.

Spreading her legs. Kody slowly began kissing her inner left thigh while massaging and caressing the other.

Winter's brain was screaming.

This isn't real. He isn't going to do this. But it feels real. Oh, so real.

Making his way towards the main event, Winter braced herself for the pleasure she would feel.

However, instead of feeling his mouth on her sweet spot, Kody kissed upward, onto her stomach, and laid a trail of kisses over her other thigh.

As he circled back around, Winter's breathing increased and she jumped slightly at the first touch of his tongue on her pussy.

"Relax," Kody commanded, tightening his grip on each thigh.

Winter obeyed, releasing a slow steady breath and allowing her legs to slump further apart, giving him the access he demanded.

The wetness of his tongue was perfection. He moved it left, then right, next up and then down.

Where did he learn to do this? Is he doing that alphabet tracing thing I've always heard about? Or writing some complicated math equation?

Whatever it was, it felt amazing. Strong sensations sparked throughout her body and pleading moans escaped her lips.

She could feel herself getting wetter, and Kody's gentle licks became firmer as he started sucking around and then directly on her clit.

Dizzy with pleasure, Winter gripped the sides of the table for support and instinctively arched her back.

"Please, don't stop," she cried.

The words were out before she could even think to hold them back. Never in her life had she felt anything like this.

Obviously, stopping was the last thing on Kody's mind. He increased the sensations by sliding two fingers deep inside her and applied pressure to a spot that Winter didn't even know she had.

The jolt of pleasure caused her to jump back. But already anticipating her move, Kody quickly placed his opposite hand behind her back, preventing Winter from sliding away.

Oh, shit!

The relentless pace Kody was using to suck on her clit, while fingering her, made her body short circuit. Her legs shook, her vision was hazy, and she was oddly aware of pressing her feet hard against Kody's shoulders.

Nevertheless, the man did not back down. If anything, he shifted closer, moving his fingers faster and sucking harder.

Reflexively releasing the table, Winter grabbed the back of Kody's head. Grinding her hips against his face.

"I'm about... to cum," she said, unable to catch her breath.

Then, unlike any orgasm she had ever had, her body erupted, bringing on waves of ecstasy stronger than she thought possible.

The orgasmic release left her pussy highly sensitive, and Winter needed a moment to regain her composure.

"Kody," she squealed, trying to back away, but he didn't stop.

He either didn't hear her or simply didn't care because he continued teasing, tasting, and toying with her.

Winter fell back onto the table, too tired to continue sitting up. Kody increased the pressure on her clit, and a few minutes later, she came again... and then again.

Finally, he slowly sat back and wiped his mouth.

"Damn, that was good," Kody said.

Winter didn't comment. She was too exhausted, too weak.

She couldn't move, couldn't catch her breath, and the world wouldn't stop spinning.

Eventually, he stood, looked down at her and said, "Thanks for the dessert. It was delicious."

Then he picked up his jacket, tossed it over his arm, and walked out of the door.

"Where do you want the tile?" George, one of Kody's employees, asked him the next morning.

The man balanced a box of marble tile on his shoulder and looked as if the effort was causing high levels of discomfort.

"Over in the corner is fine," Kody instructed.

George turned, then stopped, facing Kody again. "By the way, the cement truck is en route."

The arrival of the cement truck was wonderful news. When Winter came home this evening, the broken area in her walkway would be repaired, and he couldn't wait for her to see it.

It occurred to Kody that she may feel like he was trying to buy her with all the things he did for her. Particularly now, since he had disclosed how much money he had.

However, that was not his intention at all. He simply felt like she was his, and he took care of what was his.

Recollections of last night came back to him.

Her moans, her taste, her smell, even the feel of her thighs pressed against his face was enough to reignite him.

Damn, I need some more.

It was kind of funny because, normally, Kody wasn't big on oral sex. Yeah, he had received it a lot, but he didn't give it often.

Very few women pulled that response out of him, and Winter was certainly one of them.

Her whimpers and pleadings for more fueled his already intense desire for her and once she came undone, so did he. Kody couldn't bring himself to stop, so he didn't.

Instead, he decided to bring her to orgasm twice more. He was almost late to his meeting with Jackson because once he was done tasting her, he wanted to be inside her.

But there was no time.

He didn't mind, though; pleasing her was worth it. He wanted her left satisfied, speechless and weak from pleasure, and he'd done that.

Suddenly, his phone rang, and the display read Winter.

"I was just thinking of you," Kody said.

"Good thoughts, I hope."

Kody walked to a small corner in the room to get away from the noise of machinery and the guys talking. "Always. How did you sleep?"

"Sleep?" Winter said, as if the word sounded ridiculous. "Thanks to you, I think I was in a coma."

"I'm happy to hear that," Kody said with a wicked grin.

"I'll bet you are. How's your morning going?" she asked.

"It's alright," Kody replied, looking around. "But the good news is, I have a surprise for you. You'll see it when you get home today."

He could almost see her smiling through the phone when she said, "Really? What is it?!"

"When you get home," he repeated.

"Fine! You're no fun."

A loud engine roared from outside, pulling at Kody's attention.

"Hold on a second," he said, walking around to get a better view through the open front door.

It was the cement truck, and they were already about to back up towards the house's driveway.

"Hey, beautiful, it looks like I gotta go," Kody said into the phone.

"I understand work calls. Before you do, may I ask you a quick question?"

"Of course."

"Was last night always the type of dessert you had planned if you won?"

"Yup."

"So actual cakes and pies were not even on your radar, huh?"

Kody licked his lips, the memory still so vivid. "Not at all."

Winter spent most of her morning daydreaming about Kody—his face, his body, his touch, his scent, his voice, and all those orgasms. He had most definitely left an indelible impression on her.

Every time Winter replayed how good it felt having her legs spread wide on that table, she experienced spikes in pressure.

Those soft lips kissing and sucking on her pussy felt incredible. She needed to stop thinking about it because she was getting hot and bothered.

Hell, merely saying his name got her hot and bothered. And why wouldn't it? Kody was a good man. One unlike any other she had ever known.

She had just seen him last night, but missed him already. She couldn't wait to get home to see him after work. Then, remembering his mention of a surprise, Winter wondered what it could be.

But he has already done so much.

The generosity had to stop. Winter didn't want Kody to feel like she only wanted his money. Although, just how much money he had was a recent and shocking revelation.

Millions.

That was a lot of money, but it changed nothing. She liked Kody for who he was, not for how much he was worth.

Thinking of money and surprises reminded Winter that she needed to order the gift for Kody and her boss's niece. She'd concluded they were both getting high-quality, personalized watches.

For Mr. Sanders's niece, she chose a beautiful rose gold watch that displayed time using Roman numerals and showcased a cluster of assorted diamonds. The inscription she picked read:

> I'll always have time for you.
> Love, Uncle Cordell.

For Kody, she'd chosen a black and gold watch with a titanium band, domed sapphire crystal and anti-reflective coating. The inscription on his watch read:

> As long as time is counting, there is no room
> for doubting.

Winter remembered how happy and at peace Kody looked when he shared that story with her about his father, and she always wanted that for him.

A knock on her office door caused her to look up. It was Lisa.

"May I have the completed prop list for the Playground Horror Contract?" Lisa asked.

"I'm not done with it. They changed some of their prop requests, and I need to modify their contract. I'll be done with it before I head home today, though."

"That works," Lisa said. "Have you had lunch yet?"

"No," Winter replied, looking down at her stomach as if it could verbally agree.

"I can grab you something if you want me to. I'm getting soup or salad but haven't decided from where yet."

Winter thought about it. Soup would be a pleasant change up.

"I'll take a vegetable soup please." Winter grabbed her wallet out of her purse, pulled out $20, and handed it to Lisa.

"You sure you don't want anything else?" Lisa said, taking the money.

"No, I'm fine, but buy your lunch, too. It's on me today."

Lisa fanned herself with the money, grinning widely.

"I'll have to stop by more often when you're hungry. Thanks," she said over her shoulder, walking away.

The rest of Winter's day was devoted to meetings and preparing prop lists for several scenes.

After getting home, she showered and pulled on another pair of her beloved PJs.

The shirt on this set read, "I sleep better with you" and next to the words was a woman hugging a glass of wine.

Although the statement on the shirt rang true for Winter as well, she preferred to abandon the wine and put Kody in its place.

Having him around made a big impact on her sleep. It had been weeks since she had experienced a nightmare, and Winter hoped they were gone for good.

Kody arrived by seven and after giving him a sweet kiss hello, she asked excitedly, "Where is it?!"

Kody shook his head.

"You are like a kid in a candy store. Come on," he said, taking her hand and leading her out the front door to the walkway. "Notice anything missing?"

Winter was taken aback, her eyes widening, her mouth

dropping in shock. "That horrible hump! It's gone! How did you... no, when did you do this?!"

"I did it early this morning after you left for work."

Absently shaking her head, Winter walked closer to the freshly paved area, then stopped as if afraid to get to close.

"Is it dry yet?"

"Mostly, but see there," Kody said, pointing at two small yellow flags on either side of the walkway. "I put markers around it to ensure it not be disturbed before tomorrow."

Winter faced him with a worried expression. "How long did this take you, Kody? You didn't have to do this."

He took a step closer to her, taking her hand in his. "It was no big deal. The damaged area was already separated from the rest. We only had to dig up a little more around it and then lay down the new cement. It blended right in and only took about forty-five minutes."

"I don't know what to say. You are just too kind. Thank you."

Kody put his arm around her. "Let's go back inside out of this cold, start a fire, and we can think of a way for you to repay me."

Grinning and squeezing him closer, Winter said, "I like that idea."

Once they were back inside, and the food was ready, they settled in to eat. It was a nice feeling, enjoying a Friday night, stress-free with the music playing.

"You have any weekend plans?" Kody asked.

Winter thought about it.

"Not much besides hanging out with you," Then snapping her fingers she added, "I do have to drop off that nightstand at the women's shelter tomorrow."

They both took a moment to admire the newly refurbished nightstand with its diamond shaped crystal knobs.

"You did a wonderful job," Kody complimented. "Would you like me to load it into your car for you?"

"Always the gentleman I see," Winter replied, tossing her napkin on the table. "I'm good, though. It's pretty light."

Done with his food, Kody got up to take his plate to the sink and Winter wanted to pinch herself to make sure this was all real.

An attractive millionaire, with manners, that had feelings for her and also cleaned up behind himself?

Winter smiled. *I guess cupid has struck.*

Returning to the table, Kody took his seat, but when his eyes found her's, it was all seriousness.

"I need to ask you something," he said.

Oh shit! Maybe cupid wants his arrow back.

"Sure," Winter responded with a serene smile.

"You don't feel like I'm trying to buy you or anything, do you?"

Winter's heart got back into her chest and the sudden relief of still being one of cupid's favorite made her quietly exhale.

"No. Why do you ask that?"

"Money has a way of making things messy, and I never want you to feel like I don't think you are capable of taking care of yourself. It's more so that I am enjoying taking over that role. I love spoiling you and seeing you smile."

"Well, no worries. I don't think you're trying to buy me, although," Winter's eyes narrowed at him, "I need you to stop it with all the free work for a while. I want you with or without the money. Even though let's be honest," she said, smiling flirtatiously, "with the money is a lot sexier."

"And if it turns you on, all the better," Kody said.

Winter fanned herself.

"Stop it, Kody. I am not trying to be turned on right now."

Kody leaned in, intrigued, his voice low, his eyes intense. "But I like you turned on. You taste so good."

Winter bit her lip. The excitement of what was eventually to come that night caused her stomach to tighten.

"Speaking of... uh, that," she said, looking down at the table and recalling last night. "I still can't believe you did it."

Kody's response was simple. "Why?"

Winter shrugged, not interested in going down a long road about how selfish the men before him were. "I don't know, but you really caught me off guard."

"That was the point. The question is, did you enjoy it?" he asked.

"I think you can tell from my reaction that I did."

"True, but I want to hear you say it."

Winter locked eyes with him. "Okay then, full disclosure. I fucking loved it! I now understand what all the fuss is about, and I thank you for that."

"It was my pleasure," Kody said, giving her a wickedly sexy grin.

"What I don't understand is why did you stop? Most men would have moved on to sex, and if I'm being honest, I was definitely ready for that, too."

Kody laughed.

"Woman, you were barely conscious when I left."

"I was not!" Winter stated, trying to keep a straight face. "All I needed was a quick break, then I would have rejoined the party."

"I'll keep that in mind," Kody said. "Actually, though, I had a meeting with Jackson I needed to get to. But don't worry, tonight, there are no meetings, and I have all the time in the world."

The familiar throbbing between her legs perked up at the same time, Kody reach across the table to grab her hand.

Smiling, Winter shook her head. "I just don't get you,

Kody. Why are you single? I know you have met someone you could be with by now. What gives? Does the moving around so much really make relationships that complicated for you?"

Kody lightly rubbed his thumb over her hand. "The moving around isn't a problem. I simply rarely find what I'm looking for. But you are just as much a mystery to me. Why are you single?" Then pointedly, he added, "And you can't use your taking a break from a dating excuse you told me about."

Winter uttered a groan.

"What can I say? I choose the wrong men, or rather, the wrong men choose me. I'm sure your choices of women are a lot better than the choices I have of men to date. I feel like I can't find a good man to save my life."

"Elaborate."

"Okay," she said slowly. "For instance, a man can get several attractive, successful women who are ready to lie down, have his babies and take care of him. While many women get stuck with guys who are too old, have no job, aren't attractive at all, or already have ten kids."

Shit! Did that come out right?

Winter feared her reasoning made her sound petty or bitter, when she was neither. It was merely her opinion that women had a harder time finding good men than the other way around.

"It's kinda difficult to explain, I guess," she said in a low voice.

A new song was starting up. It was a love song with a slow and steady rhythm. Kody slowly withdrew his hand from hers, folded his arms and stared at her from across the table.

"Try to explain it," he said

Is he getting upset?

He didn't look upset, but Winter wasn't sure—his face was blank.

Searching for the words, she began, "I'm sure you meet

plenty of women who want to be with you, but you're probably too wrapped up in work and stuff to even care. Whereas I wouldn't mind something serious, but I'm barely meeting any potential, you know?"

"No, I don't know, Winter. Do you want to be with me?"

Is he messing with me?

How was she supposed to answer that? Of course, she wanted him, but it likely wouldn't work out, plus she wasn't even sure that he wanted to be with her. Finding her escape, Winter flipped the tables on him.

"Do you want me?"

Kody finally smiled and said, "I love it when you get flustered. It's cute."

Standing, he walked around to her side of the table and extended his hand. Winter took it and Kody pulled her to her feet, drew her close and began dancing.

Laying her head on his chest, Winter relaxed. The enticing scent of his cologne as she listened to the steady beat of his heart put her at ease. She could stay like this forever, lost to the world and safe in his arms.

The song ended and Winter's body protested when Kody took a step back from her. However, still holding her hand, he led her to the couch, pulling her down onto his lap.

They stared straight ahead into the fire for several moments before anyone spoke.

"Winter," Kody said, in a voice so deep and low, it vibrated through her. "I want you, and I want to be with you. But I never want anything from you that you are not ready to give me. That includes your body or your heart."

Watching the bright orange flames dance, Winter said, "I want you, too, but I can't help but feel that this..." she closed her eyes and began again. "That *we* are a mistake. Aren't you leaving soon?"

Winter braced herself for Kody to confirm a truth she already knew.

"Face me," Kody said.

Winter complied, repositioning herself on his lap until her eyes found his. The sincerity shown in them made Winter's breath catch. "I could never leave you," Kody assured her.

As if that was the push she needed, Winter kissed him. Allowing all the fears and reservations about what may or may not happen fade. She trembled as Kody slid his hand up her back until eventually burying his fingers in her hair.

"Mmm," Winter moaned softly into his mouth.

Her hands explored beneath his shirt, lingering for several minutes to appreciate the hard, smooth muscles of his chest.

Breaking the kiss, Kody yanked his shirt over his head and tossed it to the floor.

The action ignited Winter's longing.

Now more eager, she reached down to unfasten his jeans, desperately wanting to free the long, hard bulge in his pants.

However, Kody had other plans.

He gripped her wrists with one hand, halting her movement, and used the other to lift her chin. "I'm running this show," he said.

Then, putting actions to words, Kody slowly undressed her before instructing her to stand.

Winter did so, feeling overly exposed since she was totally naked while Kody was only missing a shirt.

She stood there with downcast eyes, trying to fight the annoying shyness creeping in.

"Don't do that," Kody said. "Look at me."

Winter's eyes snapped up.

It was a reaction that she didn't even think about. Kody spoke, and her body responded. She understood at that moment that not only did she want to be pleased by him, but she also wanted to please him.

"Am I making you nervous?" he asked.

Releasing a small laugh and holding her pointer finger and thumb close together, she said, "a little bit."

"I don't know why. You are the most beautiful women I have ever seen. Your body is perfect; your mind is perfect. *You*," he said with emphasis, "are perfect."

Reaching out, Kody pulled her to him and lifted one of her legs to rest on his shoulder.

She felt his breath moments before his tongue. He moved it around in a gradual, teasing manner that felt intoxicating.

Oh, I could get addicted to this.

Winter grabbed his head, urging him to speed up the pace. Which he did, and once he began sucking on her clit while rubbing and massaging her lower back, it didn't take long before she could feel the orgasm approaching.

She moaned and pulled him closer. But suddenly, he stopped.

"Is something wrong?" Winter asked, breathing heavily and looking down at him.

"No," Kody said with a grin. "I just want to change positions."

Kody slid to the floor, pulling Winter with him. They landed on the luxuriously soft rug that stretched the entire width of her couch.

Winter sat on his stomach. Palms pressed against his chest.

"Slide up," he ordered.

She obeyed, but only moving forward about an inch. Kody laughed and said, "How about you keep coming forward until I tell you to stop?"

Winter moved up, and once far enough, Kody guided her over his face, but then her nerves took over, and she stiffened.

The tension in Winter's body was unmistakable. Not only was this a vulnerable position to be in, Kody was playing a dangerous game.

What if she smothered the man? She'd never sat on a guy's face before. Hell, before last night, she'd barely gotten oral before!

Kody's hands glided down her back to rest on her waist.

"I see those wheels turning, beautiful."

"Yeah, because I like you, suffocating you isn't exactly evidence of that."

"You won't suffocate me."

Winter narrowed her eyes, and Kody grinned.

"Relax," he instructed, and guided her down the rest of the way onto his mouth.

It took no time at all for him to find the spot that not only gave her pleasure, but did indeed make her relax.

"Oh," Winter hummed quietly, spasms of pleasure consuming her, "maybe smothering you is worth it."

Kody chuckled, and the vibration paired with his swirling tongue opened the door for a powerful climax to start building.

Without realizing it, Winter began grinding her pussy on his face. Her loss of control must have been exactly what Kody wanted. He tightened his grip around her waist and sucked hard, all of his attention focused on her most sensitive area.

Her release was soon to follow. It left her shaking and calling out his name.

Kody lifted her off him and repositioned them so that she was lying down, and he was on top of her.

He began kissing all over her body—her legs, her waist, her stomach. When he made it to her breast, he gently bit and sucked on her nipples, and that familiar inner pulsating roared to life yet again.

"You aren't going to dine and run like you did last time, are you?" Winter asked.

"Not a chance," Kody promised between kisses.

His unrelenting process of delicious foreplay lasted for

what seemed like forever. He was driving her out of her mind, and the ache for him was maddening.

Winter needed him more than she needed her next breath. However, Kody's reaction to her wanting more was to give her less.

When she tried to pull him closer, he would back up slightly, clarifying that this moment was his to control.

After what seemed like endless torture, she felt him enter her. Kody moved slowly at first, ensuring she felt every inch of him.

Cries of ecstasy flowed from her lips.

Winter was in a zone. The heightened pleasure of stretching and fullness took over as Kody moved inside her, satisfying her in ways that she didn't even know she craved.

Wrapping her legs around his waist, Kody dug deeper and increased the pace. Their bodies moved in a rhythm that naturally complemented the other.

It took no effort, no thinking, just being.

Kody accompanied the physical stimulation with some mental, by telling her how beautiful she was and how much he wanted her.

Nothing, Winter thought, *has ever felt this good.*

Another orgasm approached, different from the first because this one was from him being inside her.

It was somehow stronger and made her feel as if she was coming apart.

Without restraint, the euphoric waves of her release consumed her, and her body shook and tingled with warm satisfaction.

Afterward, they lie there in silence, listening to the fire pop and crackle. Mind-numbing ecstasy and sheer exhaustion had Winter too limp to do more. She relaxed on his chest, satisfied, and completely spent.

Kody had literally fucked her senseless, just like she thought he would.

She couldn't think... couldn't move... couldn't breathe... *Dammit! I can't even see.*

Well, the last one was likely because her eyes were closed, but she wouldn't put it past Kody's capabilities.

He was extraordinary in every way.

Already Winter could feel herself slipping into a deep sleep, and her last coherent thought was that she wasn't falling for Kody because...

I've already fallen.

CHAPTER SEVENTEEN
Winter

"DID HE USE A CONDOM?"

A clanging noise in the kitchen made Winter bolt straight up. Kody was there, in the kitchen, cooking breakfast. She smiled at him.

"Good morning," Kody said cheerfully.

Winter returned the greeting, running a hand through her curly hair, that she was sure was a mess, and looked around. She was in the living room on the floor where they'd fallen asleep the night before.

Getting to her feet, Winter took a moment to stretch before going to the bathroom to freshen up.

Returning to the kitchen, she walked over to Kody and put her arms around his waist.

Taking the pan for the eggs off the stove, Kody turned to look at her.

"Hey, sexy," Winter said.

"Hey, gorgeous," he responded.

Kody gave her a quick kiss, then nodded towards the table, while he resumed making breakfast. Winter took a seat, turning sideways in the chair to stare over at him.

"Were you trying to kill me last night? I lost count of how many orgasms I had," she said.

Kody didn't even look up when he answered. "Nope, just giving you what you deserved."

"Kody! Are you still mad about my not being able to please a woman comment? You got me back for that, remember? You basically left me unconscious right here on this very table."

"I remember. Doesn't mean I was done with making you pay for it."

Winter rolled her eyes. "Well, thank you for making me eat those words."

"Anytime," Kody said, scooping eggs onto a plate.

"How long have you been up?" she asked.

"A couple of hours."

Winter's brows lifted. "I didn't hear you moving around."

"Yeah, you were sleeping pretty soundly, but I tried my best to be quiet while I showered, had some coffee and even answered a few emails all before making you breakfast."

Winter blinked a few times. "Wow! I slept through all that? What in the hell did you do to me?"

Putting her food down on the table, then sitting across from her, Kody said, "Nothing I don't plan on doing again."

Winter licked her lips. "I certainly hope so," Then, sliding her plate closer, she asked. "Wait, where's your breakfast?"

"Coffee is my breakfast. Besides, I need to get ready to go. One of my guys won't be able to pick up the things I'll need on Monday, so I have to head to the warehouse."

"Gotcha," Winter said, picking up the syrup to pour over her pancakes. "How long will that take?"

"Only a few hours. Will you be here?" he asked.

"Not sure. I'm going to head to the shelter once I'm done with breakfast. Then I have a few more errands and some things to pick up for work. Oh," Winter said, putting down the syrup, "that reminds me, would you like to come by the office and have lunch with me sometime next week?"

"That would be nice. As long as you're flexible on the day, I have some scheduling to consider."

"Fine by me."

Kody stood to leave. "Make sure you eat up. You're going to need your energy," he said, kissing her before he left.

Instantly, Winter missed him. Wanted more of his touch, his presence, and to enjoy any and everything he offered.

Looking down at the delicious food, she said, "Guess I'll have to enjoy this instead," and dug in.

"Winter! Did you bring us another one of your fancy pieces?" Mrs. Gordon asked.

Mrs. Gordon was a delightful woman in her 70s, who had been running Heart and Home, the local Women's shelter, for over fifteen years.

She always got excited when Winter stopped by and always welcomed her redesigned antiques.

"I wouldn't call them fancy, but yes, I brought a night-stand." Winter stepped aside so that Mrs. Gordon could look at the piece.

Mrs. Gordon's eyes went wide.

"Oh, don't be modest," she said, pushing her silver glasses further up her nose. "It is exquisite. Did you paint this one too and add those little shiny stones?"

"Yes, I did."

"Great job! And I know who it would be perfect for. One of the ladies just got approved for a house and has a 12-year-old daughter, and another on the way, bless her heart. I think this would go perfect in the daughter's room."

Winter beamed. "Oh, wow, that's wonderful. I am so glad I could help."

"You always do, sweetie." Mrs. Gordon stepped around

the nightstand and gave Winter's arm a squeeze. "Tell me, how have you been? Any boyfriends or maybe babies on the way?"

Mrs. Gordon made the statement with a hopeful grin.

Smiling happily, Winter said, "There is a man, but no baby."

"Well, dear, at least we have the first base covered. Don't worry, children will come soon enough."

Winter laughed. Mrs. Gordon loved babies and would have probably had a house full of them if medical issues hadn't prevented it.

Abruptly, Winter stopped laughing. The comment about kids made her mentally dive back into her night of passion.

Did he use a condom?

"You alright? You looked startled," Mrs. Gordon asked.

Winter shook her head. "I'm fine. I just realized I may have left the stove on," she lied. It was the first thing she could think of. "I apologize, Mrs. Gordon, I have to go. Is everything fine with the nightstand? Can I leave it here, or do you need me to carry it into your office?"

"No, no, here is fine. You go check on that stove. Wouldn't want you losing your place and having to move in with us."

Winter ran to her car.

She kept replaying the night, trying to locate at least one detail that would jog her memory and guarantee that Kody used protection.

But how could she remember him putting on a condom when she was lost in a world of sex?

Delicious, titillating, mind-numbing, stupidly reckless sex.

"Shit!" Winter groaned, hitting the steering wheel.

Blowing out a breath, she glanced at her cell in the passenger seat. This wasn't something you asked about over the phone.

In a few hours, she would see Kody and could ask him then.

For now, she would simply stay calm, finish her errands and work diligently to avoid prematurely freaking out.

Pulling into the garage four hours later, Winter went over the details again, drawing a blank. Which meant she would have to ask Kody if he used a condom and, in her mind, asking him that made her sound so irresponsible.

What if he said no?

Then she would have a little Kody in the next nine months, that's what. She paused as the possibility of a child with Kody danced in her mind.

Envisioning him holding a precious bundle and all the things they could do as a family made the idea not as scary as it originally seemed. It would actually be nice to have a child with a man so warm, kind, strong and levelheaded.

But not right now!

Logic was setting in heavily. This was no fairytale. A baby at this stage in her life was a disaster.

Winter was not ready for that... *they* were not ready for that. She still didn't know how they were going to survive a long distance relationship.

If we have a relationship at all, after all this.

Pushing all uncertainties out of her mind, Winter unloaded the groceries from the trunk and started a load of laundry.

To keep her mind occupied, she opened her laptop and worked on more prop lists for clients.

Kody was there an hour later on the couch watching some car show she was unfamiliar with.

"Would you ever like to see a live hockey game?" Kody asked without looking away from the TV.

"Yeah, I hear those games can be highly entertaining with the fights between teams."

"That's actually true. I haven't been to a hockey game since I was a kid, but I remember I loved it."

The mention of being a kid gave Winter the push she needed to ask him about last night. She slowly closed her laptop and said a silent prayer that this would all work out.

"Listen, last night was...amazing, for lack of a better word."

"I agree," Kody replied, eyes still on the TV.

"I can't believe I have to ask this. It's not like me to be so careless. But," Winter said, bracing herself for the worst, "did you use protection?"

Kody picked up the remote, turned off the TV, then faced her. "Yes."

Winter felt like a weight had been lifted off her shoulders. Thank God someone was paying attention last night.

"I don't even remember you putting it on," she said.

Kody gave her a knowing look. "Because you were in your own little world."

Winter smiled, slightly embarrassed at the truth. "Yeah, that was some world I'd like to revisit really soon."

"I'm ready if you are," Kody said.

Damn, he is so hard to resist sometimes.

But resist, she did, because as tempting as his offer was, another question plagued her mind.

Pushing her chair back from the table, Winter joined Kody on the couch.

"There's something else," she said, chewing on her lower lip.

"What's on your mind?" Kody asked, genuine concern lacing his voice.

"Last night, when you mentioned you could never leave me, what did you mean? Are you moving here?"

Kody thought about it, and Winter's heart sped up.

It's a no. I know the answer is no.

"Yes," Kody said, and Winter almost jumped up in excitement, however a few seconds later, she was grateful that she'd showed no response at all. "But not right away," Kody continued.

Winter stared, confused. Helpless to stop her wall of hope from collapsing.

Kody sighed. "I have a few more projects to complete first. I'll have to work out the details, but I will stop getting involved with new contracts in California and Texas and get more involved with projects here."

Winter nodded.

So far, it doesn't sound so bad.

Nevertheless, that changed when he added, "I'd only travel maybe five months out of the year instead of nine or ten."

"Travel? You mean that you might be gone five months at a time?"

"Sometimes."

"Oh, okay," Winter replied, all hope gone.

What Kody was explaining sounded a lot like a long-distance relationship. Winter didn't want that. Long-distance relationships were not ideal, not for her anyway. People always fell apart, she knew from personal experience.

Regardless, she didn't want to say that to him. Kody's company was important to him, as it should be. He had worked hard to get where he was, and pushing the issue would be rude and inconsiderate.

Besides, he is already making major adjustments for me.

Five months out of the year wasn't bad when Winter really thought about it. One measly relationship failure didn't have to imply all long-distance romance would fail... right?

"Winter?" Kody said, yanking her from her thoughts

"Yes," she replied, adding a smile that didn't quite reach her eyes.

Grabbing her hands, Kody said, "I can see that brain of yours churning away. It's going to be okay. What we have is real. It won't fade just because we will be apart sometimes. I know you told me you had a failed long-distance relationship in the past, but this is not that relationship. Plus, you can even come to see me when I do the projects anytime you'd like."

"Hmm," Winter said, getting on board with the idea, "Visiting you is fine, but I am not staying in one of those renovations. I love you, but no thank you."

Shit!

Winter could not believe she had just said that. Until the words slipped out, she had no idea that she felt that way and now that she'd said it, there was no way to take it back.

Winter closed her mouth and tried to stand, but Kody caught her hand.

"Look at me," he said.

It took effort, a whole lot of effort, but she eventually did.

"I love you too, Winter."

She stared into Kody's eyes. He was telling the truth. He loved her.

"But how? When?"

Those were the only half way coherent questions she could think to ask. Never in a million years would she have believed he felt the same.

"I think I have loved you for a while now, but I didn't want to say anything and scare you back into your shell. You may have thought I was lying if I said it too fast, but I promise you, I do love you."

If she were in one of her favorite classic movies, fireworks would burst above her head, followed by a wholesome yet romantic kiss.

However, wholesome was the last thing Winter wanted. Kody's confession of love had Winter turned on beyond measure and dirty was a lot more appealing.

Grabbing his shirt and pulling him to her, Winter decided that a repeat of last night would be much more fitting.

"There is a fine ass man here to see you," Lisa said, standing in Winter's office doorway, fanning herself dramatically.

Winter shook her head, laughing.

Continuing to fill out prop forms, she said, "Oh, that's Kody. You can send him back."

Lisa stepped further into the office and placed her hands on her hips.

"That's it! No explanation or elaboration for your favorite assistant?"

Winter dropped her pen and tilted her head. "Lisa, you are my only assistant."

Waving her off, Lisa said, "That's beside the point. I expect a full report on this relationship."

Winter narrowed her eyes and challenged Lisa's assumption.

"Who said it was a relationship?"

"Relationship, booty call, friends with benefits, late night daddy... whatever you want to call him, I want to hear about it."

"You are insane," Winter said.

"You knew that the day you hired me. Either way, that explains it."

"Explains what?" Winter asked, confused.

"Why you've been so happy?"

"I'm always happy."

"True. But you've been especially happy lately. It's a type of happy that only love and a man tapping that ass can produce."

Despite her best efforts, Winter could not stop the smile

that slowly crept across her face, causing her to sigh in resignation.

"Is it that obvious?"

"Yup. It's all over your vibe, and I'm happy for you. He's a good one, Winter."

Winter crossed her arms.

"Now, how would you know that?"

"I just do," Lisa said with a wink, and before Winter could comment further, she said, "I'll send him back."

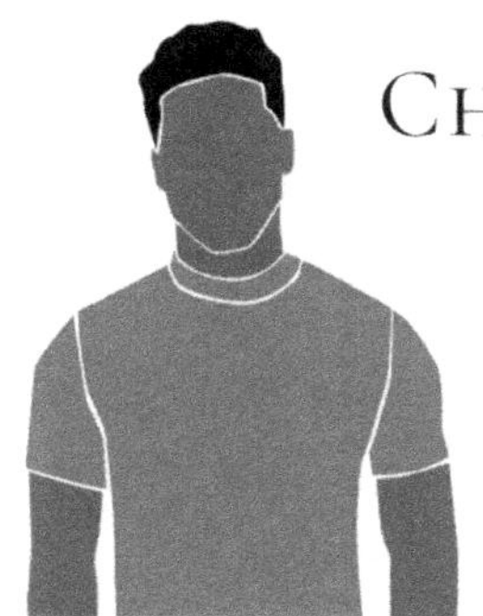

Chapter Eighteen

Kody

Winter took her time, slowly walking around the small ranch style home that no longer held any familiarity to her own.

Kody watched her marvel at the new skylight and the intricate tile design that had been recently installed in the kitchen.

"The house looks amazing, Kody!" Winter exclaimed.

And so do you.

She was wearing blue jeans, heels and a pink and yellow sweater that hugged her breasts. Her hair was down, and she looked so damn good.

All Kody could think about was grabbing a hand full of those beautiful black curls and fucking her as she was bent over the counter.

He could feel his hardness starting as the scene played out in his mind. Later, he would definitely tend to those needs.

"You have completed an incredible amount of work in such a short period. I'm so proud of you," she said.

The comment made Kody laugh.

Winter pivoted to look at him directly. "What's so funny?"

"Saying that you are proud of me. It's sweet, but that's something I don't hear often. I think the last person who told me that was my grandma about two years ago."

"Well, you should hear it more often. You do great work."

"Thanks, babe. I'll let Jackson know he needs to do a better job cheering me on."

"Maybe he'd agree," she said jokingly.

"What he'd do is call me a pussy and hang up on me, and I'd have to agree with him."

"Men," Winter said, shaking her head and moving towards the master bedroom.

Kody knew the exact moment she saw the master bath, because she let out a squeal of delight.

"I love this bathroom!"

"I figured you would," he said, joining her in the newly designed en suite. "If you'd like, I can design you something similar."

Winter spun around so fast her arm hit him in the chest, but her eyes were filled with so much excitement she didn't even notice.

"Don't play with me. I'd never leave the bathroom if I had something like this. You'd seriously do that for me?"

Kody wasn't surprised by her question. No matter how often he'd made it clear that he would do anything for her, it wasn't sinking in.

She was guarded because of her past disastrous romances, which Kody understood, but didn't like.

The simple reason that Winter never expected anything was the exact reason he wanted to give her everything.

"Winter, have I not proved to you that I would do anything for you?"

"You have, but it's just so nice!" She said, looking around the bathroom. "I love how you added the standalone tub with the faucet coming out of the floor. Then the shower has built-in bench seats on each side. It's like a spa in here!"

"And your design would be even better," he said, kissing her on the forehead.

Winter finished touring the house, oohing and ahhing at

all the luxurious touches, while Kody explained what areas were left to complete.

Stepping out onto the porch, Kody noticed a box in the corner that he hadn't seen earlier, which was odd, because he wasn't expecting anything. After a quick inspection, he located the issue. The addressed to section read:

Winter Daniels

"Looks like the mailman is at it again," Kody announced, offering her the package.

Confusion turned to understanding as Winter took the box. "Well, at least this time they got it half right."

"What do you mean?"

"This box contains something for you, even though they were supposed to deliver it to me."

Kody reached out a hand, expectantly.

"Well, aren't you going to give it to me, then?"

Winter grinned and tucked it under her arm. "I will, later."

Back at her place, Kody watched Winter grab two glasses and a bottle of wine, before joining him on the couch.

Vaguely, he wondered if there was some special occasion he had forgotten about. Between her highly chipper mood and the package that she had yet to show him the contents, Kody knew something was up.

Nevertheless, he said nothing, not wanting to spoil anything.

Winter searched for a movie to watch and immediately stopped when she found Home Alone.

"I love this movie. Are you fine watching this?" she asked, turning to face him.

Kody settled back onto the couch, pulling her with him.

The smell of her perfume was intoxicating, and he'd much rather skip the movie, but aloud he said, "Works for me."

They watched the movie and sipped their wine, laughing and commenting at all the appropriate scenes.

When the movie ended, Kody could no longer hold back. Sliding his hands under her sweater, he began rubbing his fingers up and down her sides.

The action was effective in getting her turned on, but just when Kody thought they were about to kiss, Winter put up a finger.

"I have something for you first."

Retrieving the box from the counter, she gave it to him. Kody eyed her suspiciously as he opened it. There was no need for her to get him a present. She'd already given him her gratitude.

What more could she possibly...

It was a watch.

But not just any watch. A blue and gold Seaburst, manufactured by Holzkern, a popular company that specialized in unique timepieces.

Turning it over, Kody noticed the inscription:

As long as time is counting, there is no room for doubting.

Words of encouragement from his dad. Kody was so astonished by her thoughtfulness, he was momentarily speechless. This had to have been the best gift anyone had ever given him.

"Winter," he said, looking at the watch and then up at her. "I can't believe you did this."

She was all smiles. Beautiful, self-less, compassionate

smiles. There was no way that she could understand how much this meant to him.

"Of course, I did. I love you, and you deserve it," she said.

Kody glanced at the watch again. Its intricate details and shiny outer shell.

"This couldn't have been cheap."

Laughing, Winter said, "It wasn't, but it's fine. It's not like it cost anywhere near the watch you were wearing the night you told me about your watch collection."

Kody couldn't help but smile as he shook his head slightly and stared at her.

Damn, she is amazing.

"I don't know what to say, Winter. This is very kind of you."

"You are more than welcome."

Kody grabbed her hand, pulling her closer to him. He could think of a few ways to thank her for her generosity.

"How did I get so lucky?" Kody asked.

"Oh, you haven't gotten lucky yet. But you're about to," Winter said, biting her lower lip.

"You know what that lip biting does to me," Kody growled, placing his hand behind her neck. However, once he was within inches of his lips touching hers, Winter pulled away.

"Oh, I do," she said seductively, moving the watch and packaging from his lap and then sliding to her knees on the floor in front of him. "I want you to sit back and relax while I handle the show this evening."

Not one to argue, Kody sat back and did what he was told.

The next month and a half arrived quicker than Kody wanted or expected. It was early February, and he and Winter were driving to Jackson and Erica's place for a Super Bowl party.

They were getting there before the crowd so that Winter could spend time with Erica while he helped Jackson with setting up.

The day had started off perfectly.

After having sex three times, they finally, but grudgingly, got out of bed and got dressed.

If it wasn't official before, it was now. He was head over heels in love with her.

Placing his hand over hers as they drew closer to his cousin's house, it was apparent to Kody that he needed to reconsider his work structure.

The plan was to return to California to oversee a few projects while increasing his involvement in the Georgia work assignments.

But now, he was rethinking the whole thing, no longer sure that he could be away from Winter that long.

He wanted to wake up to her every morning and fall asleep with her every night.

Appointing someone else to manage the projects was a viable option. And listing his home in California and buying one in Georgia would be easily manageable.

The biggest issue, lie in familiarity.

Kody had been working wherever he was needed for so long it was hard to let it go. He was used to seeing specific projects through to the end and ensuring that his employees exceeded expectations.

Old habits like that died hard.

After pulling up at Jackson's house and jumping out to unload some items from the backseat, Kody heard Jackson coming before he saw him.

"Didn't I tell you guys not to bring anything? Erica already purchased the entire grocery store."

"You did, but no one listens to you," Kody responded.

Jackson walked towards Kody with his arms open, as if to help grab some bags. At the last second, Jackson swerved around him and instead hugged Winter.

"Such an asshole," Kody said with a laugh.

"It's a family trait," Jackson tossed back over his shoulder. "Winter! It's so good to see you."

"You too, Jackson," Winter said, hugging him.

"Erica is waiting for you in the house. She's ready to give you a tour and start her chronicles of girl talk."

"Gotcha," Winter replied. "Kody, do you want me to take something in?"

"No, babe, I got it."

Winter gave Kody a quick kiss and went inside to join Erica.

"Little cousin," Jackson said, turning to Kody. "Are you ready to kick back, let loose and watch what better be one fucking amazing game?"

Kody pulled two bags from the truck and shoved them into Jackson's arms, who accepted it without comment.

"I think I'm past ready. Been working tons lately finishing up the house, and we've barely seen each other, man."

"It's because Winter has you wanting to spend all your free time with her."

"She does, and I wouldn't change it. Not to mention, I can see you anytime when I move here."

Kody threw out the statement without looking at Jackson, and, as expected, his cousin noticed right away.

Jackson stepped back. "Are you kidding me?! You're going to relocate to Georgia?"

"Yup." Then, in a hushed tone, Kody added, "Don't say anything to Winter. I want it to be a surprise."

"Well, damn," Jackson said, beaming as if he'd just won the lottery. "My lips are sealed, and the timing is perfect because we have a contract coming up in Rome, Georgia. It's about an hour and forty-five minutes from here. I am going to need you to go down there and take a meeting in the next week or so."

"Sounds good to me," Kody said.

Jackson was still standing there dumbfounded, dressed in a jersey that put more emphasis on his mid-section than hiding it, with a huge grin on his face.

"It's about time you came to your senses and moved here. I said it once and I'll say it again, thank God for Winter," Jackson said.

"My sentiments exactly," Kody agreed.

The Super Bowl party was elaborate and entertaining. Erica had decorated the living room and deck with bold colors and signs from her favorite team.

Truth be told, the 7,000 square foot home was possibly more festive than the stadium itself.

Streamers hung from the ceiling, a green rug designed like a miniature football field lay underneath the table and even team-inspired plates, napkins and dishes covered the tables.

Over the next few hours, more people arrived and by the time of the opening kick-off, there were over fifty screaming, excited guests present.

Kody knew a few of them, but not many. With all the moving around he did, it was hard to get to know people the way Jackson had. There were a few good friends back in California, but for the most part, his dealings were professional, not personal.

Kody's eyes scanned the room, locating Winter. She'd hung out with him for only the first ten minutes of the game before Erica pulled her away.

Now, Kody smiled at the two of them. The woman he loved and the woman that was like a sister to him, surrounded by other football fans drinking beer and cheering (or cursing) depending on the outcome of the play.

As half time approached, Kody grabbed a beer and went to the patio where Jackson was grilling.

"Need any help?" Kody asked.

Jackson was taking hotdogs and wings from the grill, loading them onto a large tray.

"First, you can get the door for me," he said, balancing the tray on his shoulder. Stepping back inside, Jackson was about to tell Kody what more he could assist with, but stopped mid-sentence when he noticed Winter approaching. "Your girl is on the way over. I think you already have your hands full."

Jackson walked away, laughing to himself, and Kody leaned back against the wall to stare at his little sexual deviant.

This was now Winter's third time coming over to "check on him." He knew what she was really doing. She was trying to start trouble.

Every time she came over previously, she would rub her breasts against him or caress his chest or arms seductively.

Then she would bite her lip and say, "Oh, excuse me," with a mischievous grin on her face.

In response to her teasing, Kody had said nothing. Opting instead to let her have her fun, and curious as to just how far she would go.

However, it never went further than the light touches before she would strut away, leaving Kody to admire how deliciously enticing her ass looked in those jeans.

Winter was trying to get a rise out of him, both literally and figuratively.

Standing in front of him now, she discreetly slid her hands down his chest and grabbed his dick, spending several seconds massaging it through his jeans.

"You look so hot standing over here. I can't stop thinking about you taking me home and having your way with me."

Releasing her grip on his dick, Winter once again turned to leave, but this time, Kody caught her arm and pulled her back to him.

Leaning down, Kody whispered, "If you keep playing with me, you will not have to wait until we get home. I'm going to take you upstairs and fuck the shit out of you and make sure everyone at this party can hear you screaming my name. So unless you want to be the star of this year's halftime show, I suggest you stop toying with me."

Winter sucked in a deep breath and Kody watched her hurry her sexy ass back over to the couch.

He wasn't bluffing, and clearly Winter knew it because she didn't tease him any more that night.

Nevertheless, Winter may have waved the white flag, but Kody wasn't letting her off the hook.

When they got home, her ass was his.

"**S**ay it," Kody demanded.

But Winter wasn't going to. What he was doing to her felt so good it should be illegal, but she had to win this bet.

"No," Winter tried to say convincingly, but the words left her lips in a breathless whimper.

"I can keep this up all day," Kody assured her, thrusting slow and deep.

Winter sighed in pleasurable frustration. She knew he could. Maybe he'd stop for a break here and there, but Kody's sexual appetite should be studied.

Giving in would have been so easy, but then he'd win and she'd lose... so no way.

Suddenly shredding her last ounce of control, Kody switched his angle and hit a spot that made the floodgates open. Winter honestly believed she was going to pass out from the glorious sensation.

Her body jolted, giving way to multiple orgasms within the span of several minutes.

"I love you, Kody," Winter said in surrender.

Kissing her neck, then moving up to her lips, Kody responded with his own declaration of love.

Winter was done for, and worse, she'd lost, which meant she'd have to cook dinner for a whole month.

In hindsight, the punishment was not a big deal. Winter loved cooking for him. Still, she didn't want the title of loser.

It started out as a joke when Kody asked Winter to make him an Indian dish he loved.

"Why would I do that?" Winter had asked him playfully.

"Because you love me."

Winter considered it.

"Hmmm, I'm not sure. I think I just say that sometimes to get my way," she replied.

"Oh, do you now?" Kody asked. "Well, I'll bet I can make you say it again. And if I win, you will cook me anything I want for a month."

"I accept your challenge, and you mark my words," Winter said, getting in his face. "I won't be saying anything."

He pulled her in for a kiss after that, which led to more kissing and then eventually sex. The sex that had made her a loser.

Lying there, basking in the afterglow, Winter confessed. "Ashley was right."

Kody had been gently caressing Winter's shoulder, but paused at hearing the sudden statement.

"Excuse me."

"The night I ran into Ashley, she told me that you are a beast in bed."

Kody hummed low in his throat. "Well, I do love sex."

"Yes, you do," she said, running her fingers over his chest. "Which surprises me that you didn't push for sex any sooner. Since you have a big appetite, how'd you suppress that?"

In the back of her mind, Winter realized his answer could be disastrous. Kody could tell her he didn't suppress it at all and had been sleeping with someone else all along.

Don't borrow trouble. Enjoy the moment.

The mental reminder gave her some peace, and Kody adjusted so that he could look down at her.

"You realize I'm an adult, right? I control sex, not the other way around. But most importantly, no matter how bad I wanted to make you cry out my name, you needed time, and things worked out better because you made the decision when you were comfortable."

See! Stop thinking the worst.

Winter stopped berating herself long enough to tell Kody how amazing she thought he was.

A few seconds later, Kody's phone rang. He glanced at the display and then quickly got up.

"I'll be right back," he said.

Winter thought it odd that he left the room since he never did when he took calls.

Is he hiding something?

Her head fell back onto the pillow. She was getting on her own nerves. Second guessing, paranoia and doubting Kody's words was exhausting.

Jumping back into the dating pool after repeated heartbreaks sucked. Nothing felt certain. She never knew when to trust her instincts and the battle of loving freely, without being foolish, was a thin and often blurry line.

Kody only had a short time left in Georgia. Surely his looming departure was the reason her fears of their relationship falling apart kept rearing their ugly heads.

The idea that he would be gone for long periods of time, creeped in every so often and forced her anxiety to rise, but remembering that they did genuinely love each other kept her focused.

Kody came back into the room and got into bed. He laid back on the pillow, dropping his phone on the nightstand.

"Everything okay?" she asked.

"Yup," he said, not being any more forthcoming. "You

want to go out for lunch?"

"I'd like that." Then, with her mood seeming to dip, Winter said, "I hate you are leaving for a few days tomorrow. I'm going to miss you."

"I'll miss you too, but I'll be back on Wednesday. This project in Rome, Georgia, looks promising. Also, cheer up, I have a surprise for you."

"Kody, I told you, no more surprises! At least not right now."

"I never agreed to that. Either way, you'll want this surprise. In addition to lunch, how about we go antique shopping?"

Winter put her hand to her heart. "Seriously, you'd go antique shopping with me? You know that is my favorite thing in the world!"

"Besides me, I hope."

"That goes without saying," Winter responded before eyeing him. "Wait. Guys don't volunteer for shopping. What are you trying to get out of me, mister?"

"More orgasms would be good," he said.

Winter laughed.

"The last guy I dated avoided antique shopping like the plague. After a while, it was really entertaining hearing the excuses he would come up with to avoid going. One time he told me he sprained his ankles."

"As in both?" Kody questioned.

"Yup. Then there was the excuse that his long-lost cousin showed up on his doorstep. Oh!" Winter said, suddenly remembering. "And the one about the neighbor's lost dog."

"Okay," Kody said slowly. "What did a lost dog have to do with him?"

"Well, who else was going to organize the search party?" Winter replied, as if his question was absurd.

Kody laughed out loud at that one. "Are you kidding?"

"Sadly, I'm not. He was a real piece of work."

Kody sat up in bed and faced her.

"I don't know. Maybe he had the right idea. If antique shopping is really that bad, I guess I better collect my payment before we leave."

"Huh?" Winter said, not following.

"I already told you, I want more orgasms out of you." Then he instructed her to roll over onto her back, placed one hand between her legs, and slid his fingers over her wetness. "So pay up."

Winter signed off on the tenth production contract for the day. She'd been at the office since 6am and had made major headway in the stack of work on her desk.

With Kody gone on his brief business trip, there was no one tempting her to spend a little longer in bed each morning and sacrifice much needed sleep in lieu of erotic activities at night.

Funny how in such a short amount of time, they'd become so accustomed to one another.

Despite all the necessary reassuring to convince her heart that Kody was a good man, Winter was finding it easier to settle into the here and now.

Mainly because now, her love life was phenomenal.

Kody belonged in her bed, just as much as he belonged in her heart, and Winter was surprised to realize that she was happy. Truly happy.

"Knock, knock," came a voice at Winter's office door.

"Lisa, what's up?"

Lisa strolled further into the room and lowered herself

into a chair facing Winter's desk.

"I have good news."

Winter moved her papers aside and mimicked Lisa's smile. "Really, what?"

"The clients you were supposed to meet with at one canceled. They rescheduled it for next week."

"Okay, but what's with the excitement? Meeting with them was no big deal. I'm actually ahead in my work for a change, so there were no timing issues."

"Yeah, yeah, but now that means you can have a long lunch with yours truly. It's been forever since we were able to go to lunch together."

"It would be nice to catch up. And you know what?" Winter said, really liking the idea, "we can go to that burger place we went to earlier this year."

"I'll grab my purse and meet you in the parking lot in five minutes," Lisa said as she jumped up to leave.

Lisa and Winter choose a booth table at the Tilted Tavern. A place well known for their delicious hamburgers and fun karaoke entertainment.

After placing their orders with the waitress, Lisa leaned in.

"Alright, share."

Winter didn't pretend to not know what Lisa was talking about. Besides, Lisa wasn't only her assistant, she was a good friend.

"Well, his name is Kody," Winter began, "and he is amazing..."

She told Lisa the story of how they met, met again and then came to be how they were today, in love and happy.

When winter was done, Lisa said, "Wow. Now that is something they should make a film about. Such a cute love story. Women everywhere would hang out in dim lit parking lots, hoping to get attacked just so that a mouthwatering, sexy, Godsend like Kody could come and save them."

"I have to admit, I agree. Well, except for the part about women hanging out in parking lots waiting to be rescued, I hope no one would do that."

Shrugging, Lisa said, "Crazier things have happened. You know how people get when they see movies they love; they want it to play out in their own lives, so sometimes they try to set the ball in motion. Like how the movie "Fight Club" made people start real fight clubs."

Winter nodded. "True."

"Anyway, lonely woman drama aside, I am so happy for you. I could tell when I met Kody that he was a great guy. It's been a long time since you dated anyone. It's good you let your wall down and let someone in."

"Yeah, well, Kody does construction, so it was kinda like he demolished my wall. Without my permission, might I add. But I'm glad he did it."

"See!" Lisa said, wiping at pretend tears. "So romantic. I need to find someone that makes me feel like that. Maybe I should take my own advice and wait in one of those dark alleys."

"Oh, stop it," Winter said. "You meet tons of men, and I know the one for you is coming along soon."

"You might be right. I did just meet this guy named Paul. Who knows, it could work out. My parents want to set me up with some nice Asian guy, but I like to find my own men, and Paul ain't Asian."

"You know, parents always want what's best for us,

according to them, anyway."

"Exactly," Lisa said. "Hey, how's Jessica and Chloe?"

"They are really good. I talked to them both last week. Chloe is preparing to go to the Dominican Republic for work, and Jessica is super busy planning an event for some wealthy wine company owner."

"I love their lives," Lisa said.

"Hey now," Winter scoffed. "You and I didn't do so bad ourselves. Working in film is fun."

"I guess you're right. It may not be on the beach, but we can always put up a beach backdrop."

"Cheers to that," Winter said, raising her cup of water and taking a sip.

Winter sat in a house that somehow seemed emptier. Navigating the early stages of this relationship was annoying because she felt like a lovesick puppy when he wasn't around.

"Ugh, get it together," Winter groaned.

But that was easier said than done. Everything reminded her of how amazing Kody was and how much she missed him.

From the smell of his cologne that lingered on her sheets, to how neatly he had stacked things in the kitchen cabinets.

Kody's way of arranging things made it so that she got a better view of all the contents and could avoid making duplicate purchases at the grocery store.

After making a chicken sandwich for dinner, Winter exchanged texts with Jessica.

A couple of hours later, she was in bed, flipping through channels, when her cell rang. She saw it was Kody and immediately smiled to herself.

"Hi, handsome," Winter said, answering the call.

"Hey, sweetie. How are you?"

"I'm good. And you? Are things looking promising for the new contract?"

"Yeah, I think the community is going to look great. They have thirty acres cleared out and want to build twenty-five, nicely-sized, single-family homes on it."

"That's an enormous project."

"It is, but I didn't call to talk about work. What are you doing?"

"Lying in bed, flipping through channels. You back at your hotel?"

"Yes, I am. I'm in bed, staring up at the ceiling."

"Hmm, are you naked and touching yourself?" she asked.

"No, and I'm not going to, but I want you to."

She laughed.

"I'm serious," he said.

Winter rolled over onto her stomach. "Why exactly would I do that?"

Kody's voice was low and deep when he responded. It was the very voice he used when he talked her through orgasms, making her melt on command.

"Because I want you to cum."

Winter sat up. She'd never done the whole phone sex thing before.

Could be interesting.

"Are you serious?" she said, assuming he was toying with her.

His blatant reply was instant.

"I think the words you are looking for are, yes, Kody, I'd love to."

Glancing over at the nightstand drawer that held her pink vibrator, Winter grinned.

"In that case, one sec." She grabbed her vibrator out of the drawer and then sat back on the bed. After hitting the speaker button and placing the phone next to her, Winter said, "Got my toy."

"Take off your shorts and underwear and then lie back. Open your legs nice and wide and close your eyes." She did as instructed, whispered that she was ready, and Kody continued. "Turn on your vibrator and start massaging your pussy with it. While you're doing it, I want you to think back to the first time I went down on you at your kitchen table. Are you with me, Winter?"

"Yes," she said, licking her lips, feeling her temperature rising.

"Do you know when I got home I could not stop thinking about how good you tasted?"

"No. I didn't know that," Winter said, moving the vibrator in a slow up and down motion.

"Oh, yes. Your sweet taste lingered on my lips and tongue as I kept replaying hearing you moan and call out my name. After your first orgasm, I couldn't stop; it was so good, I needed more, so I kept going. Honestly, I could have done that to you for hours. I hate I had to stop when I did."

Her breathing increased, and Winter began closing her legs. She needed to add more pressure to her swollen clit.

As if he could see her, Kody said. "Keep your legs open; you're more sensitive that way, and you'll get wetter."

Winter complied and shifted her free hand up to her breast.

"I wish I was there to taste you right now and then slide into you and hit that spot I know you love."

Her body jerked, an impulsive reaction to the sheer memory of the feeling created whenever Kody thrust into her. Squeezing her nipples, Winter felt her orgasm closing in.

For close to thirty seconds, Kody said nothing. But Winter

was so lost in the incredible sensations coursing through her body that she barely noticed.

Then, Kody said her name.

"Yes," she moaned, barely audible.

"Turn off your vibrator."

Winter's eyes popped open. "Huh? What do you—"

"Off," he repeated sternly.

She swallowed and did what he said. "But... but," she said, breathing heavily. "I thought you wanted me to cum."

"I do, when I'm there and inside you and not a second before. Until then, I want you turned on and ready for me. Tomorrow night, I'll call you, and I want you to do the exact same thing. When I get home on Wednesday, I will take care of the rest. Understand?"

"Yes," Winter grumbled with irritation.

Kody paid her sexually frustrated pout no attention.

"Good. Now, get some sleep. I love you."

"Love you too," she said, feeling hot and oh so terribly bothered.

The next morning, Winter decided to go in late.

Apparently, being sexually frustrated had a negative effect on getting a good night's sleep. Instead of waking up refreshed when her alarm sounded, Winter woke numerous times throughout the night with an intense need to yank out her vibrator and turn it to the max.

Finally, close to 9:30, she got herself out the door and en route to work. Pulling up to a stoplight, Winter sleepily reached for her phone when it rang.

"Hi, gorgeous. I wanted to see how you slept," Kody said

when she answered.

"Not as good as it could have been if someone wasn't so cruel."

"Don't be that way. I'll make it up to you, and you can cum as many times as you want. You can even cum; however you want, by using my tongue or my dick, your choice."

Winter laughed. "I forget how blunt you are sometimes, but I like it."

"Good to know. Hey, babe, I have to go; the client just pulled up. I can't wait to see you tomorrow."

"Me either," she said, and they ended the call.

That damn Kody. She was getting wet just thinking about the dick or tongue comment he'd made. Obviously, the man enjoyed making her squirm.

A slow, satisfied smile spread over her face.

Two can play at that game.

She'd follow his little teasing rules when he called again tonight. Admittedly, the idea of him turning her on from afar then coming home to finish the job was fucking hot!

However, once he got home, Winter would touch and tease him and see how he liked it.

Mind made up, she knew just the sexy piece of lingerie that would set the tone.

"I need that large round mirror to hang over the dining table," Winter said, assisting the staff with setup.

This scene was an argument that took place at the dinner table within a powerful mafia family. They were planning how to take vengeance on a dirty cop who had planted evidence against one of their family members.

Winter scanned the food layout. Although some of it was fake, it didn't stop the real cravings that were awakening.

The pasta, chicken, cakes and various other foods set before the pretend family made the decision that she would have Italian for lunch.

By noon, Winter was starving, and when the director yelled cut for the fifteenth time, she headed to her car.

She concluded that Vino's was the Italian place she wanted to go for her pasta fix. It also was close to the area where she met Kody.

Not wanting to waste a second thinking about the attack from that night, Winter mentally fast-forwarded to seeing Kody for the second time on her doorstep.

Thinking about why he showed up reminded Winter that she never reached out to the post office about the constant mail mix ups.

I'll get to that later.

Winter stopped at a red light as her mind continued enjoying the Kody reverie.

Yanking the door open to Kody standing there looking like a sex ad, with his beautiful eyes, captivating smile and always relaxed vibe.

Yes, that memory would forever live rent free in her head.

Winter glanced to her right and spotted the restaurant Quaint. She hadn't been there in a while and needed to make her way back for some of their yummy pastries.

Through their floor-to-ceiling windows, Winter could see couples, families and solo diners enjoying their food.

Upon further inspection, Winter noticed a couple right in front that gave her pause. They were holding hands, and although she couldn't make out the woman, she most certainly could make out the man.

It was Kody.

CHAPTER TWENTY

Winter

"YOU'RE NOT STUPID."

"That bastard," Chloe said in a rage-filled voice. Then, in an uncertain tone, she added, "That's what we're calling him, right? That bastard, because we are mad at him?"

"Yes, Chloe!" Winter shouted with exasperation.

"But why, I still don't understand? Kody is wonderful and perfect for you. Maybe he has a good explanation. You should have simply gone inside and confronted him, or at the very least, called him."

Winter stop pacing and gritted her teeth. "I don't need level-headedness. I need anger, which is why I called you first, not Jessica."

"Noted," Chloe said. "That bastard! So tell me again what happened."

Winter summarized the shocking, hurtful discovery to her best friend for the third time.

"The details haven't changed, Chloe. I was at a stoplight, turned my head and bam! There he was."

"Damn, and you sure it was him?"

"Yes! I could see him clearly, and his work truck with the Haven Construction logo plastered across the sides was sitting in the parking lot plain as day."

"Maybe there was another part of his business deal that

you didn't know about causing him to return early," Chloe offered.

She was clearly grasping at straws.

Winter spoke slowly and directly, as if speaking to a child.

"I had just spoken to him a few hours earlier. He told me he was coming back on Wednesday. Why would he suddenly be here that same day? And holding hands with some mystery woman, no less," Winter said, her voice rising with every word.

Chloe exhaled and said, "Yeah, it sounds pretty suspicious, but I wonder what happened? This all makes no sense."

Finally, sitting on her bed, deflated and miserable, Winter felt the tears start up again.

"I am so confused and hurt, Chloe. I couldn't even go back to work yesterday. I just came home and cried most of the night."

"Aww sweetie, I'm so sorry."

Winter swallowed the lump in her throat.

"A part of me hoped he would call last night, like he told me he would and we could sort this out, but that never happened. I didn't hear from him.

"Why didn't you call me?"

"At the moment, I couldn't call anyone. My worst fear had been confirmed and the pain of seeing him with her, hours after we had spoken." Winter shook her head to clear the image. "It was all too much for me."

Chloe sighed.

"I understand. Do you think you are going to talk to him soon? You know, confront the situation."

"Of course, I will. He owes me an explanation." Winter grabbed a tissue and blew her nose. "I'm so stupid, and I shouldn't even be upset because this is all my fault. Every relationship I have ends in heartbreak. I knew that and went for it, anyway."

"You're not stupid. You love him, and he had us all

convinced that he loves you, too. We all do things in love; sometimes it's just hard to see clearly."

Chloe's comforting words did nothing to soothe how naïve and helpless Winter felt.

"Regardless, I do not want to see him right now. I need a few days, but he will probably press me until I open the door."

"Hmm, maybe I can help you out with that," Chloe said.

"Are you suggesting I come and stay with you and Derek for a few days? No way."

"Actually, I'm suggesting something better. You know I have to go to the Dominican Republic again tomorrow for a few days. How about you come with me?"

"I don't know, Chloe. I'll be in your way."

"Winter, please. It's a great idea. You need to get away and clear your mind to think, and the beach is perfect for that. I will mostly be in meetings, so you'll have the room to yourself, and we can just meet up for dinner in the evenings, and that is only if you feel like it."

"No. I can't," Winter said again, less certain in her response this time.

"Come on, Winter. You said you wanted time. This is time and a vacation in one."

Winter thought it over. A quick beach getaway would be nice, and she didn't have much going on at work for the rest of the week. She could use some of those vacation days that had been piling up.

"Okay, I'm in. What time should I meet you?"

The next morning Kody had finally called, three times in fact, but Winter didn't answer.

If I had to wait, so can he.

She continued packing her suitcase with a maelstrom of emotion. Tossing in whatever clothes looked cheery, and hope that this getaway did, in some way, make her feel better.

The instincts that told her to be wary of a man that seemed too good to be true were right, and she should have listened.

Suddenly, Winter heard knocking at her front door and knew it was Kody. When she didn't answer the phone, he likely called her at work, only to be told by Lisa that she wasn't in today.

"Go away!" she yelled, walking to the entryway.

"Go away?" Kody repeated. Even without seeing his face, Winter could hear the confusion in his tone. Or was it guilt?

"Winter. What's wrong? Are you okay? I tried calling, but you didn't answer."

"I'm fine. But you won't be if you don't leave right now."

"What are you talking about? Can you just open the door so we can talk?"

Winter felt the tears, threatening yet again to overflow, but she angrily wiped at her eyes and stood tall. There would be no more crying today.

"Winter, I—" Kody stopped talking as she heard his cell ring.

Assuming he answered it, Winter moved closer to the door and listened.

"Hi Teresa, do you need me?"

It felt like a punch in the gut. Was he seriously answering the call from the mystery woman, right there on her doorstep?

He has some fucking nerve!

She'd wanted a little more time before she faced him. Falling apart and heartbroken wasn't the preferred way to do this, but he was leaving her no choice.

Outrage had her hands shaking and without a second

thought, Winter yanked the door opened ready to give him a piece of her mind, but instead was thrown off guard by Kody's expression.

He looked panicked and Winter felt a fresh wave of anger as she realized it was probably because he knew she'd heard him on the phone.

However, instead of explaining himself, Kody did something strange.

Stepping close to her, he gave Winter a quick kiss on the lips before backing away.

"I'm so sorry. I have to go. I will call you as soon as I can."

He ran to his truck, jumped in, and drove away.

Still frozen from all the emotions and the lingering feeling of his lips on hers, Winter stood there stunned, hurt, speechless, but more confused than ever.

It had been three days.

Three peaceful days in Punta Cana where the scenery and sounds of the beach with its glistening waters had welcomed her with open arms. The rampant thoughts had calmed and Winter felt better.

She'd done a lot of crying and soul searching and had finally reached a decision concerning the drama at hand. She was ready to hear Kody out. Even if she didn't like what he said, it was time she heard it.

Therefore, after work that day, she was going to put her big girl panties on and end this.

"So sorry to bombard you," Lisa said, rushing up to Winter's side as soon as she'd entered the building. "One of the clients had to reschedule again, and their only availability was this morning."

Winter's shoulders fell.

"Please tell me you're kidding."

"Afraid not. They are waiting in your office right now. So, put on a happy face. I think things look promising with them."

Lisa gave her a thumbs up, and Winter rolled her eyes.

"If we can't trust them to keep their meetings straight, I don't know if we can trust much else."

"True, but what are you going to do?" Lisa said, shrugging. "I'm going that way. I'll walk with you in case you need me for something."

Arriving in front of her office, Winter took a few deep breaths and then, per Lisa's suggestion, plastered a smile on her face.

Walking in, she turned toward the client seated and stopped dead in her tracks as Kody stood to face her.

CHAPTER TWENTY- ONE

Winter

Pulling Lisa aside, Winter said, "This doesn't look like a client to me."

"Yes, but it's more important than a client."

"I can't believe you conspired against me. You don't know what he's done or if I even wanted to see him."

"You are correct again, but what I do know is a man in love when I see one, and that man is in love."

Winter narrowed her eyes at Lisa.

"Come on, Winter, think about it. You said he demolished your walls to get to your heart. Are you really ready to build a new one so soon?"

Annoyed at Lisa's words of truth, Winter said, "I'm going to kill you later."

"Be sure to mention how cute I was on my headstone," Lisa said, walking out of the office and closing the door behind her.

Winter turned to Kody. "What are you doing here?"

Kody stood and walked towards her, stopping within arm's reach.

Winter was surprised that he made no moves to touch her. God knew she desperately wanted to touch him.

Remember, he is the enemy. Hold it together.

But did the enemy have to look so good?

"I'm not letting you avoid me any longer," Kody said.

"Brave. But can this wait until after work?"

"It could, but I've waited long enough. If I did something wrong, hiding from me is not the answer," he said.

It was at that moment that she looked at him, really looked at him. He was his usual handsome self, but in his eyes, she saw sadness and exhaustion.

Stay strong, Winter reminded herself.

Deciding to get this over with, she said, "I saw you."

Not following and pushing for her to say more, Kody said, "Saw me..."

"I saw you holding hands with some woman on Tuesday at Quaint. You know, a whole day before you told me you would be coming home?"

Kody's eyes went wide and he scrubbed a hand down his face.

"Exactly," Winter said, letting his shocked reaction speak for itself. Obviously he was guilty and that revelation burned down to her very core. Winter crossed her arms and glared at him.

"You have it all wrong, Winter."

She didn't trust it, but damn if she didn't want to hear it. Behind all the sadness and pain of the last few days, his words caused a slight spark of hope to ignite.

Tell me I got this all wrong, she silently prayed. Please say you have an evil twin, please!

Covering her desperation, Winter placed a hand on her hip and said. "How so? Were you not holding a woman's hand at Quaint on Tuesday?"

She braced for his reply, but when it came, it was much worse than she could have ever imagined.

"Jackson was in a terrible accident."

The words hit Winter like a freight train. Covering her

mouth, she envisioned the worse, and words seemed to escape her.

He wasn't supposed to say that.

Maybe that he'd cheated or learned he had a kid, hell, maybe even three kids that he didn't know about. That's what she'd rehearsed a response to. Things that seemed so frivolous compared to this.

Kody grabbed her hand and pulled her towards him; Winter moved closer without realizing she'd moved at all. Then, she said, "Oh, my goodness, Kody, I'm so sorry. Is Jackson okay?"

Wrapping his arms around her as if he could no longer take the small distance between the two of them, Kody said, "Yes, he's fine, but for a few days, we weren't so sure he would be."

They moved over to the chairs and took a seat. Now, knowing the source of the stress and exhaustion in Kody's eyes, Winter felt awful.

She gently caressed Kody's face, wishing she could take his pain away.

"What happened?" Winter asked quietly.

"Well," Kody began, "about ten minutes after I hung up with you on Tuesday, I got a call from Erica that Jackson was in a terrible accident and he wasn't waking up. I rushed back here and met her at Quaint."

A tear rolled down Winter's face as she imagined Jackson hurt and unresponsive. She really liked Jackson, and she knew he and Kody were like brothers.

Kody would have taken that hard, and because of her over-reacting, she wasn't there to help him.

Winter took his hand, and Kody continued.

"Erica was at Quaint to get Jackson his favorite pastries." Kody smiled weakly. "She was trying to be optimistic and keep busy. It was a surprise for when Jackson finally woke up."

"Poor Erica," Winter said, meaning it with every fiber of her being. "I couldn't imagine."

"Yeah, she was frantic, shaking and throwing up. It's a blur to me now, but I'm sure I probably grabbed her hands at some point to try to calm her."

Winter mentally cursed herself. All the fears and misgivings had made her abandon the first man she truly loved in his time of need.

"I really am sorry, Kody. I feel horrible for the added pressure on my end. I wish you would have just told me."

Attempting to lighten the mood, Kody nudged her shoulder with his and said, "That would have been like talking to thin air. You wouldn't take my calls, remember?"

Winter stared down at her hands.

"Don't remind me," she mumbled. "Well, when you showed up at my door, I would have listened, but you ran off."

Kody released another weary sigh.

"Yeah, that was because I'd gotten a call from the nurse informing me that Erica had fainted."

The blows just kept coming.

"Please tell me Erica is okay?"

Kody gave Winter the first genuine smile she'd seen the entire conversation.

"She's fine, great actually. She found out she's eleven weeks pregnant."

"That's wonderful!" Winter said, momentarily forgetting about all the horrors she'd just heard. But all too quickly, they came roaring back—a baby on the way and a husband in the hospital.

"Does Jackson know? Is he awake?"

"Yeah, he woke up on Friday. But by that time, Erica had been checked in because being pregnant and under such stress was causing her to have blood pressure issues."

Winter momentarily buried her face in her hands. This was a lot.

Turning to the man she loved, Winter said, "So much has happened in just a few short days. Is there anything at all I can do? Anything at all, just name it."

Kody brushed her cheek with his hand. "No, things are fine. I thank God that they are safe."

"What about you? I should have been there for you. I should have known something was wrong, I should have—"

"Shhh," Kody said, pulling her into his arms. "Everything is okay now. They are okay, and we are okay."

Winter savored the comforts of his embrace while guilt and desire flooded her heart. She had truly and utterly fucked up. It made the desperate need to do something, anything to set this right much more necessary.

Pulling back, Winter asked, "Shouldn't you be seeing about them now instead of hunting down a crazy woman?"

"Now, Winter," Kody said as if about to disagree with her self assessment. "You may be a crazy woman, but you are *my* crazy woman."

Giving him a small smile, she said, "I'm serious. I'm sure they need you. You can go, I'll be alright. I'll even come with you if you'd like."

"No need; they are in great hands. Teresa, one of Jackson's and Erica's closest friends, is also their nurse. She will call me if anything happens."

Alright, now the universe was adding salt to the wound. Teresa was the mystery woman Kody was talking to on her doorstep.

I get it okay! Winter mentally yelled. *I still have a lot of growing to do!*

She couldn't feel any worse, and Kody didn't even seem the slightest bit angry at her for how childish and horrifically wrong she'd handled this.

Why'd he have to be so understanding and calm?

"Why are you so easy on me? I know you're a nice guy and all, but I won't lie, I'd be a little annoyed if I were in your shoes."

"Because we are just finding our way, Winter. I knew you'd been hurt when we started this, which means there would be some bumps along the way."

"Ha! You call that a bump? That was more like a full on collision. I screwed up massively."

"All you did was put distance between us at what you thought was true evidence of me being unfaithful or lying to you.

"And that doesn't bother you? Or make you second guess there being an us?"

"No, it doesn't," Kody said, pulling her closer. "Yes, it's a slap in the face that you think I could ever hurt you that way, but you were only trying to protect yourself." Kody lifted her chin to see her eyes. "However, in the future, can you come to me before running away?"

"After this whole mess, you don't have to tell me twice."

"Where'd you go, anyway? I came by on Thursday because I couldn't reach you and Lisa told me you wouldn't be back until today."

Winter sighed. "Chloe had a work assignment, and I went with her to spend a few days on the beach and clear my head."

"Makes sense," he said knowingly. "The beach sounds like the perfect place for you to shake off some of that crazy before returning to me."

Winter finally allowed herself to laugh. Before she could comment, Kody kissed her with all the desire, passion and love of a man who needed his woman, and without question, she kissed him with the same.

It had been several weeks, and Jackson was getting around well. He needed crutches and couldn't stand for long, but even that was a giant leap in the right direction.

"It's my roll," Erica said, tossing the dice onto the board. "Jackson, why are you always cheating? You and Kody buy up all the good stuff before anyone else, and no one has a chance to make much money."

"Umm, it's called Monopoly for a reason," Jackson replied with sarcastic humor.

"You better be glad," Erica said, waving a finger at him.

"Glad that you love me, right?"

"No, glad that I don't want to be a single mom," she said.

They all laughed, and Erica touched her belly. Jackson leaned over to place his hand over hers, and then they gave each other a quick but heartfelt kiss.

"Hey, lovebirds," Kody said. "I don't mean to put a damper on your moment, but Erica, you rolled a four, which means you are about to owe me some money."

Erica handed the monopoly money over with fake annoyance. "I'm hungry. You guys hungry?" she asked.

It seemed nowadays Erica was always hungry. But this time, she wasn't alone.

"Yeah," Winter said. "I don't think we ate since breakfast, isn't that right, babe?" she asked, looking toward Kody for confirmation.

Kody was staring down at his phone.

"Yeah, I think you're right," he answered, only half-listening. "Excuse me for a second. I need to go make a call."

Winter watched him go. He had been doing that a lot

more lately. Leaving to make calls or excusing himself as soon as the phone rang.

She tried not to be concerned with it. It's not like she expected or even wanted him to take all his calls in front of her. It was just strange how his behavior had changed.

Asking Kody what was going on seemed like the simplest solution, but it felt too trivial when Winter played the conversation out in her head.

Jackson decided they should order a pizza, and everyone was on board with that idea. Kody hadn't returned yet, but they all figured he'd be fine with the food of choice, so Winter placed the order.

A few minutes later, Kody returned to the table.

"We ordered pizza," Jackson said. "And I'd like beer with mine, so if you don't mind, can you please grab me one from the fridge? I think I'll start drinking now."

"What about your pain meds?" Erica said with worry. "You can't drink while taking those."

Jackson looked at her with sincere appreciation.

"I stopped taking pain meds last week, baby. I told you I am feeling better, and the doctor gave me the all clear to drink if I'd like."

Erica slowly nodded, clearly wanting to believe he was okay, but still terrified at the thought of something happening to him again.

Kody stood and said, "I'll grab your beer, and while I'm at it, I'll grab one for myself too, you know, since I'm celebrating and all?"

Three sets of eyes looked up at him.

"Celebrating?" Winter asked.

"Yeah, I just got off the phone with the managers out in California and Texas. They are completely set to oversee my projects out there. Looks like my days of traveling for work are over."

Jackson let out a loud cheer while Erica clapped, and Winter looked stunned.

"You mean you no longer plan to travel five months out of the year for work?" Winter asked.

"Nope," Kody said. "I'm only going to travel as need be, which shouldn't be much at all. I'll go back to California, of course, to put my house on the market and tie up any loose ends, but my new home is here with all of you."

Winter jumped up and hugged him. She was so happy she could shout. Which is exactly what she did after laying a major kiss on him.

"I'm sorry, sweetie," Kody said, still holding her in his arms.

"For what?" she asked.

"All the private phone calls. I wanted to surprise you. I hope it didn't have your mind racing," he said, kissing her on the forehead.

"My mind racing?" she asked innocently, "Oh no, not at all."

That night, on the ride home, Winter felt like the luckiest girl in the world. She had everything she could have ever wanted.

Her phone chimed, and she saw it was a message from Jessica, asking if they were still on for their spa day tomorrow.

Texting Jessica a reply, Winter smiled as she thought about how good it would feel to get a massage.

It had been a while since her last one, and after her busy schedule at work and helping to take care of Erica and Jackson, she needed it.

But Winter didn't mind any of the work at all.

Her job was still wonderful, and she loved every minute of her time with Kody's family.

The truck was slowing, and Winter looked up from her phone to see Kody pulling over to a deserted park.

"Where are we?" she asked.

Kody put the vehicle in park before answering.

"I remember a woman once telling me on this very road that she didn't care if I pulled this truck over and had my way with her. I think it's about time I give that woman what she wants."

With a sly grin, he unlatched his seat belt. Winter smiled back and did the same.

Also by Nicki Grace

Explore the Nicki Grace Collection

Romance

The Inevitable Encounters Series

Book 1: The Hero of my Love Scene

Book 2: The Love of my Past, Present

Book 3 : The Right to my Wrong

The Love Is Series

Book 1: Love is Sweet

Book 2: Love is Sour

Book 3: Love is Salty

Erotica

His Mouthpiece

His Mouthpiece: The Prequel

<u>Women's Fiction</u>

The Beautiful Nightmare Series

Book 1: Cut Off Your Nose

Book 2: To Spite Your Face

The Splintered Doll (A Memoir)

<u>Thrillers</u>

The Twisted Damsel

<u>Self-Help</u>

The TIPSY COUNSELOR Series

The Tipsy Dating Counselor (Summary)

Book 1: The Tipsy Dating Counselor (UNRATED)

Book 2: The Tipsy Marriage Counselor

Book 3: The Pregnancy Counselor

About the Author

Nicki Grace is an Atlanta native with a bachelor's in business and a Masters in Marketing. As a wife, mother, author and designer, she is addicted to writing, spas, laughing, and sex jokes, but not exactly in that order.

Her comedic personality and unique upbringing by an illiterate but fiercely strong mother and a courageous, prideful father, made her view of the world pretty unconventional.

Luckily for you, someone gave her internet access, and now you get to experience all the EMOTIONAL, EXCITING, SHOCKING, and HOT ideas that reside in her head. She loves to have fun and lives for a good story. And we're guessing so do you! <u>Nickigracenovels.com</u>

facebook.com/nickigracenovels

instagram.com/nickigracenovels

tiktok.com/@nickigracenovels

bookbub.com/authors/nicki-grace